Scent of Danger

ALSO BY JERRY LABRIOLA

Murders at Hollings General
Murders at Brent Institute
The Maltese Murders
Famous Crimes Revisited (coauthored with
Dr. Henry Lee)
Dr. Henry Lee's Forensic Files (coauthored with
Dr. Henry Lee)
The Budapest Connection (coauthored with
Dr Henry Lee)
The Strange Death of Napoleon Bonaparte
Shocking Cases (coauthored with
Dr. Henry Lee)

Scent of Danger

A NOVEL
BY

Jerry Labriola, M.D

STRONG BOOKS

Strong Books
P.O.Box 715
Avon, CT 06001-0715

First Printing

ISBN 978-1-928782-28-5

Library of Congress Control Number 2010940701

Published in the United States of America by Strong Books, an imprint of Publishing Directions, LLC

Printed in the United States of America.

To Quincy and Jaiden
with much love

ACKNOWLEDGMENTS

I wish to give special thanks

- to the staff at Strong Books, especially Brian Jud and Ellen Gregory;

- to Susan Jordan and my wife, Lois, for their expert reviews;

- to the members of the Goshen Writers Group for their insightful suggestions;

- to Dan and Sandy Uitti for their able assistance;

- and to Dr. John Elser for his inspiration.

PROLOGUE

This is a book of fiction. But, as was the case in my last novel, *The Strange Death of Napoleon Bonaparte,* several points are worthy of mention:

- Every effort has been made to preserve historical facts.
- Nearly all dialogue has been presented in the English language to avoid the complexities of French, Egyptian and Japanese versus English.
- Most characters have Americanized mannerisms.
- The existence of Lady Beckett stems entirely from my imagination.

J. L.

BACKSTORY

What a coup for Paul D'Arneau, American historian and international treasure hunter, when he was offered a lucrative commission to solve one of the most controversial enigmas in history. There had been accusations of foul play and spirited debate over the true cause of Napoleon Bonaparte's death for nearly 200 years.

Paul accepted the challenge from the semi-secret society in France and quickly realized that his efforts to penetrate the secrets hidden in musty documents and oral histories of Napoleonic lore could cost him his life. He struggled to understand why the truth about the Emperor's death posed such a threat to the warring factions that zealously guarded their historical turf and he eventually arrived at a solution, providing concrete proof of his findings to the satisfaction of the French secret society –*Gens de Vérité*–and particularly of its chairman, Leon Cassell.

Such a story—as told in my last novel, *The Strange Death of Napoleon Bonaparte*—contains a surprise ending that will not be revealed here. But somehow, it made its way into a local newspaper and from there to the national media. They told of what Paul had meticulously uncovered and even recounted what he had initially hoped would never be brought to light again–the whole sordid mess at Yale University: how at forty-four he became the Nathaniel Bennett Chairman of the Department of History; how he wrote a manuscript suggesting that Napoleon had most likely been murdered, a view that infuriated university officials; how they accused him of being a "regressive mythologist" and no longer an historian; and how they summarily dismissed him from the faculty.

Yet eventually Paul became satisfied with the media coverage believing it provided free advertising for his eventual full-time treasure hunting. This proved to be the case. Within days, phone calls and emails poured in, all requesting his assistance in finding stolen paintings, sculptures, antiques and other assorted art pieces.

But never a missing perfume formula.

Jerry Labriola, M.D.

THE HEIST

Chapter 1

Wednesday, June 20
Early morning

Paul's study had been tagged with a dozen different names during his life-long residency at a pre-Victorian home within walking distance of the Yale University campus: "refuge", "hideout", "sanctuary". But his favorite was "The Chest Room", emblematic of its collection of neoclassic chests and cabinets—French, Italian, Egyptian, English—all dating back to the post-Napoleonic era, and given to him by individuals and museums as rewards for locating lost treasures.

There were two antique phones in the room, one for incoming, the other for outgoing calls. He hadn't heard from anybody lately and, while immersed in a book titled *The Importance of Mythology,* the ring startled him.

It was about a year after the Napoleon investigation and he was just as startled by the raspy voice at the other end.

"Hello, Paul? Paris calling."

"Leon!" Paul shouted. "Leon Cassell, is that you?"

"Indeed it is. And calling again on behalf of *Gens de Vérité.* But first, how *are* you? And how is Jean?"

"We're not as close as before, I'm afraid. A friendly split—more of her doing—something about my traveling the globe too much. But now I come and go as I please;

no explanations, no excuses, no delays. And you?" Paul asked, "All well at your end?"

"As well as could be expected. Keeping busy as much as I can."

Paul was glad the small talk was over for he was anxious to hear why Leon had called. Another assignment perhaps?

He knew that an ensuing silence was awkward for Leon, almost as much as it was for him.

Finally Leon broke it. "Well … uh … I don't know quite what to say … that I'm sorry for both Jean and you? Or … "

"No. No need for that. We've remained friends; keep in touch, especially if I need scientific help."

"She's still at the forensic lab?"

"Yes, good old forensic anthropology, though I hear she's getting tired of it. Wants to get into administration."

"I see," Leon said. "And you, Paul. You okay?"

"Just fine. Itching for more excitement but fine, considering."

"Searching for Fra Angelico's *Golden Saints,* though—wasn't that exciting?"

"You bet—for as long as it lasted, which wasn't long."

"You found it?"

"Of course. Pretty straightforward."

"Amazing. Simply amazing—but not surprising. I've said it before, Paul, and I'll say it again. You can't imagine how pleased the group is—and I personally—with how you answered so many questions about Napoleon's death."

Paul waited for more, but decided it best to respond. "Thanks, Leon. Hope it gave some closure."

"More than some."

Then, as Paul remembered, the chairman could change the subject as abruptly as a hummingbird changes course. And once again, he did.

"I'll get right to the point," he said. "A secret perfume formula, handed down for centuries and eventually retained by a French manufacturer has been missing for about a week. The manufacturer, *Perfume by Cleopatra—Cleo's* for short—well, to put it mildly, there're losing their minds down there. And can you believe this? So is the whole industry in France, including *Cleo's* competitors."

Paul finally knew why Leon was calling. He didn't hesitate. "Sounds interesting, but the obvious question is why do competitors care?"

"At this level, we aren't talking run-of-the-mill outlets. These are big-time dealers with more at stake than money alone. It's a matter of pride, of tradition. And to add to the picture, a small bit of the stuff in a tiny blue bottle—apparently from the Napoleon era—has also disappeared. The formula and the bottle were stashed in a safe in Grasse."

"Southern France?"

"Southeastern, really—near Nice."

Paul wasted no time. "And I take it that you want me to find them?"

"Yes, plus the criminal or criminals. We've already discussed it at *Vérité* and the decision was unanimous. *Cleo's* contacted us about it; our executive committee met in executive session; and you're our man. In case you're wondering, that committee is still made up of the same people you worked with last time: the delegation."

"But perfumes ... fragrances ... hardly up my alley."

"And they needn't be."

"Are you sure you want a mythologist again?" Paul asked.

"You're no mythologist."

"But that's what Yale claimed when they fired me. I think you know the story: they said I went beyond the thinking that myths are simply a teaching tool—to help understand many things before science came along to offer facts. That eventually I began believing the myths themselves. And that's just plain bull! Just because I quote mythology from time to time doesn't mean I believe it de facto. And ... but why am I going on like this?"

"Because you're still upset over it, and I don't blame you." Leon said. "Just as I don't see anything wrong with your views about an obvious teaching tool."

There was another long silence during which Paul figured Leon was consulting notes, or perhaps was trying to let the mythology issue die down. Finally Leon said, "Paul, you're considered a treasure hunter, right?"

"I suppose that's accurate."

"Well, look at it this way. Ancient perfume formulas—especially secret ones—are just as much treasures as medieval paintings or furniture pieces."

"I suppose you're right. Yes, I can see that. And come to think of it, I read recently that perfuming in general is a billion dollar industry."

"Billion? No—five billion!"

Paul, seated at a desk he rarely used, had already made up his mind to work with *Vérité* again. He asked

Leon for a minute or two to find a newspaper clipping that Leon had given him the year before. It contained part of an interview he had granted a French reporter. Specifically, it was an exchange between the reporter and *Vérité's* long-time chairman. Paul had never accepted an offer to work for a government or for any organization with strong ties to government because he believed both were too politicized. He felt that politics might stymie his efforts at what he called "maneuverability." And although he knew Leon's thoughts on the subject coincided with his own, he simply wanted to refresh his memory about *Vérité's* relationship with France in general and with any lobbying groups in particular. He skimmed through the article, finally settling on the following:

Reporter: "How many members do you have?"

Cassell: "Over a thousand. We even have some American members.

They've either worked here on long-term assignment or have moved here for good. All of our membership works to seek the truth. That's our basic motivation."

Reporter: "I see. And seeking the truth is admirable, but other than your mission project, what other things do you concentrate on?"

Cassell: "First we limit our energies to the greater Paris area. Basically we take up causes as they develop. At the heart of it is our effort to get at the truth, to go beyond the façade of political and special interest rhetoric. For example, we'll soon be taking up the cause of preserving our city's five hundred parks and gardens. Certain industrialists claim that's too many, that they hurt industrial development and the creation of jobs. Fact of the matter is that these same industrialists have histories of corruption—graft and the like. We're very proud of our work in conservation. Just as some people—like Paul D'Arneau whom we talked about before—strive to conserve works of art, we want to conserve our natural resources. Some say we're nothing more than a glorified advocacy group, but we're much more than that. Advocacy groups and governments come and go but *Vérité* remains a constant."

Paul reread the phrase, " … to go beyond the façade of political and special interest rhetoric", and felt reassured. He hurried back to the phone and, trying to curb any excitement, said matter-of-factly, "The next several weeks look clear but before I say yes or no, a few more questions, okay?"

"Of course."

"Were the police called?"

"Yes, and my main man there phoned me immediately. I suggested they keep it under wraps, that I was notifying you, and once we got our bearings … "

"Hold on, Leon!" Paul interrupted. "You sound as if you expected my answer would be yes."

"I'm afraid I did. Yes, I confess to that."

"Well, it **is** yes. The timing is perfect; I'm between cases."

"Thank you, my friend." Paul heard Leon's deep sigh. "I knew I could count on you once more. But before any more questions, let me say right up front: same monetary arrangement as before—all expenses paid, six-figure compensation, and the bonus of one million U.S. dollars if … pardon … once the formula and bottle are found and the guilty party is apprehended."

"Good. Now then, I'm sure I'm coining a new word, but unchurn my mind. When do I start? Do I work with that same *Vérité* delegation? Should I leave for Paris, say, in the morning? When and how did the theft happen, and, if you asked that it be 'kept under wraps', how could the whole French perfume industry know about it?"

"Last answer first: there had to be a leak of sorts. Maybe even deliberate. We can get into it, along with details surrounding the disappearance, when you arrive, hopefully tomorrow. I'll reserve you a room at the Meridien Montparnasse Hotel again. Call me at the usual number once you're settled. As for the delegation—yes, the same people. They'll be at the ready, including the military man, Maurice Delacroix. I'm not so sure we need military advice this time but Napoleon is sure to come up. So we have yours truly, Maurice, Vincent Broussard, Guy Martin from the *International Herald Tribune,* and, of course, Frère Dominic. Technically he's not a member of *Vérité* but I'd like to see him involved because, just like Guy, he can contact specific histarians if we need them. You remember them, don't you? 'Histarians', not 'historians'. Same as always, they'll provide key information—a piece here, a piece there—they still call the pieces 'collections'. And they'll insist on remaining absolutely anonymous, away from the public's eye and especially the media. That way, they can operate freely. They're still the same regarding phone calls. On an initial phone call with you, they'll reveal nothing regarding what they've found. Strange—it's like canon law with them. That's why you have to visit them in person. After that, some of them discuss things more freely over the phone. And like before, *Vérité* will pick up their fee—or as you in the States would put it, 'the tab.' I'm certain you recall how they work, Paul—how they can furnish information that is contrary to what history has provided—so they're aptly named. Not contrarians but histarians. As for their value to us in this new project, I'm sure it'll be hard to measure. I've said it so often but, 'Exhaustive research can change earlier beliefs,' and that's what they're known for: exhaustive research. Private collections from private collectors … from private *anonymous* collectors. In other words, our histarians never reveal their source and they always turn out to be right— right and accurate. The only possible difference this time around is that you may be consulting with an entirely new batch—especially those who understand the perfume business. And speaking of your word 'coining' a while ago, it was Guy who coined—I'd say 'bastardized'—the word 'historian', saying 'histarian' was akin to 'contrarian'."

Paul ignored all the talk about histarians—he'd heard it all several times before. Instead, he counted to a silent five before saying, "That's the complete delegation?"

"Yes. Vincent, Guy, Maurice, the prior at the Senanque Monastery, myself … that's five … let's see, I'm missing one."

"Sylvie! How could one forget Sylvie Ranet?"

"Of course. The best looking of the bunch!"

"Is she still kind of a double agent for *Vérité* and the Academy of Sciences?"

"I guess so," Leon laughed, "but both sides know it. Still, she's invaluable, as you might remember."

"Invaluable but distracting at the same time," Paul said, trying hard to constrain a suggestive grin. "And as I recall," he continued, "the Academy is a branch of the Institute of France."

"Correct. And the Institute considers *Vérité* a

rival."

"She's content to remain in the middle of it all then?"

"Most assuredly—thrives on it. Actually when you get right down to it, she's nobody's secret." Another long silence. "And Paul?"

"I'm here."

"She still has a 'thing' for you. Brings your name up all the time. It was obvious last time around, and I'm sure it will surface again. That wouldn't displease you, would it?"

"Ah ... no, not at all. I'm not attached, remember?"

"Before we leave the subject, may I ask you a personal question?"

"Shoot. I'll answer if I can," Paul replied.

"Have you and Sylvie kept in touch?"

"I figured you'd ask, and the answer is no. It was by mutual agreement: she knew I was taken and I knew she wanted the freedom to ... to ... explore. Let's put it that way."

"And you don't think any relationship you might rekindle with her would interfere with what we're asking you to do, right?"

"Right. And just to square things, Leon, the relationship last time was purely platonic. She wanted it to be more than that, but lily-white me had Jean in mind."

Paul wanted to add that such consideration was no longer the case. Instead he chose to end the conversation after stating he would leave for Paris the next day.

"One last thing though," he said, "other than the police and the delegation, does anyone else know I've been contacted?"

"No. And I think it best we keep it that way, at least for now. Don't you?"

"Absolutely. But it'll be a losing proposition, I'm sure. There's bound to be a slip of the tongue. Or we'll be noticed together in public. Or more likely, I'll be seen probing, milling around, and so on. But for as long as possible, I'd prefer to remain anonymous."

Within seconds of hanging up, he arranged an early morning flight from JFK to Charles de Gaulle Airport. One of his favorite female contacts at the terminal—also one of his favorite dates—facilitated the booking.

He then thought briefly about his usual homemade and paltry breakfast but decided to pace instead, a regular ritual whenever an unexpected and intriguing assignment popped up, or whenever he had to sift through "probabilities and possibilities." Jean had maintained the pacing was a sign of nervousness while Paul always insisted it simply helped him think—to sort out information recently received. "Nervousness, on the other hand," he once added while they were seated in his study, "that means saltine crackers if I'm at home. You've seen me consume a package in no time flat. Not too often because I don't get nervous too often. You know that, correct?"

"Uh … correct," she had answered, unconvincingly. "Just like your face. Wouldn't you say it never blotches?"

"Yeah, I'd say that."

"Then why is it all blotchy now?"

"It is? And why do you think it is, Ms. Smarty Pants?"

"Because you're getting nervous talking about your nerves."

"Oh, for crissake," he blurted, heading for the kitchen in search of crackers.

After the pacing, he would celebrate with bacon, eggs and fries at *The Downtown Nook*. He never gave it much thought but this time he did: why did he always begin the ritual at the tweed armchair in his beloved study? And this time, it lasted twice as long. His pet piece there was a standing desk constructed long ago by his father, a retired mathematics professor at Columbia University and a gifted cabinetmaker on the side. Paul dissected nearly everything requiring deep study and thought while either pacing about the room or leaning on the desk. While a schoolboy, he resisted his mother's attempts to lure him to the more conventional desk nearby. Also a retired teacher, she insisted he would eventually tire easily if he continued to stand for long periods of time while doing his homework—year after year. And year after year, he would respond with a phrase he learned while still a youngster: "That's not germane." It would be a phase identified with him throughout his life: something or other was either "germane" or "not germane."

But the study contained more than chests and cabinets. Prominently displayed were creations by Thomas Chippendale, George Hepplewhite and others who dominated the furniture scene of the late Georgian years. More recent pieces featured George III mahogany side chairs and a Regency-style chaise longue.

A powerfully built six-footer, Paul had never put his body to good athletic use except for a one-year stint on Yale's swimming team. He had jet-black, wavy hair and a smile that was basically sincere but could be flashed before a moment passed. Yet it was his eyes that arrested most observers: dark and penetrating, though not disturbing, giving the impression that all that mattered was the person or subject at hand. Many commented that his head wandered little in conversation. He once overheard a colleague combine that feature with the eyes: "They make him look like a cat staring at an invisible shadow." Paul never knew whether or not to take it as a compliment.

Since his parents moved to an Arizona condominium four years ago, he continued to live alone in that same house, vowing never to leave. Before he became chairman of Yale's history department, Paul had spent nearly all his spare time making furniture in his workshop. Several times on the cusp of marriage—the most serious to Jean—he made no secret of sharing his home with countless women, especially on weekends. He preferred those around his own age—forty-five or so—needling those others who inquired, and there had been plenty—with, "Lots of furniture packed in here, but not a single cradle."

The following morning was new and clean like polished silverware. Paul threw open several bedroom windows and inhaled the best air of the month, having awakened energized by the unusual challenge presented to him. He looked forward to working with those he remembered from the Napoleon project, trying to dismiss any favorites—for each was vital to the success of the mission—but Sylvie quickly slithered onto center stage. She was vivid in his mind's eye and he didn't know why, but the spider tattoo on her ankle loomed larger and brighter than he had recalled. Did it signify anything different? Should he be more wary? Was she even available? One thing was certain: he was no longer bound into a relationship with Jean. In fact, she didn't and wouldn't know of his trip back to Paris.

As usual, whenever he went on an extended trip, he told his neighbor, Bill Dawkins, a former Yale colleague. Bill reciprocated although he wasn't away as often, and they exchanged house keys with the tacit understanding to use them only in an emergency.

For some time now, he loathed the *process* of flying—not once seated, when he could doze or tend to some research—but the beginning and end. The checking in and checking out. Security had intensified so much since 9/11. This time he neither dozed nor researched. And midway through the flight, he began dwelling on the major events of a year before—in Paris, in Belgium, at Elba, on St. Helena—and on the characters with whom he had interfaced.

That entire venture, for which he was hired and handsomely paid, had lasted less than three weeks. Three years' worth of personalities, travel, uncertainties, threats, risk, even murder—all crammed into three weeks.

But again, what about Sylvie? She had the looks all right: petite, shapely, glistening eyes—at once green or blue, depending on the surrounding light and shadow patterns—a bewitching smile, straight raven hair whose wandering strands she pushed back from time to time, usually to capture one's attention or underline a point. And the brains: Harvard graduate; head of one of the French Academy of Sciences' most important committees, *Comite Academique des Relations Internationales Scientifiques et Techniques*; administrator of the Academy's grant proposals.

And what about her professed feeling for him? He well remembered the time, the place and her exact words: returning from St. Helena on Argus, the small Greek freighter, she had said sheepishly: "I think I'm falling in love with you." There had been a few drinks, but no lovemaking beforehand, and then that straight-out admission like a blow from a steel mallet. But why so soon? Her words had seemed genuine at the time, but they had met only ten days earlier. He remembered claiming that her words were too extreme, that she was imagining the extent of her feelings. She then countered with an understanding of his ties to Jean, but stated that if that ever loosened, she—Sylvie—would still be in Paris.

Paul couldn't resist saying, "You mean like Bogey and Bergman and, 'We'll always have Paris'?"

And now Paul knew she was still there. What he didn't know, however, was whether or not her feelings about him had changed. His mind was still filled with her and the many times they'd spent together at fancy French restaurants; about hastily called cocktail hours for two; about that tattoo of a spider on her ankle (he never learned why); and about the eventful trips to Elba where Napoleon had been exiled after his defeat by Russia and to St. Helena after the Waterloo disaster. But he suddenly found it painful concentrating on Sylvie so he turned his attention to Leon Cassell, in his late sixties and *Vérité's* chairman for thirty-five years. Paul trusted him more than he trusted anyone else in the delegation, even more than Vincent who had been his close companion and de facto bodyguard during the entire Napoleon mission.

Leon's background was in law enforcement. In his "younger and thinner days" as he would put it, he worked as a captain for both France's National Police Force and the Prefecture of Police in Paris. The past dozen years, however, had been devoted entirely to education: in turn teaching criminology at one of the city's Grandes-Ecoles; lecturing regularly at the Paris Police Museum;

and currently conducting a class on Corrections, Crime and Criminology at the Sorbonne. Over the years he had established more connections than an electrician but was known never to abuse them. A clever man, with thinning brown hair, a hawk nose, wide mouth and a wispy white mustache, he was stout of heart and stout of build. Paul had never inquired, but he was certain the chairman's six-feet-plus frame supported around 300 pounds. Yet he walked faster than Paul, who couldn't understand it, just as he couldn't understand why Leon's right thumb and index finger were so yellow when his cigarettes rarely left his mouth.

As for Vincent, he was slight of build and short, well under six feet. He had shiny black hair, combed straight back; dark brown eyes; gaps between his teeth, but an arresting smile. Only in his mid-twenties, there was a deceptive gentleness about him, but Paul remembered full well the several times Vincent had confronted certain adversaries, once staring three men down with a Beretta Cougar .45 in one hand and a Heritage Stealth 9 mm in the other. And on at least two other occasions, he had put his life on the line in defense of them both. He, like Sylvie, had studied at Harvard—four years of graduate work in history. And when he and Paul first met, he was quick to point out that some of Paul's books were required reading there, adding with a wink, "I thought Harvard and Yale didn't get along." Paul assumed that Vincent still taught at the Sorbonne.

Also at that first meeting, Vincent had explained that the Sorbonne was now called the University of Paris, that the original College de Sorbonne was suppressed during the French Revolution and reopened by Napoleon in 1808, and that as the university grew, its endless number of colleges retained the colloquial term "Sorbonne" for the entire collection.

Paul's recollections about Sylvie, Leon and Vincent left little to wonder about except for what might have occurred since the four of them last worked together. He would find out soon enough. But what about the remaining three in the delegation: Maurice, Guy and Frère Dominic? As was the case with the first three, he was just as interested in recalling their appearances as he was in the nature of their work—maybe more so, at this point. He believed it helped him remember everything important about each of them. A strange approach, but their individual faces, their speech, their body language—he judged all of it helpful in assessing what they did, or had done, not only as their life's calling but also in Paul's effort to solve the Napoleon enigma. He looked at it another way: as a group, the six represented as varied an array of individuals as he had ever conspired with. *Eclectic* was the word. He couldn't help but smile. It was *the* factor that stood out in Paul's mind and he was drawn to it because he anticipated its providing him with the most varied, most complete, and therefore most useful assistance in this new undertaking—especially the most varied. Shouldn't he cover all the bases again?

Unless things had changed. He had relied heavily on each of them before; a matter of "division of labor." Could he, a second time? But he would postpone further consideration of the last three until he met them in due course. Sylvie, Leon and Vincent had been enough for now.

Paul was growing weary of the whole review scenario and was winding it down with a sense of relief that the whole delegation spoke fluent English in contrast to a recent string of clients in Germany, Greece and Egypt.

And then he stiffened.

His was an aisle seat, two rows from the rear of the first class section and he'd been so absorbed in his recollections that he'd paid little heed to the man across the aisle. Up till now. Paul swore it was one of the three men who had waylaid him near Volterraio Castle on Elba Island! The bushy hair, the crooked nose, the jagged scar on his forehead, just below his hairline. Paul wasn't quite sure what to make of it. What was the guy doing in the States? And especially now, just an arm's length away. Any connection to his current mission? If so, was his phone bugged? Or Leon's? Or was the man's presence a holdover from the last case? There had been plenty of such instances in recent years as Paul moved among dangerous assignments. His instant reflex was to pat his left shoulder area before he realized he was on a plane and the pistol Vincent had provided him at Elba had long since been returned. He would simply stare straight ahead, only occasionally casting an eye in the man's direction. One thing was certain: he had lost all interest in resuming thoughts about the delegation. And dozing was completely out of the question. He began scratching a finger—another habit he had never curbed—and even conjured up the thought of a saltine or two.

He remained edgy for the rest of the flight, unable to concentrate, even though he knew the man he now dubbed "Scarhead" most likely had neither a gun nor a knife; and even though, in sizing him up, he knew he could hold his own if the situation arose. Still, he kept hoping the flight would end.

Once it did and passengers scrambled to retrieve their luggage, Paul was surprised at the man's behavior. Both rose in unison. The man looked straight at Paul and with a slight bow, motioned for him to go first in seeking out their luggage. Paul obliged after thanking him and wondered if "Scarhead" either didn't recognize him or was the world's best actor. The little engagement gave Paul the opportunity to study the man up close and there was no longer any doubt he was one of those at the foot of the castle.

Paul nodded for the man to lead the way down the aisle but he refused. And for the first time he spoke. It was a deep hollow voice. "No, my friend. I am in no hurry." There was no trace of an accent. Paul walked slowly, one hand carrying a small duffel bag, an over-stuffed briefcase in the other. Halfway down the aisle he turned and was surprised to see that "Scarhead" had returned to his seat and was busy writing something in a notebook. Paul quickened his pace and after all the immigration formalities had been completed, he looked around and didn't spot the man anywhere, either in plain sight or lurking around corners.

Chapter 2

Curbside, Paul hailed a cab, saying, "Le Meridien Montparnasse, s'il vous plait. And I'm late for a meeting." He always mentioned his lateness to cab drivers, an imagined code he believed the drivers understood: straight to the destination; no indirect route in order to pad the fare.

The hotel lobby had changed significantly since his last visit: less pastel in its décor; a more ornate entrance to the cocktail lounge; pleasant fragrances wafting from larger flower displays; an Edith Piaf melody in the background; two or three additional bronze statues of French war heroes. Paul circled about to take it all in. He then concluded that the local Parisians had won out after complaining bitterly about its modern rather than neoclassic design.

He checked in at the reservation desk at 1:30 p.m. and as before, was given a sixth-floor room, refusing the attendance of a bellhop.

"But Monsieur D'Armoneau," the clerk said.

"That's D'Arneau," Paul said. "I stayed here for three weeks last year, I know my way around and I can handle the luggage fine. But merci anyway."

"As you wish, monsieur."

Paul turned to leave and three steps away, was called back.

"Almost forget," the clerk said, "Gentleman was here … hour ago. Asked if you were at this hotel. I checked and told him "oui", but that you did not arrive yet. He shows me an envelope, asked if it would be all right if he put it under your door. I said "oui" again and gave him your room number."

The clerk paused, then said, "I did wrong, monsieur?"

"No, not at all. What did he look like?"

"Oh, not tall. Good suit, tie. Young, maybe thirty … thirty-five. Spoke to me in bad French."

"Did he have a crooked nose and a scar on his forehead?"

"No, I did not see that. We see so many kinds here."

Upstairs, Paul inserted the card in the slot to room 1209, pushed open the door with his suitcase and nearly stepped on the envelope. He picked it up and easily pried it open with a finger. He withdrew a small slip of paper and read a single typed line:

MIND YOUR OWN BUSINESS.
GO HOME OR ELSE

Neither stunned nor surprised, he sighed as if to utter a "here we go again" resignation. Of more immediate concern was not the sinister nature of the message but the possible—and most likely—relationship of it to his previous experience with *Vérité* in Paris and beyond. But how did the messenger know when Paul would be arriving?

After very little thought, he decided not to tell Leon and the rest of the delegation about it. One of the reasons he was stimulated by being a treasure hunter was that he was his own boss—the freedom, calling his own shots when he wanted to. Not, in contrast, to being a lofty professor at Yale and answering to the university and often to some of his colleagues. And this was a perfect example of it; he'd decided on his own to keep the note—plus the Scarhead encounter—a secret. For the time being, perhaps, but it was <u>his</u> decision. *Period.*

Such early developments, however, were solid reminders that he was about to begin the work of a detective, not in the ordinary sense, not in terms of investigating the usual violent crimes—murder, rape, aggravated assault and such—but in an attempt to locate a stolen treasure. This time, it was neither a painting, a rare piece of furniture, nor even an ancient letter, but rather, a secret perfume formula, of all things. And a blue bottle. Did that have more significance? So far, all he knew was that both had some connection to Napoleon Bonaparte and maybe to Cleopatra. He would soon find out more about it from Leon and the others.

His room was nearly the same as last time, maybe a bit larger. Once again, the view from the window contained none of the famous Parisian landmarks, which made no difference to Paul, for he had seen them all many times. Nor had he paid any attention during the twenty-mile taxi ride from the airport along Charles de Gaulle Avenue, the Avenue de la Grande Armee and onto the Champs Elysees. At the time, he was more concerned about checking for a black Citroen tailgating them as was the case a year before. He saw none.

Paul was anxious to notify Leon of his arrival, but for a minute or two he sprawled out on the bed, hands behind his head, and attempted to sort out a flood of loose thoughts. They were mostly menacing but also included those related to the familiar personalities he'd be working with, and to those new ones he'd undoubtedly come across—willingly or unwillingly. But the dominant theme was whether or not he'd be in over his head. For he knew little about perfumes, never used any, and didn't even like the smell of most of them. He concluded that he need not be a devotee of perfumery at all, that he'd been hired to locate a missing formula and bottle. He would treat his new responsibility that way. Again: *period*.

He finally called Leon. "Well I'm here and ready to go to work," he said.

"Good," Leon replied. "I'll phone Vincent and we'll meet you where? I'm tempted to recommend your room so we won't be seen together ... your face got around pretty good last time and I've created some followers through the years ... but ... "

"Hell," Paul broke in, "let's not get paranoid over all this. Sooner or later, people will find out what we're up to."

"Meaning?"

"Meaning I vote for having a late lunch at the Brasserie Lipp. I'm comfortable there and it brings back good memories."

"You got it. And by the way, notice I didn't include Guy or Maurice. Or even Sylvie. Too many at one time. I'll let them know you've arrived though, and you can set up your meetings with them separately."

"We think alike, Leon."

"That helps. See you at three, or thereabouts."

The afternoon weather had turned ominous: dark and chilly, a penetrating fog drifting about, visibility blurred.

Paul guessed the rains were near, thunder rumbles and snappy lightening crackles not far off. The air felt heavy and damp on his face and neck and he wished he were wearing his light raincoat. It suddenly occurred to him why he wasn't: he had forgotten to bring one along from the States.

From the moment he entered the front entrance of the Brasserie Lipp—arriving by taxi—he felt once more as if he were walking in the shadows of great artists and writers. Whereas Le Meridien Montparnasse had noticeably changed in appearance over the past year, the restaurant was the same, from its faint mustard and onion aromas to the Hemingway memorabilia covering many walls. On some there were a few writing samples taken from the works of Faulkner, Sartre, Camus and Simone de Beauvoir. Paul was immediately at ease, there in the place where he'd spent so much time compiling the first draft of his last book, *St. Helena: Napoleon's Final Defeat.* He knew Lipp's special history as if he were its owner: opening in the late 1800's during the Franco-Prussian War and three generations later, winning the Legion of Honor over 12,000 cafés and salons as the best literary meeting place in Paris. It was in fact why he had spent so much time there, hoping that some of the skills and inspirations of the great masters would miraculously rub off on him.

He recognized Leon at the very corner table they usually occupied during the Napoleon investigation. The place was crowded and Paul assumed he had a reservation. The *Vérité* chairman was writing in the margin of a newspaper and didn't look up until Paul approached him.

"Digesting Guy's *Herald Tribune,* I see," Paul said.

"Paul!" A few heads turned.

Leon leaped up and they embraced, each vying to utter the next words. Paul won.

"You look the same," he said. "It's as if I'd never left."

"You mean I'm just as fat?"

"Actually" ... Paul stepped back to include Leon in a complete view ... "Looks like you've lost a few pounds."

"Still the diplomat, aren't you? Actually, my weight is about the same. A losing cause ... I'm convinced."

"But you look great," Paul said.

"Aha," Leon retorted, "It's caught on even in America, hasn't it?"

"Come again?"

"The three ages of man: "Youth. Middle Age. And, 'You look great!'"

Chuckling, Paul said, "No, hadn't heard that and it's very good ... clever."

Leon removed a large black umbrella from the chair nearest him and placed it in the corner. They both sat and then Leon slapped the front page of the newspaper with the back of his hand. "See, it's no longer a secret. The whole world knows something was stolen but at least it doesn't say it was a perfume formula."

Paul wasn't sure of how to respond, so simply asked, "You usually take notes about what you read?"

"Only to keep the characters straight."

"Why did he even write it?" Paul asked.

"I figured it was coming soon, but not *this* soon. His editor knew about the crime and wanted it written, so Guy had no choice. By now, it's probably in all the other papers anyway."

In a brief silence that hung between them, Paul recalled their table as a peaceful one, despite the weighty discussions held there about a year before — and it looked like there would be more. He also remembered the waiters and waitresses as relaxed and hoped the one who hadn't arrived yet would be the same. He had a serious "thing" about those who served tables: that they could make or break a meal by their disposition, and he had no second thought about basing his eventual tip on such a factor. "Forget the taste of the food," he would think (and even say to his tablemates). "What counts more is the atmosphere the server creates."

A high-pitched voice was barely audible from behind Paul's right shoulder. "Hey you two. Like old times." He recognized it as Vincent's before rising to shake his hand. "Sure is," Paul said. "So good to see you again."

Vincent moved around to sit opposite Paul and tried to appear inconspicuous as he took hold of an opaque water bottle that was part of the table arrangement. For a moment, his eyes scanned nearby tables. He then removed a small pistol from his breast pocket and concealed it sideways against the bottle.

Leaning forward, he slid the bottle and pistol toward Paul. "Here," he whispered, "I figured you might want this. It's a Heritage Stealth 9 mm. You know — the one I usually keep in my ankle rig."

Paul had anticipated Vincent's offer and immediately felt more secure than on the plane. "Thanks, my friend," he said, "and … "

"Also," Vincent interrupted, "an extra six-round cartridge." First signaling with a head nod, he passed it in one smooth motion from his right jacket pocket to Paul's hand beneath the table.

Then Vincent repeated the entire procedure for what Paul recognized as a Beretta Cougar .45.

"You think I'll need these this time around?" Paul asked.

Leon, who had been watching closely, said, "You certainly did last time, so you never know." And, as if reluctant to continue, he lowered his voice to add, "I wouldn't be surprised though."

He slid his chair closer to the table. "You know, Paul, I was going to save this for later but I think it fits in here. Your role last time certainly had its dangers, and you were investigating mainly the reason Napoleon died. That was important certainly and I'm not minimizing it, but if you stop to think about it, there's no comparison to what's at stake here. I mean this time around. There's not only been a theft—of monumental proportions, let's put it—but millions, if not billions of dollars, may be involved. No one's sure how, but that's the thinking on the street. The whole perfume industry's upset. The formula and the blue bottle were considered … well … sacred. There's no better word for it. Someone, or some group, had the audacity to steal them. Things will undoubtedly heat up. And you're about to plunge into the thick of it all."

Leon realigned the salt and pepper shakers, then abruptly glanced at Vincent before staring at Paul. "So," the chairman said, "should you be armed? Why, that's a given."

"And one last thing, Paul," Vincent said, slowly inserting his hand into his left jacket pocket. "Here are the shoulder and ankle rigs for the guns." For some reason, he wasn't as secretive about the rigs, simply passing them to Paul over the table.

Nor did Paul try to hide them; in fact, once received, he reached under the table and fastened the appropriate rig to his right ankle. He was, however, furtive in transferring the gun to the rig. "There", he said, "ready if needed." He put the Beretta Cougar and its rig into his jacket pocket, whispering, "I'll take care of these later."

All three breathed deeply in unison, as if relieved that their favorite track star had been the first to cross the finish line by a hair.

"Just to put an exclamation point on this whole ceremony," Paul said, "are these the same rigs and pistols I had last time?"

"The same," Vincent answered.

"And they served you well more than once back then," Leon said. "Let's hope that's repeated this time around or better still, that you won't have need for them at all."

Paul crossed his fingers and shook them in full view.

"Now then," he said, "did you think I wouldn't comment on your appearance, Vincent?"

Vincent clenched his jaw. "Meaning?" he said.

"Meaning I never saw you in a suit without wearing a tie. And your hair is longer."

"Hmm," Vincent said, "Maybe I'm just generally more relaxed. Or better still, maybe I can't afford as many haircuts."

"You mean the University doesn't pay you history people well?"

"Exactly. Never did."

"I take it you're still at the Sorbonne?" Paul inquired.

"Yes. And I'm kidding about the salary. It's really not that bad. And remember, I still don't have a family to support."

Leon hailed a waitress and ordered a beer and salad. The others did the same.

Paul collected the menus for the waitress and, leaning back in his chair, folded his arms across his chest in a defensive pose. "Okay, gentlemen," he said, "I need more details and I have a bunch of questions to ask."

Vincent nodded as Leon said, "That's fine, and from here on in, let's refer to the perpetrator as Mr. X, realizing it may involve more than one person. Maybe even an entire company. But why don't you ask some questions first. Then I'll fill in any blanks."

"And when we get to that, you'll go through the companies that might have an interest in the formula?" Paul asked.

"That's simple. All of them. I can elaborate later. But for now, you already know it was *Perfumes by Cleo* that had the formula stolen from its factory showroom. They call the place *Cleo's* for short, and the perfume itself is Vintage by Cleo's."

"So let's start there," Paul said, his face suddenly hardened with determination. "Where was the Vintage formula kept at *Cleo's* and what were the circumstances of the disappearance?"

Leon didn't waste any time responding. "Let me first say there was a break-in about ten days ago and it was reported in the newspapers, but there was no mention of what was stolen. I wasn't notified about the exact nature of the theft until about 48 hours before I called you, and, as it turned out, our executive committee met in emergency session." The chairman shook his head in a gesture of disbelief. "Are you ready for this, Paul? This will blow your mind." He didn't wait for an answer. "The formula and the tiny blue bottle were kept in a leather case or packet which, in turn, was kept in one of those small portable home safes. They're no more than a foot or so square and maybe half as wide. You know the kind?"

"Yes—very popular."

"I had one when I lived in the States," Vincent kicked in. "I believe it was called *Sentry Protector*."

"Anyway," Leon continued, "I was told that for years the safe was kept in a locked upstairs closet, bolted to the floor. The closet door was forced open, the wooden floor was cut completely around the safe, and they made off with it, bolt and all. Looks like they drilled holes in the floor and then sawed it away. I can't figure out how they knew enough to bring the proper tools."

"Ah, yes," Paul sighed, "brings back memories."

"You had something stolen like that?" Vincent asked.

"No, not me. One of my clients. Couple of years ago. Jewels worth thousands. But that's a long story, with a good ending, I might add."

"Here you are," the waitress said, emptying a tray of three mugs of beer and three plates of salad. "There's plenty of dressing over there." She pointed to the end of the table.

Each man took several gulps of the beer, then seasoned and dug into their salads.

Leon broke the brief silence. "So far, Paul, sound like professionals?"

"For a heist like this? No doubt about it. Mr. X

probably paid plenty for their services. As for the proper tools, that's how professionals operate. They stack their bags with all kinds of tools, for every contingency. Anything else taken?"

"Nothing. Appears they were after one thing only."

Paul moved uncomfortably from side to side. "There's something I'm not clear about," he said. "If the whole industry knows what's disappeared and is upset about it, why wouldn't the media know precisely what was stolen by now?"

"Because I've learned there's an unwritten code among the perfumers not to talk about that … that … treasure … let's call it. The code's apparently been in place for years but, truth be known, I'm not sure *how* it got started, *why* it got started, and whether or not it's ever been violated. You may have to find out sooner or later. Guy Martin might be helpful."

Paul moved quickly to another topic without further comment on the last. "All right. Next is MOM."

"What?" Leon said.

"Motive. Opportunity. Means. Mr. X created the opportunity. He no doubt purchased the means. But what about motive? Why did he do it? Any idea?"

Leon paused to stretch a blank expression over his face, then managed, "Well one thing's for certain: it's off the competitive market now. Don't ask me why because they could have continued to produce it. But Ken, the president, was very, very upset, almost incoherent when we talked about it. He kept repeating that the formula's a relic, an antique, a reminder of times past, of the Napoleon and Cleopatra days. He emphasized that it may even have *descended* from those days—that very formula.

And that he'd rather launch a new brand than continue offering Vintage with the "stench", as he called it, of its formula being stolen. It's really a strange reaction, to put it mildly, but I've often thought they were an unusual breed down there in Grasse—those perfumers. Many's the time Ken, just in casual conversation, would refer to them as sentimentalists rather than business people."

"So," Paul said, "someone had to know Ken's make-up to assume production would stop."

"I would call that almost a given," Leon said, "plus that same someone wanted the relic very badly."

"You mean," Paul countered, "that someone— Mr. X—would go to the trouble, take the risk, not only to decrease *Cleo's* overall sales, but to take possession of a relic like that?"

"Aside from the sales, you know how it works, Paul. It's a treasure, like an heirloom. Our job is to recover the formula, not in order for *Cleo's* to resume selling Vintage, but in order for Ken to take back possession of his relic, his treasure."

Paul meekly responded, "Of course I should know about stolen treasures. It's just that I haven't dealt with perfumes before."

It was obvious that Vincent was itching to take part in the conversation. He offered: "Leon told me that in his call to you he stressed that an ancient perfume formula—a secret one—can be just as much a treasure as a medieval painting to specific individuals. And I would stress that last time you were dealing with some lost treasures. This time you're dealing with a *stolen* treasure."

"That's right," Leon said, "and you needn't have had experience with perfumes per se. That's not the issue really. Look at it this way: it's the formula's history that counts in this case."

"Plus the bottle's," Vincent said.

"Plus the bottle," Leon echoed.

Paul, like Vincent and Leon, was wearing a jacket with no tie. Paul removed his, took out an index card from its breast pocket and draped the jacket over the back of his chair. He muttered something about its being hotter in Paris than Connecticut this time of year as he scribbled down a few notes.

"So Ken is the president, the boss?" he asked.

"Yes," Leon said, "he's the one who called me about the missing formula and how the room was broken into. Name's Ken Kuroda—Japanese—real nice guy, a gentleman, and a good friend. We go back a few years ... oh, maybe ten."

"Was he the president at the time?"

"Yes, he'd just bought the business."

"From someone who's Japanese?"

"No, French. I forget his name."

"I see," Paul said, making another notation on the card. "How old is this Kuroda fellow?"

"I'd say about fifty."

Paul tapped his finger on the card. "What else was kept in the room?" he asked.

"Practically nothing. It's kind of a tiny corner closet. I believe Ken said there was a building deed and a few old perfume catalogs in there, but they weren't touched."

"He has the only key to the room?"

"I assume so, but I'm not sure."

"Why the delay between the time of the break-in and calling you regarding the packet?"

"I asked him the same question and he said he wanted to mull over whether or not to go this route. I mean with *Vérité*."

Paul put down his pencil and squared himself for emphasis "Now, Leon," he said, "don't get me wrong. I know this Ken guy's a friend of yours, but is there any chance he's faking the whole thing?"

Paul was surprised at Leon's initial response: "I knew you'd take that into consideration and would be bringing it up. The answer is no, I can't imagine it. For one thing, what's to be gained?"

"Publicity."

"I doubt it. He's not that sorta man."

Paul's eyes became mirthful crescents. "I've come across many 'non-sortas' in my line of work. They never fit the mold but I must say, I trust your judgment." He checked his watch. "He knows you called me?"

"Yes, and of course he knows all about your success in the Napoleon adventure."

"I'd like to meet with him."

"Of course. I'll set it up. For tomorrow?"

Paul pointed at imaginary times in the air. "Let's see," he said. "No, make it the next day. Tomorrow I'll spend with Sylvie, Guy and Maurice." He reached back into his other breast pocket to remove another index card. It was covered with brief notations. "Now, are you game for more questions?"

"Absolutely," Leon said. "I … we'll … answer what we can."

"Let's see," Paul twisted the card around, checking both front and back, as if having trouble deciphering his own words.

The waitress appeared with the bill. Leon took it while Paul and Vincent nodded to him.

"Which reminds me," Paul said, "is it fair to inquire about where my fee is coming from?"

"Fair enough—and simple enough. *Cleo's* is putting up your fee plus whatever we pay the histarians. And they're adding $250,000 for *Vérité.*"

Paul flashed a triumphant smile. "Not a bad arrangement, I'd say, at least from our perspective."

"Well, recovering the formula means a lot to them," Vincent said.

"Yes, indeed," Leon chimed in.

"As I said, let's see," Paul repeated. "What's left to bring up during this first of many encounters, I'm sure?"

Vincent seized the initiative. "For me," he said, "two things. One: my role. Like before, I hope—accompanying you wherever you like. Especially the driving. I'm looking forward to it. And two: here's a list of phone numbers for the delegation members, including their cell phones. I don't believe any have changed over the past year." He checked with Leon who shook his head approvingly. Vincent handed Paul a sealed envelope.

Paul thanked him and added, "And, of course, protecting my life as necessary. Let's work it the same as last time. I do know my way around Paris so I'll just use taxis most of the time. But I can call you whenever?"

"Day or night."

Leon waved to a man and woman as they left the restaurant, dismissing the interruption with, "Some old friends." He paused to allow Vincent more time to continue but received a "your turn" look. "No, you go on," Vincent said.

"Now Paul, you plan on seeing Guy, Maurice, Sylvie, Ken, and who or what else? Or am I pressing you too much?"

"Not at all. I'm as anxious as you to get to the bottom of this. I'd like to take a look at *Cleo's*, which can be done when I meet Ken. And good old Frère Dominic. Still wants to be called 'Dom' and still a top histarian?"

"Yes, still active, but wants to talk to clients in person, not on the phone. That's why you have to go to Gordes."

"I've got to see him. How is he anyway?"

"Fine. As spry as ever. He knows you're here and expects to see you. I'll definitely arrange it. And that reminds me. Dom's ties are to the histarians in France. If you plan to consult with them elsewhere, Guy's your man."

"I do remember that."

"My light plane, the German *Breezer*, will be available for you at any time. As will its pilot. You'll need it for the visit to Dom down in Gordes. Unless you combine it with your trip to Grasse. Either way, you'll have to fly. Then, too, I have my helicopter. That's at your disposal."

"Very good," Paul replied. "And I have something I want to clear up. I'm aware that *Vérité* and The Institute have had their disagreements. They won't try to block anything, will they? I mean once things filter out, and I'm sure they will."

"No way!" Leon shot back, taking out a silk handkerchief and dabbing around his mustache.

"Next question then." Paul measured his words. "Why do you need to have Sylvie as a spy at the Academy?

I recall asking you the very same question once before, but refresh my memory."

"Certainly. In a sentence: to see what the whole Institute is up to regarding discrediting *Vérité*. And as I indicated last time around, we're doing it through Sylvie's branch. Maybe it would be helpful to go through the organizational set-up again. The Institute has five branches, all of them academies: Fine Arts; Ethical and Political Science; Inscriptions and Belles Lettres; the Academy of Science, which is Sylvie's branch; and the French Academy which is merely a collection of intellectuals trying to impress other intellectuals." Leon rattled off the branches as if he'd done it on a daily basis.

"Thanks," Paul said, grinning. "Someday, I might be able to recite the very same thing to somebody."

"And to review the financial issue one more time, Paul," Leon said. "$200,000 has already been deposited in your name in the Union de Banques Suisses: the Union Bank of Switzerland. And there's another million in escrow there for you upon the successful conclusion of this case. Then too, it goes without saying that we'll pick up all outside expenses. As for a contract, we can dispense with that, based on our mutual trust, which, in turn, is based on the ordeals we shared a year ago—wouldn't you say?"

"It all sounds fine and very generous, Leon. Plus— and this is also based on how we operated last time—I'll try to contact you each day so we can compare notes."

"Perfect," Leon said.

Paul was the first to rise, saying, "I guess it's a wrap for today, gentlemen. Excellent start."

At the front entrance, they looked at one another and then at the rain pelting down, its drops heavy and boisterous. The spray from passing cars reached their hoods, torrents rushed violently along the gutters.

"I can't believe it," Paul said.

"It's unfortunate there's no 'raindrop size' game in the Olympics," Leon said. "Paris would always win!" He alone laughed but, with the door open now, Paul could hardly hear anything other than the rain.

"Look, Vincent," Leon said loudly, "Take my umbrella and get your car. We'll drive you to the hotel, Paul."

"No, you two go ahead. I'll phone for a taxi."

The first thing Paul did upon returning to the hotel was to reserve his room for a full month. He anticipated some flights via commercial airlines and this would ensure a place to store the guns.

Upstairs, he slowly opened the door to his room, his eyes casting about the floor. His face felt wooden. The threatening note was still fresh in his mind. There was none this time. He raced to the bathroom sink to rinse out his mouth. Though exposure had been minimal, he could still taste rain—surprisingly disagreeable, and he didn't know why. French wine, yes—French rain, no!

He sat on the edge of the bed in a vague funk. He was delighted to be engaged again in his favorite line of work in one of his favorite cities, with the same financial remuneration of a year ago. On the other hand, there was the lingering doubt about his ability to work within the perfume industry, even though Leon had assured him it was a formula that had been stolen "Forget perfumes, scents and fragrances if it makes you more comfortable," Leon had said. "Tell yourself you're not even after *a formula*. Think of it as a purloined manuscript if it makes you feel better."

The clock on the nightstand read 5:35. Paul threw off his clothes and headed for the shower. He heard the phone ring and doubled back to pick up the receiver. He couldn't remember the last time he had answered a phone call totally nude. It wouldn't surprise him if he felt his face turn red.

"Yes?" he said, his voice empty of expression.

"Paul? It's me—Sylvie!"

"Omigod!" he exclaimed. "I mean, if you could see me now ..." His next words were inarticulate until he got to, "Sylvie! How are you? I didn't expect ..."

"Are you okay, Paul?"

"Yes, of course. Thanks for calling."

"And alone?"

"Yes, why?"

"You sound funny. Should you sound funny?"

"Yes, and I'll explain later. Nothing serious."

"And nothing intimate?"

"Intimate? Well, in a manner of speaking but, as I said, I'll explain later."

After a prolonged silence, she said, "Can later be tonight? I'd love to see you."

"You should see me now." He regretted the comment.

"I've *got* it!" Sylvie shouted. "I've figured it out."

"What? Figured what out?"

"You're naked. I caught you naked!"

Paul couldn't clearly make out her following sentence, a pitch or two higher than normal. But he was quite sure it resembled something like, "Which is better than ever before."

Disguising his enthusiasm, he agreed to see her later

that evening.

"But Paul," she said, "I have some key work to complete at the Academy and won't be available until around … let's say eight-forty-five. Hope that's not too late for you. You must be tired after your trip and all. Leon briefed me on your talk with him and Vincent today."

"No, 8:45's fine."

"Incidentally, I don't know whether it came up at your meeting," Sylvie said, "but I've moved. Further south, closer to my work. And there's a nice place to dine right nearby: the Atelier Maitre Albert Restaurant. Within walking distance of my apartment. Maybe you've eaten there before?"

"No, can't say that I have."

"It's on the Left Bank, in the Latin Quarter, just across from Notre Dame in the 5th Arrondissement. One Rue Maitre Albert. It has new chefs and great cuisine."

"Fine," he said. "I'll be there. There's no sense in your driving north to pick me up. I'll take a taxi."

Chapter 3

Paul calculated he had more than two hours before leaving. He took a slow shower, shaved for the second time that day, and called for a taxi to pick him up at eight. He unpacked his suitcase and garment bag, then tried on several combinations of clothes, settling on a turtleneck, jacket and trousers in different shades of brown. He made sure—checking and rechecking—that the Stealth 9 mm and Beretta Cougar were secure in the rigs he'd carefully applied to his right ankle and left shoulder.

He watched television for a while, grew increasingly restless, and decided to have a wine in the small bar just off the lobby. There, his thoughts centered not on perfumes and the crime he was hired to investigate, but on Sylvie. After a full year and now unattached, he was anxious to see her and convinced himself that she felt the same. Otherwise, why the phone call and invitation on his very day of arrival?

Time seemed to crawl; his sips of a single wine became smaller; and, with thirty minutes to go, he returned to his room and watched more television. Finally at eight sharp, the phone rang. It was the concierge who stated that his taxi had arrived.

The weather had improved somewhat but not enough

to quell a steady drizzle and an occasional thunder clap. Overcast in solid blacks and grays, the moonless sky seemed close enough to touch through swirls of steamy air. A thin night fog blurred a side exit from the hotel and Paul slipped on a sliver of soggy grass by the pavement and couldn't help but limp to the taxi.

Halfway to the restaurant, the intermittent massaging of his calf muscle had worked, his leg finally pain-free. Paul asked the driver about the restaurant: its food, its atmosphere, its popularity. In halting English, the driver was positive about all three.

"Do you take many customers there?" Paul asked.

"Oui, many, many." But he went on to explain that for the past two weeks, cars were not allowed complete access to the restaurant, that street improvements were being made on the two blocks this side of it, and that he would have to walk those last two blocks. Paul was glad he had massaged away the pain and that he had brought along a small collapsible umbrella. He wondered why the taxi driver hadn't mentioned a possible approach from the opposite direction, but he let it go, believing the short walk might do his leg some good.

Ten minutes later the taxi stopped outside a crumbly brick barrier blocking the street. The driver indicated he could go no further, and that a walkway was open on the other side of the barrier. Paul got out, paid the man and squeezed through a gap in the barrier. Broken mortar, wood and other debris were piled high for ten feet or more on each side. Beyond that, the street appeared spanking new.

The walkway turned out to be a wooden jetty with a low cement parapet on his left that ran as far as he could see. It had narrow recesses in it at regular intervals. To curb construction costs? To help fishermen? A few yards away, the sign on a stanchion indicated the restaurant was two blocks ahead. Its light cut through wisps of vapor usually seen at daybreak. Paul hadn't expected to hear a foghorn in that location but one sounded—a single dull moaning that was longer than he was used to hearing. He felt as though he were in a nightmare, dark and shadowy.

And then he heard footsteps. Footsteps that echoed. He glanced back and saw a man in a wide-brimmed hat not far behind. Though difficult to size up through the fog, the man looked to be solidly built, wide in the shoulders, no neck, and hands in the pockets of a long raincoat. Rarely had Paul's collar felt wet—he was sure it had nothing to do with the rain. And he didn't know why but *Jack the Ripper* popped into his mind—the murder of at least five prostitutes on foggy nights. By tensing his leg he could feel the gun at his ankle. At the same time, he patted the bulge near his left shoulder.

Next, without warning and in complete silence, car headlights materialized in the front, coming toward him at a slow but steady pace, nearly blinding him. And an old nugget of advice flashed through his mind: if confronted by armed men who want to drive you somewhere, you will eventually be killed, so never cooperate, even if you're staring at the muzzle of a gun. Fight them on the spot at all costs. History has taught that many of those shot before entering a car will survive, whereas those who are brought to a remote location will never make it alive. All this before the car even reached him! The nature of his assignment with *Vérité*; his worry that Sylvie was having the same difficulty in reaching the restaurant, though he hoped she'd driven; the man on his heels; the car up ahead; the shear brutality of the weather—had conspired, he thought, to make his day an unforgettable one. And all for the wrong reasons. He anticipated the worst.

The car, near him now, swerved into half a U-turn and came to a stop, sideways in the road, its motor still running. Steam rose from its hood, as if it had traveled a long distance.

Suddenly a shot rang out. Instinctively he ducked, threw down his umbrella, crouched into one of the recesses and whipped out both guns, thrusting them high enough for the car's occupant or occupants to see. He concentrated hard on whether or not he'd been hit, concluded he had not, and almost without thinking, fired shot after shot at the car's left front tire. It began to deflate. Was there any rationale to what he had just done or had he hoped to stun the car's driver?

In any event, to his surprise the car behaved like a startled and wounded mortal, finishing its U-turn and hobbling away.

Meanwhile, Paul spun around to check on the man at his rear. Seeing no one, he eased back, guns still drawn. One stanchion away, the man lay sprawled out, both legs at improbable angles, his hat crooked over the front of his head.

Paul kneeled over him and took his pulse. There was none. Using the tip of the Beretta, he flipped the hat over. There was one bullet hole smack in the middle of his forehead. A small trickle of blood was inching toward his right ear. He didn't recognize the man who was bald, unshaven, dark-complexioned and appeared to be in his mid-forties.

Paul's first inclination was to phone Leon immediately; however, on further consideration, he decided to wait until he reached the restaurant. What he understood about forensic science included maintaining the integrity of the crime scene, so he wrapped a handkerchief around his hand before he unbuttoned the victim's raincoat and groped in the area of his back pant's pocket. He withdrew a decrepit wallet but refrained from examining all its contents, except the uppermost card in each of two compartments. One was an identification card containing only the name, Rico Cretelli, and a Paris address marked "temporary." The other was a faded business card with the inscription:

Ahmad Khalil, Senior Vice-president
British East India Company

Paul stood dumfounded! In his last investigation for *Vérité,* this company had played a key roll in terms of its activities and particularly, its own personnel and those with whom it had once done important business, including Charles Maurice de Talleyrand-Perigord, Elihu Yale, Napoleon Bonaparte and one Lady Beckett. During the course of his flushing out all he could about such characters—and others—he had incurred the wrath of certain relatives of theirs.

Was this whole assault aimed at himself? A carryover from before? But why shoot that other guy? Who was he, anyway, this … this … Cretelli?

He thought better about what he was about to do but did it anyway. He put the card in his own wallet.

He made it to One Rue Maitre Albert ten minutes before Sylvie was to arrive and in its vacant vestibule, headed straight for a corner farthest from the cascade of chatter and background music emanating from the main dining areas. He still recalled Leon's cell phone number but checked it on the frayed index card folded in his wallet.

Leon answered in a matter of seconds and Paul described the entire jetty episode in great detail. He was caught off guard by the chairman's initial silence but then almost visualized the ensuing emotional outburst of *Vérité's* leader, the kind he was accustomed to seeing and hearing in the past.

"And we haven't even started!" Leon barked.

"Meanwhile," Paul said, "there's a dead body two blocks from here and I suppose I'll have to repeat what I just said to the police."

"Your contact with them was minimal last time, remember?" Leon said. "I'll take care of it, same as always. If they have questions, there won't be many and it won't take up much time." With reference to more than size, Paul had come to picture "the giant" as one with the "highest connections at the highest French levels", and this was another indication of it. Like flicking a switch, he seamlessly shifted into a lower gear: unemotional, definitive, resolute.

"Have a good dinner with Sylvie," Leon said. "She called me about it. And try to relax. Ha! No really, Paul, you need your nourishment and rest. We'll talk more tomorrow."

After thanking Leon, Paul's reaction to the encouragement was one of measured relief—and he still had Sylvie coming up. He felt just shy of giddy that he was about to reunite with her. Why on earth hadn't they kept in touch?

And then she appeared at the front door. They stared at one another for a mere moment. He remained motionless as she came toward him. An Eau Couture fragrance came with her. Their embrace was brief, but not their kiss. Paul stepped back an arm's length and with a hand on each of her shoulders, said, "Here, let me have a look at you." It didn't take long before he followed with, "You look exquisite and enticing." He thought it over. "But are those words too strong?"

Tears glistened in her eyes as she searched for a tissue in her handbag. "No, I like them, Paul," she answered, sighing happily. "You can repeat them as often as you want. Any woman who just reached forty likes to hear talk like that."

She wore a gray pleated silk-chiffon dress that ended slightly above her knees, a hunter green scarf—wrapped twice around and tied in the back—silver peep-toe pump shoes and a plain black silk coat that was unbuttoned. She carried a tiny green umbrella that matched her scarf.

Paul was so overwhelmed, he was nearly lost for words and settled for, "Did you walk or drive?"

"Drove, even though my place is a stone's throw away. I hate rain—no, actually I like rain as long as I'm under cover. It's rain and fog that I hate."

They hadn't yet approached the desk where the maitre d' stood and Paul got a chance to look around, temporarily released from the heaviness of the call to Leon, the jetty, the parapet, the steamy car, the shot, and most of all, the body. The vestibule was adorned with flowers in shallow vases of green and silver.

"See," Paul said with a rush of what he thought was spontaneous cleverness, "they match your outfit. Did you plan it that way?"

"Hardly," she said.

"Any new tattoos anywhere?"

"No, just this silly one of the spider." She lifted her heel off the floor and pointed to a small dark spot on her ankle, barely visible through her black silk stocking. "Why I allowed it to happen, I'll never know."

"Last year when I first saw it," Paul said, "I did some research. Did you know that superstitions surrounding spiders date back to Egyptian times when they were associated with riches? And that Napoleon had a pair of gloves made from spider webs?"

"No. Maybe I should have a web tattooed around the spider."

"*That,* I'd have to see," he said. "And the Napoleon influence doesn't seem to go away, does it? Perfumes, spiders—what else?"

Sylvie took hold of his hand and kissed the back of it. Looking up, she answered softly, "Lovers?"

Paul searched for a response until he found one. "Is that a question or a declaration?" he asked.

"I wish I knew," she answered with obvious doubt. Her smile was coquettish as she turned to march up to the maitre d' while Paul sauntered off to the side and peeked into a moderately-sized dining room straddled by a smaller one and the main one. All were filled to near capacity. He never considered himself an aficionado of décor but was impressed by the skillful mix of modern and traditional tables—both glass and mahogany—and by the marble floor areas and carpets in various shades of red, brown and rust. Even the walls and ceilings were a mixture of limestone and furrowed wooden beams. Again, flowers were everywhere. The music was orchestral and featured old French and American classics.

"Charming," he said when Sylvie joined him

"Wait till you see the fireplace," she said. "It's no doubt the most beautiful in all of Paris. And aren't the aromas in here simply delectable?"

"Yes indeed—'delectable.' Haven't heard that word in years."

They followed a waitress as they angled among the tables in the direction of the main dining room, Sylvie occasionally pausing to address other patrons.

Upon nearing an immense, ornate fireplace spanning an entire wall and consisting of three separate hearths— only the middle one was lit—Paul was speechless but his eyes told of his disbelief. "Guess you're right," he said.

"Dates back to the thirteenth century," she said proudly. "Aren't the flames and crackling sounds comforting?"

"Yes, very."

They sat at a table for two, near the fire.

"You come here often, I take it," Paul said.

"Quite often. I like the food and the atmosphere. And I live close by. I'd say twice a week."

"Twice a week you live close by?"

"No, darling. Twice a week I come here." She looked at him adoringly.

Following an awkward silence, Paul said, "So here we are. Did you ever think we'd meet again?"

"Yes, I knew we would ... some day ... somehow."

"Are you glad?"

"Can't you tell?"

"I hate to sound sentimental, and I haven't even had a drink yet, but I feel the same way." Paul thought he could have said it better.

"I can't believe we never even wrote to each other," Sylvie said.

"Or a phone call now and then."

"I guess we both got caught up in our own responsibilities. Well no matter, do let's not work it that way again. We shared so much last time for it to have ended so abruptly. I promise. Do you?"

"Promise. But who says we'll separate again?"

Sylvie hesitated and didn't answer.

The waitress returned and he ordered a scotch and soda, Sylvie, a Chardonnay.

"Back to our relationship, or lack thereof," Sylvie said. "Of course, Jean was in the picture."

"Yes. Leon no doubt told you we split. But we're still friends."

"I'm sorry and to tell the truth I'm not sorry. I mean about the split. And I want to get back to that before we call it a night. Is that okay?"

"Okay. But let me ask: are you serious with anyone?"

"No, not at all."

Paul was tempted to express his relief, instead saying, "So that makes two of us."

"I know," Sylvie said, contentment in her voice.

She pointed to the smaller dining room. "See that one," she said. "That's for the children of parents who want to eat alone. But this place has a policy. If the kids become too loud or unruly, the family is asked to leave as quickly and conveniently as possible."

"Hmm," Paul said. "But doesn't that hurt business?"

"Not in the slightest. In fact it helps. People are impressed that management sticks to its guns."

Paul paid only slight attention to the waitress who came with their drinks and asked if they had looked at their menus yet. He requested she return in a few minutes while they thought further about their choices. The waitress complied.

Paul bit his lower lip and said, "That's as good an opening as there is."

"Come again," Sylvie said, her brow furrowed.

"Guns. It reminds me—not that it would take much to do so." He then apologized for bringing up his recent ordeal so soon and plunged straight into what had transpired "less than an hour ago." He spent over ten minutes on the issue.

She listened without uttering a word. When he had finished, she reached over the table, gathered both his hands in hers, and squeezed them tightly. "Oh, Paul," she said. "Are you sure you're up to this kind of business again?"

"Why not? It's exciting. The pay isn't bad. And I'll work with you again."

Sylvie did a double take "Wait! Hold it now. Give me that again!"

"The excitement, the pay …"

"No, no—about working with me again. You mean it literally?" She dabbed at a trace of mascara beneath her eye.

"Yes, why not? You, Vincent and I made a great team. If it ain't broke, don't fix it, right?"

Sylvie leaped up, crossed over to his side, wrapped both arms around his neck, kissed him and returned to her chair. They raised their glasses and toasted each other and the team, in that order.

"Paul, my Paul, I accept the invitation!" she cried. "We'll be traveling places, just like before?"

"Just like before, but not all those Napoleon places necessarily—you know, Elba, St. Helena and the like—but mainly to confer with the histarians that Leon and the prior at the Senanque Monastery down in Provence will clue us in on. I'm hoping they can help. I'll also want to visit Grasse while we're in that area—and, naturally, check out *Cleo's*. Then, depending on what develops, I'm sure we'll have other places to go."

"I hear you."

"Now Sylvie, what's germane here is your being able to get the time off. I figure about two weeks, maybe less, maybe more."

"No problem, unless some emergencies arise. I'm pretty much my own boss now. And besides, the grant proposals have all been assigned through October." Her breathing and speech had become heavy. "Oh, Paul," she murmured.

Paul eyed the waitress walking toward them and they both hurried through the menu. She chose roast duck, preceded by soupe a l'oignon. He ordered the same though he wasn't particularly fond of duck. He was preoccupied with his next sentence.

"I plan on meeting with Guy and Maurice tomorrow. Which reminds me, when you met in executive session, the robbery at *Cleo's* was discussed at some length, I take it."

"At *great* length," she said.

"The Vintage formula, the blue bottle, the leather packet, the locked closet, the safe, the way it was cut out, Ken Kuroda, his heritage, his giving up on selling Vintage?"

"Yes. Challenging case."

"So you're well acquainted with it."

"Completely."

Out of nowhere, Paul brought up a subject they had discussed over a year ago. He dwelled on the dangers of chasing down stolen art treasures—170,000 of them world-wide. "And of those," he said, "166 are Rembrandts, 167 Renoirs, 175 Warhols and 200 Dali's. But how many are perfume formulas? *None!*"

They then touched on his most recent cases and the nitty-gritty of her work at the Academy.

The food came and each picked at it. They ordered another drink apiece. Paul checked his watch—nearly 10 p.m. His cell phone rang. It was Leon. Paul listened intently, the phone in his left hand, his other half blocking his right ear.

"The police just called," Leon said in a stern voice. "They couldn't find the body."

"What?" Paul exclaimed. "No! I can't believe it!"

"They scoured the area. There's no dead body within a mile on either side of where you said. But, Paul, these things happen. Somebody might have picked him up and taken him to a hospital. They're calling around right now."

"Or dumped him somewhere. I can't believe it!"

Paul wanted badly to pace, but cramped by the space, merely rose and walked around their table one time, then sat heavily back onto his chair.

"You're still at the restaurant?" Leon asked.

"Yeah, we're still here." Paul stirred in his chair, his face contorted in a deep frown.

"Well, later on, get a good night's sleep. I'll call you around nine or nine-thirty in the morning. And one other thing. They don't need to question you. I took care of it. And they'll keep it out of the papers."

"Well that's something to be thankful for anyway. With the mood I'm in, I'm not even sure I could *give* an accurate account of what happened. Then there's the business of being incognito for as long as possible. I realize the police already know I'm here on the perfume case, but the more in touch we are, the more likely it becomes public knowledge. At least that's been my experience everywhere else. And I'm not criticizing police at all. It's just a question of being spotted in their company … eager reporters and the paparazzi and so on.

"So thanks for that, Leon." Paul paused, unsure of whether he should share his next thought with the chairman. But he did. "Wish I knew if that whole jetty scene fits in with the bigger picture," he said. "It's bugging the hell out of me."

"It may take some time, but we'll see." Paul reckoned it was the chairman's only logical response.

After relating what Leon had said, Paul stared at Sylvie and repeated for the third time, "I can't believe it."

"But, Paul, it's not your fault. They'll come up with an answer—eventually. Maybe someone threw him it in the water. Who cares? It probably doesn't matter in the greater scheme of things."

He gulped down the rest of his drink and suggested they skip dessert and leave. When they reached the vestibule, Sylvie took hold of his arm and said in a hushed voice, "May I ask you an unrelated question?"

"Sure," he replied, his face somewhat calmer.

"What did you mean when you said I was 'enticing'?"

Paul first studied her eyes, then her lips. "I meant I want you," he said.

"Your place or mine?"

"Mine."

"Good, I'll drive."

THE NAPOLEON CONNECTION

Chapter 4

As promised, Leon phoned Paul at 9:30 the next morning. "Feeling better?" he asked. Paul rolled around in bed to check that he was alone.

"Much. Sorry for my reaction last night, Leon. It's just that the news caught me by surprise. Did the police call back about the hospitals?"

"Yes. No sign of him. So let's let it go for now. But Paul, something's been nagging at me. If whoever was in the car was out to get you, why did they shoot the guy on foot? And was he really tailing you in the first place?"

"I'd *swear* he was. Maybe they thought he was my bodyguard."

"Of course. I never thought of that."

"It could be that the whole thing wasn't connected to the *Cleo* heist at all but was a holdover from last year. You know: the Talleyrand and Lady Beckett stuff."

"I see," Leon said. "But then again, it may not. So you don't need me to remind you to be cautious. And I'd advise you to have Vincent nearby as often as possible."

"Definitely."

"That brings me to today's schedule. You said you wanted to spend some time with Guy and Maurice. Last night you took care of Sylvie … er … sorry … I mean you consulted with her."

Paul cleared his throat.

Leon went on. "That leaves Ken at *Cleo's* and Frère Dominic, not too far from there. Which means you can fly to Grasse tonight if you wish. Or wait till the morning. Whatever time you think you'll need. Remember, my *Breezer* and its pilot can be ready within an hour at most. I still keep the plane at that little airstrip east of here."

"Ah, yes. The one with no official name until you dubbed it de Gaulle Junior."

"Right on," Leon said. "Now I hate to do your thinking for you, but I would guess you don't need Vincent along for the Maurice or Guy visits later, but that he should accompany you on the flight south." It was more a statement than a question.

"Sounds about right," Paul responded, still sleepy.

"And speaking of Maurice, he's an expert on Napoleon history as I'm sure you learned last time, but coincidence of all coincidences, he's just as knowledgeable about perfumes. Napoleon used a lot of it, as you may know, but also Maurice grew up in Grasse. He might agree to give you a brief tutorial about the history of perfumes and the perfume industry. If you want my opinion, I don't think it would hurt. You never know if you might pick up some pearl that could throw light on the task before us. Your opinion?"

"My opinion?" Paul rubbed his eyes. "I agree, except I don't think Maurice can give *a brief* tutorial about anything." He bit his tongue over the comment. "I mean he's a bit long-winded and ... oh, I don't know what I mean."

Leon reacted quickly. "As I've heard so many of your citizens put it, 'I get your drift.' And I agree, but listen to him carefully. He's been around a long time—and all in the right places. You might find that pearl among his blither and blather."

"Amen," Paul said. "I'll definitely ask him about perfumes. God knows, I'm completely in the dark on the subject." He rubbed his chin. "And in case you're wondering, the reason I want to meet with the two of them is simply to touch base as well as learn about the perfume business and get updated on histarians—which I assume is still in Guy's domain."

"Yes, his and Frère Dom's."

They both said nothing for a full fifteen seconds. Finally, the chairman said, "I take it you're wondering whether to fly tonight or tomorrow?"

"You're too much, Leon," Paul said with a polite laugh, "but you're exactly right. Look, let's make it tonight. Maurice and Guy aren't going to take up the whole day—one this morning, the other, early afternoon. So, yes, let's do it that way. Would we fly into Avignon like before?"

"No, make it the international airport in Nice—closer to Grasse, maybe a thirty-minute drive."

"Good, we can stay overnight and meet with the *Cleo's* people—especially Ken—first thing tomorrow morning. It's a Saturday. That wouldn't present a problem, would it?"

"I doubt it, but I'll find out. I can call Ken and let you know. Since here to there takes about three hours, maybe you should leave our airstrip … say around four this afternoon? How's that sound?"

"Perfect. And you'll alert your pilot?"

"Yes, and Vincent. I'll take care of that."

"One other thing, Leon. I'd like Sylvie to come along.

I promised her she'd be part of the whole operation like the last time around."

"I have no problem with it, Paul. In fact they're a great addition, those two—lots of brains."

"And fortitude."

"That, too."

Paul grinned to himself. "So that's it," he said. "We each have our calls to make; I'll meet with Guy and Maurice; and either you call me or I'll call you when—about noon?"

"Yes. I'll call *you*."

Paul phoned Sylvie first. She was overjoyed and said she'd be ready. Next he phoned Maurice and Guy who both agreed to meet with him separately at the Café de Flore, at the corner of the Boulevard Saint-Germain and Rue St. Benoit. It was the place Paul had recommended for two specific reasons related to his prior Paris visits. Reasons that gave him great comfort. First, in conjunction with his former position at Yale, he had written extensively about existentialist philosophers like Kierkegaard and Nietzsche, and this café had once been at the heart of the Existentialist Movement. And, second, authors and philosophers Camus, Sartre and Simone de Beauvoir had met there regularly.

Maurice said he would arrive at eleven, Guy at twelve-thirty. Paul decided to forego breakfast and use the upcoming first meeting as brunch. As he showered, he ran through all he recollected about the military man.

As far as he could tell, most who knew Maurice considered him a legitimate expert with long stints in the French Foreign Legion; as teacher and advisor at the Special Military School of St. Cyr; and with the Gendarmerie

Nationale, the country's military police force. He was of average height and stooped, with tremorous hands, and appeared in his mid-eighties though Leon had said he was sixty-six. A black beret was his constant companion as was an elaborate cane. Thin and somewhat wasted, his face was perpetually blank with wizened pockets beneath both eyes. Loose-fitting horn-rimmed glasses seemed fastened halfway down his nose. He spoke deliberately, teasing out each word as if never having uttered it before, and staring as if trying to impress someone behind you. Once started, he usually capitalized on the opportunity to ramble on about various Napoleonic military battles, the process seemingly endless as he detailed the same things over and over from different points of view. Paul diagnosed the condition as perseveration (an uncle had been assigned such a diagnosis) and had quickly learned to interrupt the flow as soon as he grasped what the man was trying to explain. But he didn't understand why Maurice never slurred his speech despite the alcohol on his breath. Was the intermixture of fast aging, tremors, perseveration and even the breath, some kind of illness—a central nervous system syndrome? Nonetheless, Paul assessed Maurice's mind as sharp. A year had passed, though. Leon would have mentioned it if he were worse. Paul would find out soon enough.

He took a taxi to the café and walked under its white awning a little before eleven. The classic Art Deco interior of all-red seating, mahogany and a myriad of mirrors hadn't varied a bit since he was last there. Nor—for practical purposes—had it ever since World War II, he was once informed.

Within minutes, Maurice came limping in, seemingly

none the worse for wear. If anything, his walk was brisker and his smile broader than Paul remembered. He made sure his own smile conveyed a sense of appreciation for the old man's willingness to meet. Neither spoke as they exchanged handshakes and an embrace.

Maurice was the first to speak. "Welcome back to Paris, my friend," he said. "Yes sir, my *good* friend, and I don't have many anymore—the way they're passing away. In droves, they are, just suddenly passing away, like opening up your fist." He made a fist, and did just that. "And another thing, thank you for accepting this new challenge. It's simply awful, it is, the nerve of whoever—I mean whomever—to make away with something so important to that there Mr. Ken, or whatever his name is. Simply awful."

Paul knew immediately that he'd be interrupting at a speedy rate before their meeting was over. As Maurice inhaled to start another sentence, Paul said, "Good to see you again, Maurice. Leon tells me you were born and raised in Grasse. That's where we're headed tomorrow, to see the crime scene at *Cleo's* and meet with Ken."

"Ken?"

"Yes, Ken the owner, the one you just mentioned."

"Ah, of course, and why not? It's the smart thing to do. Now getting back to my upbringing … but pardon me, Paul, you game for sitting out there on the terrace? All I want at this hour is a coffee and croissant. My real lunch I have at two. Hope I make myself clear. I don't have two lunches. It's at two that I have my single lunch. In fact, I already prepared a sandwich before I left. It's in the refrigerator. You game? I mean, sitting on the terrace?"

"That would be fine. Then I could ask you some

questions about perfumes, okay?"

"Okay. But first, getting back to my upbringing, and I'm quite certain you know that Grasse is the perfume capital of the entire world. It was just about that way when I was in grade school there. So perfumery and my early years go hand in hand. In fact, perfumery shaped my entire life. Shaped it, it did."

Paul gently took hold of Maurice's arm and led the way to the terrace where a waiter assigned them a table among the many that were filled.

"In what way did perfumery shape your life?" Paul asked.

Without hesitation Maurice replied. "First off, you know about my understanding of Napoleon and his military talent and his ways. Ways with his ambitions, ways with the women, and—surprise—ways with perfumes."

"Your understanding? Absolutely, but not of the perfumes as related to him. I'm also vaguely familiar with the fact that Napoleon fancied perfumes, especially the one called Vintage by Cleo's. It supposedly dates back to him, as a user. And to Cleopatra. That's how the company got its name. At least that's what they advertise, and it's the extent to which I understand the connection."

Paul had deliberately made his explanation somewhat vague and circuitous, hoping that in Maurice's corrections, the pearl that Leon had referred to would show up.

"And it's true," Maurice stressed. "It's true advertising. Which is rare nowadays. Anyway, oh yes. Yes, indeed. It's well documented that the emperor and his entire court were mesmerized by fragrances. He, himself, used more than sixty bottles a month because he believed the smell stimulated his brain. And stimulated the women, too.

His Josephine—she was Creole, you know—but that's a different story. She developed a passion for penetrating scents and as a result got the nickname 'muskfool'".

No pearl yet.

"And speaking of stimulating his brain," Maurice said, "so did arsenic. He intertwined the fingers of both hands. "Now don't think I've gone daffy—at least not completely—but, as you know, arsenic was used in his day as a recreational drug when taken in small quantities. But what if someone wanted to poison him by sneaking larger quantities into his food or drink? Enough to do the job but so small he couldn't tell the difference. This, my friend, would be a form of bioterrorism."

"Of what?"

"Bioterrorism. It's a distinct entity today and I've been reading up on it. Yes sir, it would have been considered a form of bioterrorism against one man. But who equates Napoleon with just one man? Why, he was the equivalent of several armies, for heaven's sake. But getting back to arsenic, they found some of it in his hair samples. But who's to say the hair was definitely his? Makes no difference though—he used or was given arsenic, period. And if he was fed it unbeknownst to him, then it was a biological thing—bioterrorism.

"As I told you once before, Paul—or was it twice? Napoleon was a different person during the last of his battles. His judgment was erratic or better put, 'son etat mental'—his mental state. Once the arsenic accumulated— it tends to do that, you know—then *pow*." He pounded a fist into his other hand. "That was it. He started to make error after error. Take the Russian campaign, eighteen and twelve. Errors you'd never dream of. What happened to his brilliant diamond-shaped formation—eighteen and six against Prussia? His square battalion? His spider web tactic and his envelopment attack? All gone, or poorly carried out. What am I leading up to? I'm not sure exactly, except to advise you to keep bioterrorism in mind. I have a sneaking suspicion that you'll come across it in your travels—not necessarily the act of it but the subject. In fact I'd bet heavily on it because all countries are turning their attention to it. It's the wave of the future."

A waiter appeared and Maurice ordered his coffee and croissant, as did Paul, who also asked for orange juice. As Paul gazed around the terrace, he happened to spot a man seated alone six tables away. The man had just lowered an open newspaper from a position that hid his face. He glanced at Paul, then quickly returned the paper to its original position. Paul recognized him at once. There was no doubt. Scarhead! In Paris?

Paul looked away for a few seconds, trying to appear inconspicuous. When he looked back, the man was gone.

"You just turned pale," Maurice said. "What's wrong? You sick or somethin'?"

"What?" Paul replied, distantly. "Oh no, just a little indigestion I guess. But getting back to perfumes. You said perfumery shaped your life. How?"

"Thought you'd never ask, old buddy. First of all, there are two things that compete for the world's oldest professions and they both start with the letter 'P': prostitution and perfumery. I call them two "P's" in a pod—and they're really that close. I mean they often work together, or I should say they 'go' together. The same with Napoleon and perfumes. Now throw in another. Me. Are you with me so far?"

"Well, yes, except for the last part."

"It'll come together. I'll make it. I come from a perfume family in Grasse. My parents, my brothers, my aunts, my uncles, my cousins—they all worked in the same leather and perfume factory there. By the way, early leather and perfumes go together too. In the old days lots of people didn't like the smell of leather, so manufacturers soaked it in perfume. Then the same people got sick from the perfume, especially if it got on their hands, so the saying went, 'Take your gloves off before you shake hands.' And I didn't make that up; it's true. Now where was I?"

Paul had finished his croissant. He rested his elbows on the table, his closed fists on either side of his chin. "You said your whole family worked in the perfume factory."

"The same? No, nearly the same. I mean there were two of them, across the street from each other."

"So it was almost the same." Paul wanted Maurice to remember he was still there.

"The point I'm leading up to is that I worked in one of them, too—summers, when we were off from school. I learned all about the industry: that perfumes have been around for more than four thousand years; that it was first used by the Egyptians as a cleansing tool by burning incense; that they used it as medicine, specifically in skin treatment and that eventually they realized its worth as a cosmetic and a seduction device. They said Cleopatra used it to conquer the Romans and Bathsheba, used it to seduce King Solomon. Speaking of Cleopatra, she was influential in spreading its use among the Greeks and conquered Romans. In fact the first actual perfume factory was built in Greece. Then about five hundred years ago, France—our France—became the center of the industry. I already mentioned its use on leather gloves, but it was also applied to clothing and furniture. And medical uses came back into the picture: doctors, considered smart over this, went around claiming that scents like lavender and rosemary could ward off the Black Plague. Not to mention today's aromatherapy, a questionable practice in my opinion—but hey, if it works, it works."

Maurice took a breath. "Shall I go on?" he asked.

"Please do. You haven't gotten to how it shaped your life."

"Oh that? Yes, of course. That's what I started to say. But first I need to cover one or two more things about perfumes and I'll just skim through it. What constitutes a perfume? A mixture of alcohol, essential oils, a fixative and in the modern era, chemically created scent. And what's a scent? It's the same as 'fragrance'. Some know-it-alls make a distinction. I think they're the same thing. So 'what are some of the common fragrances', you ask? No, you didn't ask, did you? But I'll mention a few anyway, if you don't mind. Rose, frankincense, orange blossom, spice, sandalwood, jasmine, sportif ... let's see ... you've heard of Eau de Cologne? That's one, too. It happens to be the longest-lived fragrance on the market today and was one of Napoleon's favorites. And the last thing I'll say about perfume itself is that there's no legal protection for a perfume formula. So theoretically anybody can mix a batch of ingredients and come up with a beautiful blend the same as somebody else's, and is not guilty of copyright infringement. There's no such thing. I refer to it as the third 'P' in that pod: piracy. So there are plenty of copycats out there—and it's all legal. Now, whether or not this has anything to do with the incident at *Cleo's*, I can't say. One thing I *can* say though—and it's related to what we've … I've … been talking about—is that in the old days, the perfumers hardly ever looked at a formula even if they had one. They knew it all by heart. It was automatic."

Paul wrinkled his forehead and released his fists from his face. The pearl?

"So, finally—why all this background influenced my life. Very uncomplicated; very simple. While learning all about the business way back then in Grasse, Napoleon was mentioned practically every day because of his fondness for various fragrances. He even took loads of perfume onto the battlefields, you know. It was as if he became the industry's spokesman even though he died in 1821. Well, one thing led to another: I studied him, his many campaigns, his love affairs and so on. I was led, thereby, into the military field."

He then embarked on a review that Paul had heard before, the one about the Foreign Legion, the Special Military School, and America's West Point Academy. Paul listened patiently.

"To think it all started with perfumes," Maurice said. His face was solemn.

Each checked his watch. Two minutes to twelve. Paul's cell phone vibrated at his hip and he answered it. "Hold on," Paul said. He cupped his hand over the phone and whispered to Maurice that he would handle the bill. Maurice got up and extended his hand. Paul shook it and said he would be in touch. They thanked each other and Maurice left, his gait stiffer than an hour before.

It was Leon on the phone and Paul briefed him on the meeting, indicating that it was a valuable one and one in which he may have picked up a pearl or two but didn't specify. As agreed upon last time around, it was a given between the two of them that only *definitive* information would be shared. Other kinds of information in various stages of development might be temporarily withheld. But Paul did call attention to Maurice's discourse on perfumes, flowers and Napoleon.

"That's ironic," Leon said. "I was about to tell you: I got word that there's some kind of silent rift in Grasse between *Cleo's* and the town folks—about *Cleo's* not favoring local growers for the company's perfume production. Maybe you should make some subtle inquiries."

"Will do."

Leon then said all was ready for the four o'clock flight to Nice and Paul indicated he'd be at the airstrip on time.

"Vincent will pick me up?"

"Yes, he'll be in the lobby at three-thirty."

"And Ken for tomorrow?"

"That's all set too. He'll be at *Cleo's* at nine and he's anxious to meet you."

"The feeling's mutual," Paul said, "and that's in spades."

Paul had about thirty minutes before Guy arrived. The day was clear, windless and humidity-free. He decided to take a walk to clear his mind in preparation for what he was certain would be a wholly different type of meeting, and in deference to that preparation, he promised himself he would postpone any dissection of Maurice's words and ideas. Plus he had time to spare. He paid the waiter, gave him a generous tip and indicated he would return in half an hour for a second meeting, requesting the same table.

Paul walked away with no destination in mind. He would work it the way he always had whenever he had an engagement, but time to spare, whether having driven or walked to the agreed upon location. The thought of simply sitting and waiting, reading a book or magazine, was counter to his make-up. Rather, he would start a slow walk or drive, using up exactly half the time, then turn around and head back. However, it never panned out as designed and he was unable to figure out why. He would still show up early because the trip back always took less time. Or so it seemed. He would never concede that he drove faster or walked faster. A short time later, the waiter ushered him to the same table at twelve-twenty-two and he waited for Guy.

As he'd done prior to his appointment with Maurice, he reviewed in his mind's eye all he could recall about Guy. There would be just enough time.

Compared to the military/perfume man, Guy Martin, the newspaperman, was quite a different story. For years an investigative reporter for the *International Herald Tribune,* he knew more about France and its history than anyone Paul had ever met with the possible exception of Leon. But there was more to Guy than that. Like the chairman, he had connections at the highest levels; came close to Maurice in terms of Napoleonic lore; but most significantly, had direct and quick access to a worldwide network of histarians.

Paul admired the reporter—and trusted him, which is not to say he didn't trust the others. But in Guy's case, there was the addition of substance, of complete credibility, of his having no reason to bend or otherwise modify the truth. And Paul doubted that this would have changed.

He also associated Guy with the sidewalk cafés of Paris, particularly the *Brasserie Lipp,* the site of yesterday's meeting with Leon. It was there, last year, that Paul and Guy had first met and "wined" their way through a prolonged conversation about Guy's professional background and his experiences with the histarians. It was that experience that had played such a vital role in the resolution of the Napoleon case, and Paul was counting on its playing a similar role this time around.

He didn't know the reason why but he looked around for Scarhead, saw no one even resembling the man and forced himself to drop the still disturbing thought of his presence in Paris. Except for one last, "Why?"

In fact all his thoughts began to trail off, and none too soon, for he noticed Guy approaching the terrace from the side and greeting the waiter.

"Oh, it is you, monsieur," Paul heard the waiter say. "Welcome, welcome. I believe I have the right table for you. An American?"

Guy nodded and rushed over toward Paul who rose and met him halfway. "Well, hello, stranger," Guy said.

"Stranger? It's only been a year," Paul countered. "But you're right. I love Paris and all you guys. I really should come over more often—on business or whatever." Their handshake was firm, sincere and prolonged. Paul then put his arm around Guy's waist, leading him to their table.

He was a chunky man, a head shorter than Paul, with

a poker face until he smiled, pale cheeks, flint hair that appeared ironed, a pencil-thin mustache, and occasionally a brightly colored beret. A chain-smoker, he puffed rapid-fire, in harmony with the cadence of his speech. He wore a dark shirt with sleeves rolled up to the elbows, matching pleated trousers and a polka dot bow tie. Always a bow tie.

"So," Guy said, slightly short of breath. "You're about to flirt with the unknown once again."

Paul winked at him and replied, "Danger might be a better word."

"Other than that, how have you been?"

"Busy and sometimes bushed, but holding my own. And you?"

"About the same. I could call it a 'year of sameness', I suppose."

The pleasantries over, Paul couldn't wait to ask the next question. "You still have your band of histarians scattered about?"

"Oh yes, to be sure. Only more of them, and I believe even better informed than when you last dealt with them."

"That's possible?"

"Well, maybe not *better* informed, just informed about more things."

The waiter returned promptly. They each indicated that neither was very hungry and would settle for splitting a ham and cheese sandwich to go with their coffees.

"Now then," Guy said, spreading a napkin on his lap, "before you bring it up, I wrote the article about the stolen formula not because I wanted to but because my boss wanted me to. Somehow he had gotten wind of it. But I simply reported it as a theft. I never mentioned its being cut out—safe and all—just that it was missing. How would I know about the extent the perp or perps would go to steal the packet? I called Ken Kuroda for some background and he told me—but, as I said, I left the cutting part out."

"The article's perfectly okay, Guy. Doesn't affect anything I have to do. Whether the perp—incidentally, we're calling him or her 'Mr. X'—whether he had a key to the safe, or blew it up, or cut it away—doesn't change anything. The end result is that someone had the nerve to commit that sort of crime."

"Good. That's out of the way. You mentioned things you have to do. Any specific requests of me? What can I do to help at this point?"

"It's a very early point, so nothing specific … not yet anyway. Although I'll get to a general issue in a minute."

"Care to share how you plan to proceed?"

"You won't print it, will you?" Paul replied, a twinkle in his eye.

"Hell, no. My boss doesn't even know we're conferring."

"Well, most of this you know, I'm sure. I've met with Sylvie and Maurice and at length with Leon and Vincent. Leon's scheduled me with Dom and Ken for tomorrow—I'll fly south with Vincent and Sylvie. I'm hoping Dom might have some inside information already, but in any event, I'll ask him to arrange meetings with French historians. That is, if he feels that's important at this stage."

"But they'll learn all about the theft."

Paul scrutinized Guy from the waist up. "Guy, it's

been in all the papers."

"Oh, of course. I guess I meant how the theft occurred."

It was the first time Paul recalled hearing the reporter on the defensive, but pretended it was no big deal.

"When I see Ken in Grasse, I'll have a chance to visit the crime scene … and oh, here's something I hadn't thought of … something you could look into."

"Name it," Guy said firmly, no doubt trying to compensate for his earlier blunder.

"Not that I'm a forensic expert, but I've had *some* experience. If you could get your hands on any official documents dealing with the crime—photographs, police reports, forensic reports and so on, I'd like to take a look at them."

"Consider it done, if they're available to me. I'll try, but if I have no luck, you might ask Leon. With his police background throughout France, he's probably the one with the most clout in that area."

"You know, you're right," Paul said sheepishly.

Guy flashed a knowing smile.

"I guess we're even now," Paul said. "Let's put it this way: between the two of you, while I'm traveling here and there, maybe those official things can be obtained. It's really not that urgent. Come to think of it, after examining the crime scene and meeting with Ken, I may not need them after all."

"Whatever. I'll look into it."

"Good! I'm glad that's over. Sorry I screwed up what I'd intended to say."

"No you didn't. Take the things on your mind about the case; dealing with the delegation members; wondering about whether histarians can help; and probably more concerns I don't even know about—add them all up, and you're entitled to screw up a bit which you didn't."

"Thanks, Guy. And for meeting with me like this. I forgot to tell you that before." The waiter returned with the meal. Paul consulted an index card and made an abbreviated notation.

"Okay then," he said, "about the general issue. No matter how we view it, whether it was a crime among competitors, an inside job, or a reflection of something we haven't even encountered yet, Napoleon and Cleopatra seem to enter the picture—the whole mix."

Guy nodded judiciously.

"Because of that, I might have to visit some Napoleon landmarks — his grave or graves, maybe Elba, hopefully not St. Helena … too far, and Cleopatra's haunts in Egypt. If so, and if necessary, can you arrange for me to meet with some appropriate historians? Some who might shed light on the relationship between perfumes and these two giants. I realize they both savored fragrances of all sorts, but maybe we could extract some clues related to the theft that might be lingering somewhere—though this might be far-fetched."

"I still have my histarian alliances and I'd be happy to narrow them down to the one or two who live in those areas and might help the most. So let me know if the need arises."

The conversation continued between bites for another ten minutes. Guy's cell phone sounded, a melodious and large sound, probably louder than necessary. Heads turned their way.

"Sorry, Paul. Hello."

Guy listened for a minute at most and said, "Yes, I do remember. Vaguely. I'm on my way. And Helen? Thanks."

He returned the phone to its case. "Sorry I have to rush off," he said. "Some kind of deadline at work. Can I have the bill?"

"No, I'll handle it, and thanks for taking the time. We'll be talking."

When Paul stepped off the terrace, he noticed a string of taxis parked along Rue St. Benoit. He started casually in that direction. Two other vehicles caught his attention: a bus parking across the street from the stationary taxis and a taxi that screeched to a halt at the head of the line. One man emerged from the bus and walked toward Paul. He was dressed in black—jacket, shirt, trousers. His right arm was crossed over his chest, his hand buried under the left side of his jacket.

At the same time, another man leaped from the newly arrived taxi. He wore nearly the same-colored clothes except his shirt was gray. But his hand position was identical to that of the man who'd stepped off the bus.

Paul's eyes jerked from one man to the other, knowing what the hand position signified. He turned and ran as he yanked his own pistol from his shoulder rig and transferred it to his side pocket. The two men came at him, one on the same sidewalk Paul was negotiating, the other from across the street.

He never had an opportunity to check their faces as he bolted from store front to store front. One pursuer gained on him, and then the other. Neither said a word. The action stimulated mid-day observers, some joining the chase themselves at a safe distance, their voices crescendoing. Faces suddenly appeared at second and third-story windows. Cars stopped, bumpers touched, horns blew, drivers gawked. Some shouted obscenities. Paul ducked down a narrow steep alleyway that reeked of exhaust fumes from passing cars above. He ran at full speed nearly its full length, his feet making crunching sounds on broken glass, loose cobblestones, brick pieces and other assorted rubble—but now he had no choice.

And then the shot! It reminded him of the one at the jetty, only clearer, more resounding, less muffled by soupy fog. He wasn't hit but feared more. None came. He continued his run, looked back for a split second and seeing no one, slithered behind a heap of barrels. He pulled out both pistols and peered around. He detected nothing strange at first but as he wiped sweat from his eyelids, he spotted one of the men spread-eagled on the ground about forty yards away. His gun lay nearby. The other pursuer was nowhere to be seen, but Paul was reluctant to assume less than the worst. Was the supine man a decoy?

Paul eased out half-crouched and, leading with his pistols, inched back up the incline and sidled up to the motionless man. He stared at his face and recoiled in horror. It was the unmistakable face of Scarhead!

He returned his guns to their rigs and scampered up the side steps of a building complex, onto an enormous esplanade. Amidst a crowd of people, munching meals at metal tables, talking in groups, or walking every which way, he mingled among them, shoulders hunched, hands limp in the side pockets of his trousers. He wondered if it had all been a dream. He pinched his cheek and almost said aloud, "This was no dream, folks!" After a few minutes, he found a taxi to deliver him back to the

Meridien Montparnasse.

In the lobby, the desk clerk—Henri, Paul had learned by now—signaled him. "Monsieur," he said, "the same man as before ... he asked if you are still registered here. I said, 'oui'. I asked if I might please have his name so I could inform you. He said, 'I have no name to give out.'"

"Thanks, Henri," Paul said, with an outward show of disinterest. What now?

As expected, on the floor by the door of his room, he found another neatly typed note. It read:

FAULT ROSETTA STONE AND ELGIN MARBLES
UNLESS YOU DO NOT MIND A TURNAROUND

He stood flabbergasted, mouthing, "First I'm warned to clear out of the city, and now this cryptic message." He shook his head as if to dislodge water from his ears. But why pick these British Museum pieces?

Scarhead killed, two notes, the jetty scene, a dead and lost body. Paul didn't need his fingers to confirm he'd been in Paris only forty-eight hours. It seemed like forty-eight days.

Chapter 5

Paul had intended not to notify Leon about the existence of the first note, but the second one, along with Scarhead's death, changed his mind. Leon hadn't even known there *was* a Scarhead.

Paul and Vincent arrived at the airstrip at four sharp. They both agreed that the weather conditions were ideal for flying: the sky a cloudless blue, very little wind, no storms brewing anywhere between Paris and Nice.

Leon and Sylvie were already there. Ansel, the pilot, was in the light plane which could be seen not too far off on the compact runway.

After Paul had kissed Sylvie and shaken Leon's hand, he signaled for the group to gather together for some information he'd withheld from them, without going into the reasons why. In addition, he said he wanted to share some recent news. He first covered the whole Scarhead story, from the man's appearance on the flight to Paris, in the Café de Flore and finally as a dead body in "the damned smelly alleyway." He then commented on Scarhead's killer, referring to him as "Shooterman". But he spent more time on both notes left under his hotel door.

All speculated on various aspects of the revelations, Leon labeling them in pithy sentences: some expected, some unexpected, some to be taken seriously, some probably pure bluff. He put his arm around Paul and continued with a brief commentary. "Hang in there," he said. "Let's not let it deter us. We have an important schedule ahead of us. I'll think on what you just said, and I'm sure you have and will continue to. We'll get to these questions when you get back. Who knows: maybe some answers will show up after you talk to Ken and Dom."

Sylvie was less stoical. "Just be sure Vincent's with you as much as possible," she said, obviously trying to curb her emotions. She looked at her colleague. "Right, Vincent?"

"Right," he answered. "And keep those pistols on your person—or under your pillow at night."

Paul smirked and said, "Well, those developments are off my mind. Ha! So let's get going." All but Leon hurried out onto the runway.

Three hours later, they touched down at the Nice International Airport, their plane dwarfed by the airliners of Air France, Alitalia, American Airlines and Virgin Express. It was 7:15 p.m. Ansel negotiated Leon's light plane with ease, taxiing off to the side and bringing it to a standstill. He was tall and blond, neatly dressed in a blue blazer, blue shirt and red and gray striped tie. He spoke for the first time.

"You know what name Leon gave this aircraft?" he asked, patting the back of the empty seat next to him. *"Little Mongoose*. It's tiny but fast."

"Good job," Paul said. "So smooth I slept."

The others chimed in with their own versions of kind words.

The hotel where Leon had made reservations, the Hotel Campanile Nice Airport, was nearby on the

Promenade des Anglais. He had mentioned it was across the road, a five-minute walk from the airport. They did it in less. As they entered the lobby, Paul reminded the others that the meeting with Ken was set for nine in the morning, to be followed by the one with Frère Dominic at the Cistercian Abbey Notre-Dame-de-Senanque in Gordes, ninety minutes away. That one was scheduled for two o'clock.

"So, Ansel, tomorrow we could leave here at, say, four or five, and make it back to Paris by eight at the latest. Is that about right?"

"Right on the nose," the pilot responded.

At the modest, nondescript hotel, they learned that the reservations were for three rooms. It seemed obvious that what Leon had in mind was individual rooms for Paul and Sylvie and a shared room for Vincent and Ansel. They so divvied them up.

The desk clerk said that *Perfumes by Cleo* was in the center of town, about a twenty-five minute drive away, and that shuttle buses left every ten minutes.

"We also have an appointment in Gordes tomorrow," Paul said. "Is there a bus or do we have to rent a car?"

"Will you be returning here?" the clerk asked.

"Yes." Paul looked at his watch. "I'd say we'd like to leave from Gordes at about three or four."

"Then renting a car would be your best bet. I can arrange it for you."

Paul checked with the other two before saying, "Please do. We'll take the shuttle to town here but use the car for our Gordes trip."

None of them was particularly hungry so they ordered sandwiches "to go" at a small coffee shop just off the lobby, but agreed to meet there for breakfast at seven-forty-five a.m.

After Paul opened the door to his room, he checked the floor without even thinking—a habit that had formed quickly and was likely to continue for the foreseeable future. He saw no notes this time and breathed the biggest sigh of relief he could muster.

The bus pulled to a stop on one of Grasse's side streets at a few minutes before nine a.m. But the driver didn't refer to it as a street. "This is the square you want," he said.

"How beautiful!" Sylvie exclaimed as she disembarked. "The setting, the fragrant aroma." She inhaled slowly and pointed to large slabs of old stone underfoot, low cinderblock walls strategically placed for sitting, and rows of alternating trees and black designer lampposts. Lavender plants surrounded everything that could be surrounded.

"Oui," the driver shouted, "we enjoy it every day. And there—over there—is the building you asked about."

Sylvie called Paul aside and said, "Vincent and I have discussed it and decided that you should consider both of us as just tagging along. We'll give input only when you ask for it, unless we feel you're not picking up on something, and if so, we promise to be discreet about it. We figure we can help by taking notes. In fact we flipped a coin to see who would do it, and Vincent won."

"So, he'll take notes?"

"No, I will."

They chuckled and then Sylvie returned to the heart of what she was saying. "That way you can proceed uninhibited except by your own standards. After all, you're the pro at this, not us." She jabbed Vincent in the side and Paul noticed.

"Thank you," Paul said. "But stay alert."

She led the way, followed by Vincent and Paul who carried a briefcase. Ansel had stayed behind at the hotel assuring the others that he would find plenty to do, if only to nap or browse around.

The *Perfumes by Cleo* factory was ahead of them, forming the end of a dead end street—or square—which technically wasn't a square at all, for it flared out into the shape of a flat tuba. Paul wondered aloud why such a building and others they'd passed were called factories.

"They don't deserve it," he said. "Especially this one. Doesn't look like any factory I know of."

It was an elegant, two-story structure with yellow siding, shuttered windows and balconies of patterned wrought iron. The roof was flat with a cupola at its center. The square's lampposts continued over into a massive grass courtyard with features one could not ignore. Off to the side was a large freestanding stone sign, lavender on white. It read:

PERFUMES BY CLEO
SINCE 1888

Below the second line was a design of a triangle with one word in the middle: "Cleo's". A similar sign graced the roof directly above the main entrance. A tall bronze statue of a smiling woman with outstretched arms was positioned next to the sign on the grass. Hugging the entire front and sides of her body were four rows of shelves stacked with bottles. Her hands held tiny sacs of perfume ingredients, and towels were draped over her arms. The statue's pedestal bore its own sign:

THE COSTUME OF A PERFUME-MAKER

The building's main entryway was plain, large and directly in line with the cupola above. Its door, level to the ground, was topped with thick glass, curved to resemble an arch.

"This is it." Paul opened the door. "In more ways than one," he added as an afterthought.

An attractive receptionist sat at a counter in the middle of a large round room. The fragrant scent was stronger than it was outside, but not offensive. Soft music was barely audible. Behind her, one wide oak door was contoured into the cement walls of the room. On the right, empty perfume bottles of all sizes, shapes and colors lined three tiers of shelves that rimmed half a wall. A bottom shelf contained rows of soaps stacked like scented bricks. On the left were tables of bowls laden with fresh flowers of every color.

Vincent motioned for Paul to draw near and then whispered, "Either nothing's being manufactured in this place or those walls are soundproof."

"I heard you, and I agree," Sylvie said softly.

The receptionist looked up and said, "Sorry but I heard you, too, and there's plenty going on back there. Our workers are just quiet—and efficient. But greetings. Warm greetings to *Cleo's*."

She rose to a height as tall as the statue outside. With probing eyes she said, "My name's Camille. May I ask if you might be the delegation to see Mr. Kuroda?"

Paul's first impression of the woman was not a nice one and he felt like saying, "You got it, sister." Instead he answered, "Yes, indeed. I believe he's expecting us."

"Correct, and that's why I asked," she said. "If you go through that door … ," she pointed over her shoulder with a thumb … "his office is the first on the right."

"Thank you, ma'am," Paul said, giving a snappy salute.

He opened the door and the trio walked in. Their collective eyebrows shot up as they viewed the expanse before them: groups of blue and gray metal barrels with metal tubes emerging from them and circling overhead to areas not visible—hundreds and hundreds of them; glass plates covered with fatty material and variegated flower petals; packaging tables again in the hundreds—with automated machinery working their magic on boxes, bags and pouches; huge side rooms, some with running conveyer belts and enormous vats, all partially visible; in others, men in shirt sleeves, busy at computers. But most amazing was the *depth* of the space, as large as an American football field. One never would have guessed it from outside.

As for personnel, there were perhaps seventy-five or eighty, mostly women in white caps, gowns, masks and plastic gloves.

This was the extent of their observations before Paul knocked on a door with a gold plate: "Kenneth Kuroda, President".

"Please enter," a voice said from inside. It was a soothing voice that Paul and presumably the others would grow fond of in the next hour.

Ken Kuroda was slowly rising from his desk chair as Paul opened the door a segment at a time. Their caution gave way once each side saw the other, both suddenly beaming. Paul was quick to introduce Sylvie and Vincent. There was a round of handshakes but not before Ken had bowed three times.

"Please," Ken said, motioning them toward several chairs positioned in front of his desk. They sat in unison.

The office was austere at best: sparsely furnished with the desk, the straight-backed chairs, single bookcase, a computer and printer and a photograph here and there on two walls.

Ken was about what Paul had anticipated only taller and thinner. Obviously oriental in appearance, his straight black hair was combed back, his eyes slanted only slightly and his skin was dark with a yellowish tint. But his teeth were whiter, even brighter than the others in the room. Head-on, his cheeks were concave, as if he were constantly sucking on sour candy. He wore an open-collared blue shirt and black pants with a belt that bore a buckle bearing the *Cleo* design.

The president took the initiative. "Now, may I call you by your first names?"

All three nodded.

"And," he continued, "I realize you're here primarily to inspect the infamous corner room upstairs." He spoke perfect English.

Paul remained silent for a moment or two, then said, "Yes, and thanks for having us. The corner room? Of course. Plus we ... I have a few questions to ask before we go there."

"That will be fine," Ken responded, "but even before that, I'd be most appreciative if each of you would read through what's on these cards." He shuffled three of them as he spoke. "It's in lieu of showing you around the plant or demonstrating how we operate here. Of course if you'd like a tour, I'd be glad to accommodate."

Paul looked at the other two who shook their heads almost imperceptibly. "No need to bother," Paul said. "But what's on the cards?"

Ken handed them out. "Simply a condensation of what I would have said on a tour. I've taken the liberty of borrowing it from the International Museum of Perfume here in Grasse and, to be quite honest, it says it better than I can. I've never done it this way before with any other visitors. You're my experiment, I suppose."

It took less than two minutes for them to read the cards:

Grasse is the most important center of the perfume industry, not only in France but also in the whole of Europe. The material from which the perfume is extracted is provided by the large flower plantations and lavender fields of the surrounding area. In and around Grasse about 30 large firms process throughout the year several million kilograms of blossoms (orange, rose, jasmine, thyme, rosemary, mignonette, violet, etc.). For the manufacture of perfume from natural raw materials three main methods are used: the first is the old-fashioned distillation process by means of steam; the second is an extraction process in which the perfumes together with fatty deposits are extracted by using alcohol; the third is a method of solution whereby the scents are extracted by chemical means. For example, to obtain 1 kg of ethereal oil, 1,000 kg of orange-blossom are necessary. To obtain oil of lavender, the plants are picked (either by machine or by hand), allowed to dry for a week and then treated with steam in vats. After the mixture has cooled, the particles of lavender oils which have a lighter specific gravity, float to the top of the brew and can be removed. About 40 kg of lavender plants are necessary to obtain one liter of oil of lavender. Most of the perfume factories in Grasse have set up sales rooms and operate guided tours.

Three heads nodded in approval and three pairs of eyes focused on the president.

"I should stress that I like to think of our *Cleo's* as an automated perfume processing plant, not a factory," he said. "And just to give you an idea—because so many visitors ask about the process when they come through here—all the vats you may have noticed out there? Well, certain so-called dosing valves are controlled by computers individually arranged on each vat. We prefer to call them reservoirs. The conveyer belts contain mixing vessels and the computers are programmed to a certain perfume code signal from a scanner on each moving vessel. So the conveyer belts and the dosing valves work in harmony to make sure the exact amount of substances is deposited in the mixing vessels—all to give a desired perfume result. As you know, only yours truly knows the code by heart. That's why I haven't needed to open the packet that used to be locked upstairs—at least for two years or so."

Ken appeared smug as he continued. "I should also point out that at the New York City Headquarters of International Flavors and Fragances—that is, the IFF—master perfumers experiment with new smell combinations. They spend $185 million U.S. dollars annually in research, all to develop new smells, not only for perfumes but also for shampoos and deodorants and to create fresh flavors for drinks and packaged meals. They have over 5,000 employees. We at *Cleo's* have representatives there on a regular basis. That's how important we think ongoing research is."

The president slid back in his chair and waited. Getting no reaction, he slid forward as if he thought they hadn't digested what they had just read and heard. "So what do you think?" he asked.

"All very informative," Paul said. "It makes perfumery seem more complicated than I thought. Or am I wrong?"

"Yes, you are quite right, but experience negates a complicated process and makes it simpler, wouldn't you say?"

Vincent craned forward, Sylvie made several notations in a notebook, and Paul lightened the push of his foot on the floor.

"Absolutely," Paul said, "and we appreciate the card you prepared, and all that. You can tell that we admire your facility … your plant, but we're principally here to investigate a crime. I'm what most might refer to as a 'treasure hunter' and the packet, as you call it, is what I'm commissioned to find—with the help of my colleagues here. So if you don't mind, may we get to it?" Paul wondered whether he'd been too abrupt, too direct. But Ken appeared to admire Paul's forthrightness and answered in the affirmative.

"Yes, of course," he said. "My apologies if I delayed things. And I imagine you'd want to begin with questions before we visit the 'bottomless closet' as I think of it now."

"Not necessarily—except for something that's been bothering me since I learned about some of the details of the case."

Ken raised one eyebrow in a questioning slant.

"And that is," Paul went on, "if you were an outsider hearing about your reaction to the theft—that is, discontinuing offering Vintage to the public—wouldn't you consider that rather unusual?"

"Maybe, maybe not. My mind is stuck on the fact that Vintage has been defiled ... stained ... tarnished ... however you want to put it. But even though I can run through the formula in my sleep, I want the original back, on the original paper—and the blue bottle—the whole packet. I consider them my relics, as I'm sure my friend Leon told you. It's as simple as that."

"So the bottle was *in* the packet, not separate from it?" Paul asked, as if surprised at what he'd just heard.

"Yes. It's a tiny blue bottle, but it means so much to me."

"I understand, and actually I'd rather hunt for a relic than a criminal, although they often go together." Paul rose from his chair. "Well, shall we go upstairs now?"

The others followed suit and Paul motioned for Ken to take the lead. The door to the second floor was nearby, and halfway up the stairs, Paul said, "You should be aware, Ken, so we'll all be on the same page, that we've been referring to the culprit or culprits as 'Mr. X'. How did Mr. X gain entrance to the plant?"

"He somehow jimmied the lock in a side door to our plant, just as he did with the room ... er ... the closet upstairs."

They stood in a circle surveying a cluttered second floor, about a third the size of the first. Bottles, baskets, packing containers, broken tubing and other assorted materials were strewn about. Chairs were piled high on each other as were desks and tables, all in a disorderly fashion. "Please excuse the mess up here," Ken said. "As you can see, we use it mainly for storage, but I really think it's all junk."

A musty smell dominated any fragrance from the square outside or even from below. Overhead light fixtures were simply exposed bulbs and half were dead. In the dim light, Ken pointed to the far right corner. "Over there," he said.

As they headed in that direction, Paul bringing up the rear and Ken already a dozen steps ahead, Sylvie turned to Paul and whispered, "I don't know about you but I thought he was more interested in getting across how they make perfume than in his losing his precious treasure. Those cards, for example ... I mean he wanted the whole perfume story to be totally accurate. If he told it off the cuff, he'd be afraid that any slip-ups might make him appear what—dumb? Vulnerable? Guilty?"

"I wouldn't go that far," Paul said. "In fact, I don't get the connection. Guilty of what?"

"I'll explain later," Sylvie said, writing down a few more notes. Her expression reflected disappointment over Paul's reply.

At the corner, Ken waited for the others to arrive and then gradually opened the closet door. The other three vied for positions to peer in.

The empty space inside was hardly a closet, much less a room, no more than four feet wide and three feet deep. In the center of its floor was a rectangular hole, about a foot long and six inches wide. Its edges were ragged with oblique cuts here and there as if a saw had periodically run off-line. Incomplete round holes were present at each corner of the cutout.

"Look how it was cut exactly between the joists," Paul said, leaning forward.

"Probably had some experience with carpentry," Sylvie said.

"Or just reasoned that the bolt was between two joists," Vincent added.

Paul looked at Vincent and said mockingly, "Very good, Sherlock! Very good!" Then Paul straightened and stepped back where there was more light. He consulted another index card and the questions and answers poured like ticker tape.

"Any prints lifted?" he asked.

"You mean fingerprints?"

"Yes."

"No, I don't think so."

"I'd suggest it."

"Where?"

"At the edges of the hole."

"Just there?"

"No. On the doorknob. On *all* doorknobs. On all the junk as you call it. Any DNA analyses?"

"No"

"I'd suggest that, too. And speaking of doorknobs, how did Mr. X know which room had the packet?"

It was the only moment either man had an opportunity to take a decent breath.

"The only one locked, I suppose," Ken finally

responded.

Paul regarded the president curiously. "You mean this closet had the only locked door in this entire plant?"

Ken didn't delay his answer. "Yes," he said. "We have a very open and honest community of employees here. No other room in the plant is kept locked. Nothing's locked up."

"Except an ancient formula and bottle," Sylvie said.

Paul stifled a laugh. She's still on some kind of a kick.

"Yes, that is entirely and utterly correct," Ken said, enunciating each word distinctly without looking at Sylvie.

"Did you ever report the theft to the police?"

"Yes, but they said they'd keep it quiet, at my request."

"Did you tell them about the floor being cut away?"

'No."

"Did you inform the media about the theft?"

"No."

"But I hear the whole perfume community knows."

"Word gets around, but all of perfumery is discreet."

"Why didn't you want the police to act?"

"Too embarrassed, I guess."

Paul took a breather before resuming. "So no one knows about the floor being cut away?"

"No one, except you three now."

Paul had seen enough, heard enough, and overall, had learned nothing new. Later, he would review all that had taken place, as was his custom in other cases.

Yet, back in Ken's office there was another barrage of questions and answers:

"There's a key for the closet and a key for the safe, right?"

"Yes. They're on the same key ring."

"Where do you keep them?"

"Locked in a desk drawer in my home."

"The blue bottle. Was it empty or full?"

"Empty."

"Then why did you keep it?"

"I liked its shape, its feel, and the fact it was a relic, just like the written formula."

"Was it inside the packet or outside?"

"As I said before, inside."

"So it must be fairly small."

"Yes, it's tiny and very light."

"What was the formula written on?"

"Plain parchment-type paper. It's flimsy and the ink is faded, but it's readable."

"How many pages?"

"Three."

"When did you last refer to it?"

"About two years ago."

"Why?"

"Why two years ago?"

"No, why did you refer to it when, as you said, you knew the formula by heart?"

"I finally knew it by heart two years ago, but I had read it over many times before then."

Sylvie's note-taking accelerated.

Paul had been sitting on the edge of his chair during

the questioning while Ken lounged back, seemingly relaxed and enjoying the proceedings. Paul's face which hadn't changed its somber expression as the questions continued rapid-fire, suddenly turned serene.

"Ken," he said, "I hope you haven't minded the questioning because ..."

"No, not at all. In fact I'm enjoying it. And if it helps solve the mystery, I'm all for it."

Paul perused his card again. "So are you willing to answer one or two more?"

"Certainly."

"Do you have any close friends in the business? I mean here, in the Grasse area."

"Friends? Business allies? Yes, fortunately I have several I consider very close. I hope they feel the same way." Ken paused and scanned the ceiling. "I suppose the closest one—even though we're competitors—is the president of the *Remsington Company*—most everyone calls it *REMS*. Name's Yawashita—Junzo Yawashita. Our families are Japanese, born in Tokyo. Junzo and I were born in San Francisco. We moved to France at about the same time—fifteen years ago.

"Then there's the president of *Perfumes by Pierre,* Tomi Morita, also Japanese. We were friends at the same college, drifted apart, then became friends again at a perfume convention about five years ago. Good guy, just like Junzo."

Paul wrote down the names as did Sylvie and Vincent who had taken out his own card.

Then Paul said, "Two last questions: Was the key ring ever out of your possession?"

"No, never."

"Did your friends Junzo and Tomi ever examine the packet?"

"Oh, maybe six months ago. Junzo, Tomi and I had been talking about relics of all kinds and I said that I had one dating back to Napoleon's time—and who knows, maybe even Cleopatra's—and I described what was in the safe. Anyway, a day or two later, they wanted to know if they could see the formula papers and the bottle because they'd never seen relics like those before. I said yes and I went up to get the packet for them the next day."

"Did they accompany you?"

"No."

"And how long did you let them have it?"

"Oh, just a matter of minutes, maybe five."

"Were you present when they looked it over?"

"No, I left the office for about those five minutes."

For the first time during the interview, Ken appeared agitated. "Now wait a minute!" he exclaimed. "If you're suggesting they would do … whatever … take pictures of the formula, try to memorize parts of the document, forget it. First of all, they aren't like that, and second, there wasn't enough time. I think they were sincere and when I came back, they were… what?… gushing with appreciation for my letting them see what was in the safe."

"I'm sorry if that question offended you, Ken, but it had to be asked. Think about it for a second. Let's switch places. Wouldn't you ask it?" Paul had been in this kind of situation many times before in conjunction with his treasure hunting, resorting to hypothetical role reversal. It had worked for him all over the world. And it worked again.

"I see your point," Ken said. "Yes, that makes sense.

I see your point."

Paul placed his finger against his nose, wondering if he should ask two more questions before leaving. They were underlined on his card. He decided to ask them straight away.

"Tell me," he began, "you mentioned those flowers a while ago. Are they all grown around here?"

Ken's eyes took on a wounded look. "No," he said, "elsewhere too."

"Where's that?"

"I'm really not at liberty to say. I'm sorry, but we have an internal policy here: there are certain aspects of our operation that must remain secret."

"I see. And last one, Ken … you've been so helpful … was there something else in that packet?"

"Like what?"

"I don't know."

"Something else? I doubt it. That's nonsense."

"But you must know for sure. You have the key."

Ken's face flushed. "Look, I know what I put in there two years ago—only a perfume formula and a blue bottle—but I didn't check since."

"But your friends did—six months ago."

Ken's facial color deepened. "Then go speak to *them*!" he commanded.

He straightened some papers on his desk, faked a cough, then said, "Sorry for the outburst. Maybe we've conferred too long, especially when my nerves have been shattered for a week now."

Paul's eyes met Sylvie's and Vincent's and they rose stiffly as if bothered by bad backs. It was apparent they were about to leave.

"But, Paul, before you go," Ken said, his manner smoother but hurried. "I hate to sound formal, but I take what's transpired—that is the theft, plus the money exchanged in retaining you, through Leon and *Vérité* of course—I take it as a most serious matter. Therefore, it's incumbent upon me to bring up something you never addressed." The president's tone had an air of retaliation. "And that is, if I may mimic you and bring up that something in the form of a question: 'Have any attempts ever been made to steal the formula before?' And the answer is yes, numerous attempts. At least it appeared that way. Each time I found the closet door broken into, but the safe intact. And each time that same side door to the plant was also found broken into. I can't tell you how many times we had to replace the lock. And there's more, probably unrelated but more serious … ah … incidents … that I can't get into at the present time."

Paul walked over to Ken, took his hand in both of his and said, "Thanks, I understand. I do hope we're not ending this initial get together on a sour note."

"No, not at all. I just misread you for a few seconds there. My fault. I appreciate your coming and I wish you—and you, Sylvie and Vincent—I wish you all much luck."

"I can call you if need be?" Paul asked.

"Anytime—either here or at my home or on my cell phone." He took out his wallet. "Here's my business card. It has all three numbers plus my email address." In unison, the trio uttered variations of, "Many thanks."

Once again, Ken bowed three times, and the trio left.

Outside the plant, at just after ten, Paul was tempted

to ask Sylvie what she meant when she used the word, "guilty," but he wasn't in the mood to hear her answer. And she didn't bring it up. Instead, she said, "Very interesting. Lots to digest. But I still come back to why did he go to all the trouble to explain their operation? He knew why we were there. And why the secrecy about flowers?"

"I can't answer that yet. But the answer to your first question is because he's a proud man," Paul replied.

Vincent looked around, evidently to ensure they were alone, then said, "You used the word 'yet', Paul. You know, about the flowers. 'I can't answer that yet.' Why the 'yet?'"

"Because I intend to find out the answer. To that and to his reference to 'incidents.' They could be very important in the overall scheme of things or he wouldn't have expressed it that way. I'd even bet he's kicking himself right now."

They were walking as they spoke. Paul stopped abruptly, faced the other two and said, "You know, I never would have thought it in the beginning, but as it all went along, he changed dramatically, as you saw. Toward the end there, I began thinking he might be caught up in something. Is 'hiding' too harsh a word? He's not a very good actor."

The others agreed.

Chapter 6

The rented car ride to Gordes took less than the estimated ninety minutes. Vincent drove and Ansel again stayed back at the hotel, assuring the others he wouldn't be bored.

Paul remembered the area well, a medieval village perched on the southern border of Plateau de Vaucluse with dry-stone bories tightly set against the base of cliffs that had served the Resistance well during World War II. Visiting there yet another time reminded him of the wide coverage he'd given the Resistance in one of his books. They paid little attention to signs as Vincent, familiar with the winding road from before, proceeded for two miles through valleys and forests, eventually coming upon the Cistercian Abbey Notre-Dame-de-Senanque. The surrounding fields of lavender had not reached their most radiant hue, that of a month to come.

As was the case during their last visit, the place looked deserted. Vincent parked the car and the trio went directly to the dome-topped entrance marked "South Wing." Again, the door was unlocked. And again, inside, Paul thought that the mold of centuries and the loud ticking of a clock detracted from the rotunda-like space with its frescoed masonry walls and sheened oak floors.

"Once more, no monks anywhere," Vincent

whispered to Paul.

"Another prayer meeting in the auditorium, I assume," Paul said.

In the upstairs anteroom, Frère Rudolph, the same middle-aged sub prior, appeared out of nowhere, saying "Aha, the Doctors D'Arneau and Broussard! Welcome back. Welcome back indeed. Frère Dominic is expecting you. And I see you've brought along a woman this time. Welcome also, Doctor … er … "

"That's Ranet," Sylvie said, curtsying. "But you can call me 'Sylvie'."

"Thank you," the sub prior said, the top of his nose wrinkling as if he'd never seen a curtsy before. He opened the door to a large book-lined office.

Paul didn't expect Frère Dominic to have aged so, to have become so stooped. There were no words exchanged until Paul had rushed over and embraced him, being careful not to squeeze too hard.

The first words out of the prior's mouth were a repeat of last time, "Please call me Dom. Everyone else does. And it's so good to see you."

"Dom it is," Paul said.

"Now then," Dom said, still seated and staring at Sylvie. "I spent a good deal of time on the phone with Leon, and you I know, Vincent … and of course, you too, Paul. But you, young lady? I know your name is Sylvie and I'm totally impressed with your background." He had a folder of notes before him but never looked down at it. "French Academy of Sciences within the Institute of France; head of grant proposals; member of *Gens de Vérité* for many years. Yes, most impressive."

"Thank you," Sylvie said with a curtsy more demure

than the one two minutes before.

"As for you, Vincent, any friend of Paul is a friend of mine. And what you did to save him—yes, you saved him—at the Volterraio Castle, was simply … well … heroic. What more can I say? And do sit, please. There are three chairs there." They complied.

Dom was a thin man, almost wasted, with bushy white hair, a high-pitched voice and facial skin that appeared tight and remarkably wrinkle-free as if it had never experienced the sun. But it was his nimble smile that was even more unusual, at one time rich and full, the next second gone.

The picture of him behind the desk had never left Paul's mind, especially with regard to the clothes he wore: white collar and lavender blouse tucked into black pants. And the cross—the oversized silver cross that hung from his neck. Paul was tempted to believe that it alone contributed to the prior's increased stooped condition.

There was a brief but awkward silence broken only when Paul finally said, "Looks like the number of your books has increased, Dom."

"Naturally. I never liked the designation 'history buff' because people might believe I read in the nude, but I suppose that's what I am." Paul and Vincent, who had heard this response before, affected a smile but Sylvie laughed out loud.

"Eventually we'll get to what you're here for, according to Leon," Dom said, as if he couldn't wait. He fashioned an expression that was just as eager and said, "But I believe the Napoleonic era is one that bears on so much, and especially at this time and especially since you mentioned my reading, that I should expound on the following for your benefit. And let me preface it by saying I'm well aware that I covered much of it a year ago, but it's still important and it's still the best lead-in to what I want to stress to you. And incidentally, things worldwide have gotten even worse since then."

If there was any doubt in Paul's mind what was coming, he never let on. Nor was he disinclined to listen intently; neither was the prior when Paul preempted him with a brief summary of the subjects covered at *Cleo's*.

Dom's turn came. "I've read the importance of the Stone Age through developments in ancient Egypt and in the civilizations of Mesopotamia and Sumeria and Babylonia; in the battles of the Hittites and the Persians and the Assyrians; through the glory of Greece and the grandeur of Rome, as they say; and on into the Middle Ages.

"And I've read and reread the sad details of terrible wars—revolutionary, civil, worldwide; the rise and fall of the Hitler and Stalin dictatorships in Europe; anti-colonial sentiment in Africa and Asia; flaming battles for independence in Kenya, Algeria, Mozambique, Angola and Rhodesia; the Mao Tse-tung cultural revolution in China; Israel's six-day war in Egypt; internal turmoil in Russia, Nicaragua and the Philippines; skirmishes in the Falklands and Granada and Northern Ireland; ethnic cleansing in Yugoslavia; the rise of terrorism and the 9/11 attacks; Iraq, Iran, Afghanistan; and now, most of all, the whole issue of Islamic Fundamentalists—you know, those extremists. It's those extremists we have to be leery of. They are bad ... bad ... bad!"

Though Paul and Vincent had heard a good deal of those very words on their last visit, they forced a most polite and studious face throughout the repeat rendition. Sylvie, however, appeared legitimately transfixed. Paul, in addition, wondered why the prior had so emphasized extremists. And why say *those* extremists and not simply extremists? But he dismissed his concern about such a distinction as splitting hairs.

"So what am I driving at?" Dom asked. "Just this. I don't simply read for reading's sake. I analyze. And my analysis, as it pertains to Napoleon and perfumery in general—again based on what Leon and I discussed—is that he, Napoleon, although a master military commander for the most part, had some weaknesses directly related to perfume. He just loved pleasant aromas, pure and simple. He was especially fond of citrus and herbal smells and used several bottles a day. And everyone knows that he inspired many perfumers down through the years. In fact there's one popular perfume today called Napoleon and its manufacturer maintains that its fragrance is tenacious, lively, deep and sensuous, as was the emperor.

"In this connection, what about his wife Josephine? Well, with her West Indies background, she preferred exotic scents like vanilla, clove and cinnamon. Also history reveals that in the early 1800's, there was an official perfumer assigned to French royalty and, upon Napoleon's coronation, that individual was appointed her official perfumer and was ordered to create a special perfume for Empress Josephine, one that had a strong civet component. And get this: around that time, Napoleon approached another master perfumer and commissioned him to make two scents, one for himself and one for Josephine. The perfumes were designed so that if Napoleon and Josephine were in the same room, her scent would dominate, but if the two came together, the two perfumes would merge to create a whole new unique fragrance. He went so far as to make a rule that the 'combined' perfume formula was not to be released for 200 years after his coronation. And, if you're wondering, yes, it was released in 2004. But that's enough on perfumes. I just wanted you to know that he spent hours and hours on other things besides military battles and perhaps perfumes—and women, of course—headed the list.

"Now, I should point out that I'm not a betting man—or should I be in my position, I suppose—but if I were, I'd bet that when you spoke to Maurice … my dear Maurice who's probably failing quicker than I am. We call it a contest to the end. At least we get a laugh out of it. Now where was I?"

"When you spoke to Maurice …" Paul said, gently guiding the conversation.

"Oh, yes, I'll bet he gave his lecture on flowers and such. I've heard it myself, on one or two occasions. But speaking of bets, he's right on the money in what he says. I would further bet that he spoke of fragrances. Well, because I believe the flower issue is maybe the most important one we'll take up here … the four of us … you see, Leon and I discussed it at length just yesterday … I want to add to what Maurice told you. If that's all right with you."

"More than all right, Dom," Paul responded. "It's so strange, I was going to bring up the subject myself: flowers, perfumery and how Napoleon fits in. And even arsenic."

"I'm sure he spoke of that and called it bioterrorism against Napoleon."

"Yes, he did just that. And what's your theory? If biological agents were available back in Napoleon's time, do you think he would have used them in his battles?"

"Without question. He'd have had no choice because others would have."

"Makes sense," Paul said. "And if they *were* around then and continued to be used right up to the present day, what would be the condition of the world now?"

"Hmm … awful thought. I'd say we'd have less countries, for sure. More cases of mental illness and chronic anxiety reactions in existing nations. More money spent on research, development and specialized medical care. Less on education. So we'd have a global society that was sick, dumb and broke!"

"Not a very inspiring picture," Paul said, "and I can't help but think that with biological weapons available all over the place, such might be the picture 200 years from now."

"Indeed. I hate to imagine it, but that's for our descendents to grapple with."

They both stared off into space.

"So," the prior said, "did the subject of flowers actually come up at *Cleo's*?"

"Yes. Ken Kuroda, their president, said the flowers they use aren't all grown in Grasse. I think he put it, 'elsewhere too'. When I asked where that was, he refused to say. Said it had to remain an internal company secret."

"He's of Japanese heritage, I hear."

"Yes, and so are his closest friends, Junzo Yawashito and Tomi Morita." Paul had read from one of his cards. "They're presidents of other companies in Grasse but apparently are good friends."

For the first time, Dom consulted his notes, leafing through the pad before him. "That would be *Remsington* and *Perfumes by Pierre.*"

"That's right."

"How do I know? Well, when Leon and I spoke yesterday, the subject of flowers came up and after we hung up, I began contacting some of my histarian friends, those I thought could help us the most. And do you know who heads the list?" The prior didn't wait for an answer. "Clive Weaver!"

Paul flinched. "Clive, over on Elba?"

"Yes, on Elba. The same histarian you consulted when you were there last year, no, more than a year now."

"Flowers never even came up then."

"At the time, he was concentrating on Napoleon's will, on Talleyrand, on Lady Beckett and all that, not on flowers. But he happens to have the largest collection ever in his gardens there. The largest I know of, anyway. He's well into his eighties and he's been at it maybe sixty years. Supplies perfumers and aromatherapists around the world. Especially with exotic varieties. So, among our histarians, he's by far the expert on the subject. You *must* go see him, Paul. Make sure he includes what he knows about Napoleon's relationship to it all. And *Cleo's*. Get his take on them. I wouldn't be surprised if they were one of his customers."

The entire trio flinched this time.

Paul nodded deferentially. "There's no question. We'll go," he said.

"Excellent. I gave you a pamphlet about the island

last time. Maybe it would be good for you to brush up on its history and all but ... ah ... of course, it's probably back in the states. Here's another one." Rummaging through his top drawer, he located another copy and handed it to Paul.

"And in case Clive doesn't get to this, let me superficially cover the following. It might ring a bell during your journeys and help you in the task you face. I doubt it, but you never know. And speaking of your task, I don't envy you—that's for sure. But I do admire your—pardon the expression—your guts."

Dom made no effort to conceal glancing at his folder now and again, at first combining it with a comment directed at Sylvie, "I see you're taking notes, so I'll go through this slowly. I'll simply skim the surface about what's called 'Fragrance Notes' and about 'Olfactive Families'. That's 'fragrance' and 'olfactive'.

"Borrowing from the musical vocabulary, there are three sets of fragrance notes or scents: top, middle and base. Manufacturers, mindful of the evaporation process of perfumes, craft these scents with great care. Top notes or scents are perceived by the applicator immediately and disappear just as fast because they evaporate quickly. This doesn't diminish their value, however, particularly from a commercial standpoint, because they create the very first impression of a perfume in a potential buyer's mind. That's why top notes are sometimes called 'head notes'.

"A middle note, on the other hand, is the scent body of a perfume and makes its appearance as the top note evaporates. A middle note or scent must also be one that's timed to mask the oncoming unpleasant olfactory sensation experienced when the base note kicks in. This latter sensation improves with time. Middle notes are often called 'heart notes', as you might expect. Am I going too fast, Sylvie?"

"No, not at all. I'm getting down the important points so far."

"Okay. That leaves the base note. This combined with the middle note is what's referred to in the business as the 'main theme' of the perfume. They give it its depth, and this usually doesn't appear until at least a half-hour after its application. And that's about it as far as Fragrance Notes are concerned."

Dom scrutinized two pages in his folder, no doubt to be sure he hadn't left anything out, then continued to speak with broad, sweeping gestures.

"Now in thinking about it, my friends, perhaps the terms I've cited might become the most valuable part of what I've said if you find yourselves in a discussion about perfumery. Terms like 'notes', 'evaporate', 'first impression', 'head note', 'scent body', 'heart note', 'base note', 'main theme', 'depth' and so on. As I've said, this kind of information might come in handy for you.

"As for Olfactive Families, this can get a bit technical and there's a lot of overlap. So I'll just read some lists from my folder if you don't mind. Again, just so you'll be familiar with the terms. Most are self-explanatory. First, the classical classification ones that arose around 1900:

Single
Floral
Floral Bouquet
Wood
Amber
Leather
Fougere

Chypre. Maybe I should comment on this one. It means Cyprus in French. A famous example is *Mitsouko* which is the Japanese word meaning girls.

"Finally, there's the modern classification, instituted in 1945:

Bright Floral, combining the Single and the Floral of the classical version.

Green

Citrus

Fruity

Aquatic

Gourmand. I have no idea what this means. Let's see. It says here: 'scents with edible-like qualities. Often contain scents like vanilla or synthetic flavors resembling agreeable food flavors.' Now I get it. Gourmand? Gourmet."

Like a machine that had stalled while another suddenly ignited, the prior said, "I'm sure you have better things to do than spend more time than necessary with me but one last thing. And that is: don't forget to bring Napoleon into the discussion, the debate, the exchange of ideas — whenever you get the chance. Whenever one talks of fragrances, one has to include him. He loved aromas, especially the citrus and herbal kinds. And he was known to use several bottles a day! He recognized what he called 'perfume power' early on, using it to seduce women and — would you believe — his influence in negating the value of men's fragrances endured until the 1960's! Can you believe it?

"And I may be way out in making something of it, but the word 'oriental' seems to keep popping up in all of this, Napoleon or not. When it came to men's perfumes, he spoke harshly of oriental components like amber. Then there's that *Mitsouko* brand I already mentioned. And let's not forget the three Japanese perfumers in Grasse. They're clearly at the heart of the problem you face, Paul, or at least the *Cleo's* guy is."

Paul acknowledged Dom's taking the time to brief them on what he termed the "perfumery language" and to point out the "Japanese linkage". He peered at his colleagues, then at the prior.

"You look exhausted, Dom. Do you ever take naps?"

The prior responded with a half-smile. "I always look this way," he said. "But to answer your question: 'only the one I take all night long.'"

Paul considered laughing but thought better of it as he observed Dom pushing on the desk to lift himself off his chair. He limped toward the front and walked his visitors to the door. There, after handshakes and initiating a round of loud thanks, he turned and limped back toward his desk.

Chapter 7

At the very beginning of the return drive to Grasse, Sylvie said, "What a sweet man, and well-informed."

Now taking his turn at the wheel, Paul stated, "All the histarians are."

"Sometimes he sounded so much younger," Vincent said. "Even his language—hardly what you'd expect from an octogenarian."

"Don't let him fool you," Paul said. "That mind of his doesn't age."

The rest of the trip—ninety minutes—was a relatively quiet one. Paul wanted it that way as he attempted to sort out all that had transpired in the preceding six hours. He was hardly successful, however, both interviews having been crammed with details and innuendoes, some of them disjointed, some not. Yet all in all, it didn't disturb him very much, as he planned to digest later what he had learned, when he was alone in the *Hotel Campanile*. There was so much, but it would keep. And while in a semi-meditative mood, he felt reassured he hadn't minimized the whole jetty scene or the shooter chase or Scarhead's murder. But in the midst of his more recent pursuits, he wanted to compartmentalize these past occurrences for the time being, no longer considering them as "holdover things"; rather as *Phase One*. He had gone this mental route before on other case*s*. It was apparently a way of clearing his mind temporarily of issues that could keep, for in the past, there had never been a *Phase Two*! In a related vein, he convinced himself—and he wasn't sure why—that the two cryptic messages under his door were not connected to his past case, as he had previously thought, but to the present one.

Also later, before leaving Nice, he would phone Leon to bring him up to date. Perhaps talking with him would make his overall analysis easier. But as he tried to shift to other thoughts, he was almost positive about one thing: Leon had already heard from the prior.

Not surprisingly, Leon was waiting for the three travelers at the airstrip on the outskirts of Paris. It was 7:47 p.m.

"You made good time," he said.

"Yeah, I think our pilot cuts corners."

No one laughed, probably because Leon was waiting to hear Paul's version of their meeting with Ken and the prior. And the other three were tired. At least they looked that way and said they were. Paul turned to Ansel and asked, "How can you be tired when all you did was fly an airplane?"

The pilot answered the question with a question: "Do you think it's easy napping behind a flower pot in a hotel lobby?" This time they laughed. Paul chalked it up to post-fatigue giddiness. And he was correct in his guess that the prior had already called Leon.

"You've got plenty on your plate—that's for sure—but I believe you're up to handling it all," Leon said. "Funny how similar this is to your last case with us. Different scenarios, different characters, but the same kinds of roadblocks and threats, the murders, the many questions to follow-up on."

"I'm used to it, Leon. I've never put it this way before, but I crave it. It's a far cry from the academic life—even if I *was* in charge of history there at … what's its name? … oh, yes, Yale. But through all my searchings—for paintings and sculptures and manuscripts and jewelry and furniture pieces, and even an antique car—it's never ceased to amaze me that the same story line structure emerges: you learn something here and it sends you there; you learn something else there and it sends you to another spot. And so on. Sometimes I've felt as though I were trapped in a wild goose chase. For example, I now have to return to Elba based on what I learned in Gordes. I'm not complaining, mind you, just … well I suppose I *am* tired after all, rambling on like this. But before I stop, I have to admit that the only difference is that I never had the advantage of historians until last year."

"Your success rate has been admirable though, with them or not. That's why *Vérité* learned of you in the first place. Now why don't you get a good night's sleep. You're entitled. Put this aside for eight or nine hours and call me in the morning. We'll start by trying to figure out what that blasted Rosetta Stone—Elgin Marbles message was supposed to mean."

Once in his Meridien Montparnasse room, Paul ran through Sylvie's notes in a cursory fashion for he had remembered most everything, even though he didn't know how to put it all together yet. Then, following the chairman's advice, he fell into a dead sleep within a minute or two.

At 7:30, the morning looked so inviting through the window that Paul stepped outside even before his shower and shave. He believed strongly that contact with nature was therapeutic—*any* contact, whenever he had the time. So having donned Bermuda shorts, a polo shirt and sneakers, and just in case, inserting the smaller of his pistols in his back pocket, he walked around the block twice, little sun notwithstanding. He also believed such a stroll satisfied his frequent need to pace. The air was clear, traffic noise minimal, birds just beginning their chirping for the day, and a gentle breeze tousled his uncombed hair. Invigorated, he headed back toward his room to ready for the day ahead and, upon opening the door, stopped short. Another message! This time without an envelope. It read:

I'M TALKING POISON

He almost crumpled it up and tossed it in the wastepaper basket, but decided against it and put it in his pocket. He was determined to remain calm. There had been other messages, hadn't there? But he did note the use of "I'm" and not "We're."

His shower was deliberately unhurried, the shave perfunctory as usual. He put on a dark blue shirt, seersucker trousers and a light blue blazer and tie. This time, he armed himself with the usual pistols in the usual locations. Without any fresh thoughts or preparation, he phoned Leon.

"Good morning, Mr. Chairman," he said. "New man here. Emotionally settled. At least I awoke that way, but we have something new."

"Oh? Can it wait? Have you had breakfast?"

"Yes and no. I mean yes to the first, no to the second."

"I can be over in half an hour. I like the coffee shop there and you can tell me about it." Leon spoke like a father consoling his son.

Paul wandered down to the lobby and could have ended up at the small shop simply by following the smell of coffee and bacon. He sat at a glass-topped table for two, waved off a waitress, saying, "Expecting a friend," and couldn't avoid noticing the back of a man seated at a counter stool not thirty feet away. He was short and stumpy and had shiny black hair gathered in a sloppy-looking ponytail. The man appeared to be finishing a cup of coffee or tea and periodically turned in Paul's direction, giving a poor imitation of one looking over Paul's head, when in fact his steely eyes were giving him the once-over. Was he the one who had left the note?

In turn, Paul made like he hadn't noticed, mostly staring into a heavily flowered courtyard nearby or up at the ceiling with its glass panels rising to a center point. Actually he became fascinated with patches of dew that rolled downward, dispersing into new patterns, seconds at a time.

Leon arrived and Paul showed him the note. He casually looked over and the man was gone.

"I'm talking poison? Strange," Leon said, looking around the room.

Neither could make any sense of it, but both admitted it might presage something sinister.

"All we can do, Paul, is wait and see. So you slept

well, I take it," the chairman said, an obvious attempt to lighten the situation.

"The best in weeks. And you?"

"Not well at all. That Rosetta Stone thing kept me awake half the night. I can't figure it out. What's the Stone got to do with perfumes and flowers anyway? Of course, we're not personally familiar with its English translation, are we?"

The waitress returned and they both ordered orange juice, coffee and whole-wheat muffins.

Leon resumed the one-sided conversation: "To show you why I couldn't sleep, I made a copy of some things I got off the web and read word for word. I think it would be helpful if you read the key parts I underlined. Not now, of course. Maybe back in your room. Then, the other thing last night: I remembered that we have an histarian in Egypt who knows about the Stone backward and forward—I mean what the inscriptions say. I'll give him a call, maybe save you a trip. Of course, he won't tell me the exact content over the phone, but he'll say whether he knows or not. I'll ask him if he thinks there could be some kind of clue there. As for the Elgin Marbles, I'd vote to wait on that. Take one thing at a time."

"Good idea."

Leon gave Paul several sheets of paper which he folded and put in his pocket. "I'll be sure to read what you think is important," Paul said. "Maybe even more."

The waitress delivered their food, both men commenting that such breakfasts were deliberately "skimpy"—as were their lunches—to compensate for "gargantuan" evening meals. Considering Leon's size, Paul doubted his veracity on the subject.

"So what's your plan for Elba?" Leon asked.

"I'd like to leave early this afternoon, by two if possible, and meet with Clive tomorrow. Takes about five hours to get there, as I remember."

"Yes, and leaving at two would be fine. I'll contact Ansel. Like before, you'll land at Airport Marina di Campo after refueling in Marseille."

"We'll stay at the same hotel?" Paul snapped his fingers. "Hotel … what?"

"Hotel Fabricia. In Portoferraio, ten minutes from the airport."

"I liked it."

"Good. I'll make all the arrangements including setting up the meeting with Clive. I'm sure tomorrow will be fine. I'll notify Vincent, too. You'll call Sylvie?"

"Yes, I will."

As they finished the last of their coffee, Paul was tempted to mention the man at the counter but decided he'd rather clear his mind of the whole episode. The man's behavior might have been just his imagination anyway. What wasn't his imagination, however, was the man's hair. Why not add another moniker to the list: "Ponytail Man"?

"I'll be in touch as soon as possible," Leon said. "You'll be in your room?"

Paul said yes, indicating he wanted to read the Rosetta Stone material and bring his notes on yesterday's meetings up to date. "I have this strange feeling that there's already some kind of thread hiding in what we have so far."

Chapter 8

In all past cases, there came a time when Paul felt compelled to list current developments in order to keep them straight. The more interviews he had, the more he was apt to mesh one with the other, and he never wanted to get ahead of himself in understanding what was going on. Merely listing them was sufficient; he needn't add meaning or interpretation, necessarily. This was one of those times.

At the desk, he compiled the lists longhand, not wanting to chance that someone somehow might tap into one of the lobby computers. He wrote:

<u>Subjects Brought Up at Cleo's with Ken</u>
— Handed me cards re importance of Grasse as perfume capitol and how perfume is made.
— Continued to explain perfumery.
— Mentioned upstairs packet.
— Further explained process of perfumery at his plant.
— Said Cleo's has representatives at NYC Headquarters of International Flavors and Fragrances.
— Said he considers original Vintage formula and the blue bottle as his relics and feels as though the perfume has been "defiled" by the theft.

—Said that bottle was in the packet , not separate from it.

—I indicated we consider perp or perps as Mr. X.

—Explained how Mr. X gained entrance.

—Viewed second floor. Junk all over. Cut-out hole of closet in far right corner.

— My questioning started:

Any fingerprints, DNA studies?

Was closet the only locked room in the plant?

The key ring.

He likes the blue bottle.

What kind of paper was formula written on?

When did he last look at it?

Any close friends in the business?

He mentioned Junzo Yawashita (Remsington) & Tomi Morita (Perfumes by Pierre).

When was packet out of possession? 6 months ago. Gave to above men for 5 min.

Re flowers. Refused to say who besides locals supplies them.

Lost temper when asked if something else in packet.

Mentioned other attempts to steal formula.

Secretive about other kinds of "incidents".

Subjects @ Friar Dom's

—I summarized events at Cleo's.
—Per usual, he expounded on wars.
—This time, included Islamic Fundamentalists ("those extremists")
—Pointed out Napoleon's weakness for perfumes.
—Asked if flowers came up for discussion at Cleo's.
—Indicated Ken's refusal to say who else supplies flowers.
—Pointed out Ken's Japanese heritage.
—I said Junzo & Tami also Japanese. Dom named their companies.
—Mentioned Clive Weaver (Elba) as master flower supplier.
—Said Cleo's could be one of Clive's customers(?)
—Stressed imperative of meeting with Clive.
—Discussed types of fragrance notes & olfactory families.
—Stressed I should bring Nap. into discussions wherever.
—Pointed out "Japanese linkages".

It was nearly ten when Paul finished, plenty of time to familiarize himself with what Leon had given him about the Rosetta Stone. But first he read through the lists even though he believed he'd included everything. He locked the two sheets in the small safe above the room's refrigerator.

He took the "Stone" sheets from his pocket, began to read, but soon found it difficult to concentrate. He decided to call Sylvie instead.

"Hi, it's me," he said. "I didn't wake you, did I?"

"Are you kidding? It's already ten. I haven't slept past eight since I was a kid."

"And that was a long time ago."

"Ha ha–what's up?"

"Elba. Leaving at two today. Leon's in favor and will take care of details. You game?"

Paul thought he heard a gulping sound followed by a moment of pure silence, and then he definitely heard, "Paul, my darling, you made my day!"

"So it's a yes?"

"Of course! We had our adventures there, didn't we? And learned a lot. Volterraio Castle where you nearly got your head blown off; Napoleon's will; the East India Company; all that Talleyrand and Lady Beckett stuff. And Clive Weaver—what a doll! Just like the prior. In spite of the castle scare, I really love that island."

"I've been thinking, Syl …"

"So now it's 'Syl'?"

"Sure, why not? 'Sylvie' takes too long to say."

Paul waited for some kind of retort but none came. "As long as you brought up Lady Beckett," he said, "I think we'll eventually have to pay her casket a visit up at Beckett's Gardens."

"The gardens in London?"

"Yup. Not sure yet, but probably."

"Why?"

"I'm not sure of that yet, either, but I've been mulling over her possible ties with the East India

Company—remember she was an executive with them; Talleyrand; those threats on my life, as you mentioned; Napoleon; those characters in Grasse; perfumes ... what am I leaving out? ... Flowers! Good old flowers! But as of ..." he looked at his watch " ... 10:05 today, Sunday, June 24, there are still some pieces missing. We'll see. So Leon's calling back and I'll let you know when we'll pick you up."

He returned to the "Stone" pages, leafing through them and deciding he wouldn't read them all word for word. Instead he began by focusing on those sentences underlined by Leon and then noticed a second article that he felt was not too technical, yet would be sufficiently informative for his purposes: to gain an understanding of the Stone's history. This article he *did* take the time to read word for word, initially making note of its curious last sentence. It read: "You may freely reprint this article or place it on your website by adding this statement: Courtesy of www.kingtutshop.com." This was preceded by the following literal account:

The Rosetta Stone is very famous for it provided the key to solve the ancient Egyptian language. [It] was carved in 196 B.C. It was discovered by the French soldiers who came with Napoleon. The Frenchman, Jean Francois Champollion, is the one who cracked the code of the stone. The discovery of the stone of rosette later called the Rosetta Stone is an interesting story.

The stone was discovered by the

French troops in Napoleon's military expedition in 1799 in Lower Egypt, when they were digging the foundations of an addition to a fort near the town of el-Rashid (Rosetta) in the Nile Delta.

It was discovered near the town of Rosetta (now Rachid) ... about 40 miles northeast of Alexandria, by a Frenchman, Pierre Bouchard, on 15 July, 1799. Captain Bouchard, an engineer officer in Napoleon's expedition to Egypt, was supervising the reconstruction of an old fort, as part of the preparations for defending the French from attacks by British and Turkish forces in the area. The Rosetta Stone came to light during the demolition of a wall in the fort. Captain Bouchard saw that the polished black basalt stone contained three sections of different types of writing, and recognized its significance immediately. He sent the stone to Cairo, to the scholars who also accompanied the French expedition to Egypt.

In 1801, after two years of warding off attacks by the British, and after their defeat at Abuquir Bay, the French forces in Egypt surrendered. Under the terms of the Treaty of Capitulation, all antiquities in the possession of the French, including the Rosetta Stone, were ceded to the British.

The stone is a compact basalt slab [measuring] 114 x 72 x 28 cm. [It] contained words in three types of writing: Egyptian hieroglyphs, Demotic, which is a shorthand version of Egyptian hieroglyphic writing, and Greek. By translating the Greek section, scholars were able to learn what the hieroglyphs meant. This enabled them to translate inscriptions inside the Egyptian temples.

The inscription on the stone was a decree passed by a general council of priests which assembled at Memphis on the first anniversary of the coronation of Ptolemy V Epiphanes, king of all Egypt. The text concerns the honors bestowed on the king by temples of Egypt in return for services rendered by him to Egypt both at home and abroad. Priestly privileges, especially those of an economic nature, are listed in detail. Because the inscription appears in three scripts, hieroglyphic, demotic, and Greek, scholars were able to decipher the Egyptian hieroglyphic and demotic versions by comparing them with the Greek version.

The representation of a single text of the three mentioned script variants enabled the French scholar, Jean Francois Champollion (1790-1832) to basically decipher the hieroglyphs. Furthermore, with the aid of the Coptic language (language of the Christian descendants of the ancient Egyptians), he succeeded to realize the phonetic value of the hieroglyphs. This proved the fact that hieroglyphs do not have only symbolic meaning, but that they also served as a "spoken language".

Another British physicist, Thomas Young, worked on the translation of the stone with the French Egyptologist ... Champollion. Thomas Young was the first to prove that the elongated ovals or cartouches in the hieroglyphic section of the stone contained a royal name written phonetically, in this case, that of Ptolemy. Champollion went on to correct and enlarge Young's list of phonetic hieroglyphs and lay the foundations of our knowledge of the ancient Egyptian language in a paper which was read to the Academie des Inscriptions et Belles-Lettres in Paris in 1822. It was this discovery—that the Egyptian hieroglyphic writing system used a combination of ideograms, phonetic signs, and determinatives—that provided the breakthrough in the translation of hieroglyphic writing, And this ability to read the ancient hieroglyphs in turn opened the door to the history of ancient Egypt and gave birth to the new discipline of Egyptology.

Paul was tempted to reread the entire article until it dawned on him what it was that stood out. It was the sentence, "This enabled them to translate inscriptions inside the Egyptian temples." He underlined it in red ink.

What inscriptions? Did this have special meaning for his undertaking? Was it truly a clue?

And something else had caught his attention: the article failed to indicate that, in 1802, the Rosetta Stone was transferred to London's British Museum where it is still on display. He wondered why this important fact hadn't been mentioned. The questions were piling up. He shook his head as if to clear the way for a more important concern.

This time, he had no hesitation in utilizing one of the computers down in the lobby. He gathered up the materials before him and raced to the elevator. It was too slow to arrive so, in his excitement, he bolted down six floors to the lobby. Fortunately, two computers were available and, catching his breath, he searched for "Egyptian temples" and wrote down the names of five that were located near one another: Luxor, Karmak, Esna, Edfu and Kom Ombo. He pledged that when he had time in his schedule —sometime after Elba—he would pay the temples a visit to check on their inscriptions, but then he remembered Leon saying there was an histarian there who was an expert on the subject.

At the elevator, he couldn't stop scratching his finger as he wondered if he were making too much of the sentence. Or was he onto something?

He reentered his room as the phone was ringing. Leon said Vincent would arrive at one-fifteen. Paul, in turn, called Sylvie back and informed her they would be at her place at one-thirty. He didn't mention the "clue".

He removed the two lists from the small safe and, together with the Stone material, put them in the briefcase he would take to Elba and waited for the concierge's call.

As was the case during their flight to Nice, Paul deviated from his usual routine of reading up on the history of a particular destination. The memory of their trip to Elba a year ago was still fresh, and what's more, he knew more than most about the tiny island's background. And especially its place in Napoleonic history. Preoccupied with what many would label a mishmash of recent events, situations, possibilities and newly met characters, he resorted once more to his habit of "listing". It always worked for him in lessening the confusion. Only this time, he didn't write out a list, but ran through one in his mind, much like running through the alphabet to recall a person's name. He even differentiated between two types of reviews and had given them names: "written listing" which contained more detail, and "reflective listing" which was more superficial. It seemed he was forever making them—one type or the other—during all his treasure-hunting assignments. This time it was reflective and it applied to Elba and Napoleon. It only took a minute or two but what came up was a series of bullets:

— French invasion of Russia marked a turning point in Napoleon's career.

—His army had been seriously damaged, never fully recovering.

—A year later, he lost again at Leipzig, the largest battle of the Napoleonic wars.

—Next year, France was invaded, Napoleon was forced to abdicate and was exiled to Elba.

—He was made emperor of the island and remained there for ten months, establishing a close relationship with the people and the land itself.

—He escaped Elba and managed to return to power.

—He was roundly defeated at the Battle of Waterloo in 1815.

—He spent the last six years of his life in British confinement on the remote island of St. Helena.

He had had enough of this series and though he had included Dom's Elba pamphlet among the papers in his briefcase, he never referred to it. Nor was there much conversation in the plane throughout the flight, each of the passengers either reading magazines or napping. In Paul's case, he munched on some saltines he had taken along.

After landing at 7:10 p.m., they took a taxi to the Hotel Fabricia, ten minutes away. Once again, Ansel stayed behind—at the Marina di Campo Airport—stating that his friend there, an employee named Rosalia, would find things for him to do. He assured the group that he would be at-the-ready to return to Paris whenever they completed their business on the island, and that Rosalia or one of her co-workers would inform them of his whereabouts.

A year ago, the hotel receptionist had arranged for a car rental, but Paul's agenda on this trip was confined to a give-and-take conversation at one of the Napoleon Museum Buildings. Clive had been the curator for fifty-two years, Paul recalled.

The following morning, Paul asked a taxi driver who had arrived at the hotel, "I'm sure you know of Clive

Weaver?"

"Si," the driver said. "Very famous. Curator of two Napoleon buildings. Long time there. One here. Portoferraio. One in San Martino."

"We'll just want the one right here, where his office is," Paul responded.

They were on their way, a short taxi ride but too long to walk. The morning was breezy and warm, as were most days on the island, they were told. And each of them wore mid-summer clothes: the men sporting print short-sleeved shirts with no tie and light blue slacks, Sylvie, just the reverse: light blue blouse and print skirt.

The ride provided the same sights and sounds as before: gray cliffs silhouetted against a pale sky; sea breezes rocking all varieties of boats; greens and blues reflected in surrounding waters; lemon-yellow buildings; a large number of older pedestrians, nearly all smiling; and mostly, the scent of wildflowers. Ordinarily such a scent would have passed Paul's notice, but not under the circumstances of his mission. And he puzzled over the many smiles, just like last year.

Such sights and sounds evoked many memories, most of them pleasant, or at least informative, including details about Napoleon's will; about Lady Beckett's many secret liaisons with the emperor; about an illegitimate baby she had, reportedly by Napoleon; about Charles Maurice de Talleyrand-Perigord. Paul grinned as he imagined that with a full name like that and, in keeping with the immediate past history of Shooterman, they should have called such an individual "Talleyman." This led to Paul's last thought about the past visit, one that would never leave him: his assailants on the cliffs of Volterraio Castle, one of whom had been Scarhead, now dead. This time, the castle was not on Paul's agenda.

The curator's office was in a small one-story annex attached to the two-story main building. Old and weathered, both were architecturally structured in typical Tuscan style. Clive's longtime secretary, the amiable but mellow Miss Sarcodina, gave the travelers a most gracious and animated greeting.

"Well, I'll be!" she exclaimed, "We expected you, but I never thought it would be so exciting. More exciting than last time, but of course, we'd just met you then."

"Same here," Paul said. "You've been well, I take it?"

"Oh, yes. An ache here, a pain there. You know." From behind the counter, she gave each one's upper half the once-over, then said, "I take that back. You *don't* know, but you'll see."

She came around to the front saying, "Here let me lead you to the office. The curator will be so happy to see you again."

They walked down a winding hallway and, once again, Paul's imagination took hold. He tried to picture Napoleon taking the same steps, at once brooding and no doubt plotting. Did he have his last defeat on his mind? The possibility of commanding at Waterloo? Lady Beckett? Flowers?

Clive Weaver appeared younger to Paul, who didn't bother with a greeting, saying, in its place. "You must be taking megavitamins, Clive!"

They exchanged drawn-out handshakes before Clive's response: "Thanks for the compliment. You're no doubt referring to how I look, but I had nothing to do with it. It's aromatherapy.''

"Aromatherapy?" Sylvie questioned.

"Ditto," Paul said. "What's that all about? You mean you're receiving it?"

"Receiving and giving. I'm an official aromatherapist now. Have been for almost a year. But I'll explain later.''

The basics of his physical appearance hadn't changed appreciably but there were some definite differences. Quite tall, he stood more erect and the previously loose neck folds were gone. His head was still a near-perfect circle, his complexion less pale. Beady eyes and a narrow pointed nose gave him the pinched features of a barn owl. Only his mouth was of normal size and shape, and his lips had lost their quiver. He gesticulated with thick wire-framed glasses and another large ring had been added to his other middle finger. He loosened his tie and rolled up the gartered sleeves of a white and blue striped shirt.

Sylvie prepared to take notes.

Like so many historians Paul had consulted, Clive could switch to a new subject before the previous one had been fully covered. "Do sit," he said with a decidedly British accent. "I've been in touch with the prior and, of course, with Leon." He lowered himself gingerly into his chair. "So, let's get started, shall we? I know there's the subject of a perfume formula theft, some threats you received, the perfume business, questions about the Rosetta Stone, Napoleon and other things, not the least of which is flowers. Ah, near and dear to my heart. We didn't talk about it when you were here last, although we referred a little bit to our gardens. Truth is, I have quite a few of my own and, by hook or by crook, I manage most of the others. I seem to have inherited looking after their welfare—sort of the island's administrator of flowers, don't you know."

"So Elba flowers and your aromatherapy kind of make sense," Paul said. He was searching for words.

"I suppose you could say that. Now what's on your mind? I'd like to get your own version, so you go first."

Paul settled into his chair and said, "Well there's so much. I don't know where to start …"

"Start anywhere. We'll get it all in. You've come a long way for my take on things. I'll listen first. If I interrupt and go off on a tangent, give me royal hell." Vintage Clive, Paul thought.

He took out an ever-available card filled with notes and gave it a quick once-over. "What you specified as topics fairly much matches what I have written down here," he said. "So, the stolen perfume formula … let's start there."

Paul summarized the essence of the theft itself, Ken Kuroda's explanation of it, the small closet room, the strange cut-out, and anything else he could think of relative to *Cleo's* long history and current standing within the perfume business. He further gave an opinion of Ken himself: self-centered; probably a manipulative president; smug; and certainly short-tempered. And you've heard about the three messages at my door?"

Clive nodded and jotted down a few words on a sheet of paper.

"It's the second one that has me baffled: "Fault Rosetta Stone and Elgin Marbles Unless You Do Not Mind A Turnaround.'"

Paul alluded to the Stone pages that Leon had

given him, emphasizing the sentence he felt was highly significant: "This enabled them [scholars] to translate inscriptions inside the Egyptian temples."

"Doesn't that sound important?" Paul asked.

Clive, elbows at his sides, hands spread and facing upward, replied, "I'm not saying a thing until you finsh. Then I'll have my turn." The curator looked momentarily sheepish before following up with, "I think that's the best way to cover the most ground." He raised the piece of paper. "You see, I have my own reminders."

"Good," Paul said. "So while on the subject of the Stone, how do the Elgin Marbles fit in? Or, for that matter, Lord Elgin, himself? And let's not forget Cleopatra. Relevant in all this or not?"

"Sparkling," Clive said softly with a measure of guilt.

Paul hardly heard the comment. "Okay. Next thing," he continued. "What can you tell me about Napoleon and perfumes? I realize he liked them—used them to excess—but beyond that, anything meaningful? Truly, Clive, this is at the heart of our visit." He studied his card for the last time.

"I'd better summarize: Napoleon and perfumes … and let's not forget flowers; Rosetta Stone … that is, your read on it; Elgin Marbles and Lord Elgin; Cleopatra; the three perfume presidents back in Grasse … Leon must have touched on them; Lady Beckett … haven't even mentioned her yet; nor the East India Company. And that about does it." Paul's summary was partly a duplication of what Clive had brought up minutes before and Paul acknowledged it, concluding with, "It's like a broken record, but I guess we're on the same page. And please excuse the clichés."

"Yes, I think we are. But aren't we always?"

Paul put his card away while Clive kept glancing at his paper. Up to this point, neither Sylvie nor Vincent had uttered a word. Clive asked if either of them cared to add anything.

"No, sir," Vincent said, leveling his shoulders.

"No," Sylvie said, "other than this should get even more interesting. Or should I say 'sparkling', Mr. Curator?"

"Clive, please."

"Or Dr. Aromatherapist," Vincent said. His eyes turned blank. "Sorry ... ah ... Clive. I couldn't resist. It's just that you wear so many hats."

Clive gave a constrained laugh and said, "You're forgiven. And you know what? I've never been called that before. A bevy of other things, but not that. Sounds ... uh ... sparkling."

Now they all genuinely laughed.

Clive was the first to stop. "All right," he said, "my approach will be threefold: One, answer your questions as best I can. Two, tell you what I know or have found out. Three, indicate what I believe you should do. I may combine the three in a single sentence or two. And let's work this a little differently from when you had the floor, so to speak. Don't hesitate to interrupt me as you see fit, either to have me elaborate or to add something you forgot to point out.

"So first, about that sentence in the paper Leon gave you. You asked if it's important. My answer is '*extremely* important,' and you should definitely go to some obvious Egyptian temples to check on inscriptions that might be pertinent."

"First interruption," Paul said. "I've already compiled a list of five or six, all south of Cairo."

"Excellent. Next: Is Cleopatra relevant to all this? Absolutely. If only because in honor of her, *Cleo's* got its name; and the stolen formula may have been handed down not only from Napoleon, but perhaps from as far back as the Cleopatra era. It may very well be a re-creation of one that the queen allegedly concocted for herself. So it's undoubtedly been around for a long time—centuries. She was well versed in the creation and use of perfumes. It was she who perfected the balms and scents that were available back then, ones she herself used to conquer Julius Caesar and Mark Antony. And listen to this. Regarding Mark Antony? When she sailed to Tarsus to meet with him, she perfumed the sails of her barge!

"And the blue bottle?" Paul asked.

"Just thrown in as a bonus."

"By Napoleon?"

"Yes, that's the likelihood."

Paul hoped that his brief scowl didn't show.

"By the way, Paul, you should know that Leon spent much time with me, going over *Cleo's, Remsington,* and *Perfumes by Pierre.* A strange lot, indeed. Their leaders are all Japanese and have ties with certain rainforests in Japan—yes, Japan does have rainforests. Not that that has anything to do with anything else. Or does it? One has to concede, however, that the main source of *Cleo's* flowers is not Japan, and bear with me. I'll get to that subject—I mean the flower source—in awhile. I've got another histarian friend working on the Japanese connection and also on the past histories of those three gentlemen. We'll see what comes up. The historian lives in the town of Rosetta in Egypt. What a coincidence! Incidentally, I hope you're planning on going there. I can set up a meeting with him. Name's Nadim Maloof."

In his own mind, Paul agreed, even contending that Clive was sounding more and more like the prior—and even Maurice—who when given a chance, would carry on about the simplest of ideas. But Paul justified Clive's style by believing none of this was simple.

The other thing that interested him at this point was that both historians he had consulted—Dom and now, Clive—had spoken of what he, Paul, had termed a "Japanese linkage."

"Let's move on though," Clive said, "and I'll try to be less ... less expansive."

In an effort to help Clive do just that, Paul said, "How about if we consolidate three or four things? I think they're all related to begin with: Napoleon and his perfumes, Lord Elgin, Lady Beckett and the East India Company."

"Good point," Clive responded. "Let's see, where to start ... let's take the two men. The emperor was by far one of history's most talented field commanders, but he was naive when it came to trickery in human relations—I guess that's the best way to put it. Especially bribery. He learned about that in dealing with Lord Elgin. They *hated* each other, but in exchange for Napoleon's supplying flowers, perfumes and particularly the one handed down that's the center of your investigation, Elgin agreed to help him in securing women. Many, many of them. I mean in addition to Lady Beckett.

"You know, most of the key points about the importing and exporting of women today applied back in *those* times, too. For example, unlike drugs, a woman's body can be sold over and over again. It takes only a few days to move a teenager from country to country and in the process, her identity is obliterated by destroying all travel documents she may have. I'm not certain what they had then, but there must have been some sort of identification paper. Anyway, there are usually payoffs in the transit—maybe the girl herself for a night or two—but she's eventually delivered to her final destination, after being transformed into a commodity with net stockings and stiletto heels. Then she's delivered to a buyer who often beats and tortures her into compliance." Clive paused, apparently to determine if he'd left anything out. "Sorry," he said, "I tend to go off on tangents."

Paul thought Sylvie looked more disturbed than Vincent, and he knew why.

Clive continued. "In this case, we're talking flowers, not money. The flower shipments started when Napoleon lived here on Elba and somehow their destination spread to Grasse—whether through Lord Elgin or not is unclear. And the exchange simply kept up. Not all flowers, mind you, just certain ones that gave *Cleo's* perfumes their unique fragrances. That is *Cleo's,* in particular.

"And somewhere along the line, you probably learned that Elba as a flower source was kept secret. The reason? You heard this, I believe. Because the town folks in Grasse wouldn't take kindly to flowers being imported. They were, and still are, proud of their own flowers. So am I. Honey, in its wide variety of flavors, is quite a specialty in these parts. Avocado, chestnut, berry, eucalyptus, heather, wildflower, orange blossom and many others. They kind of symbolize the perfumes of the island

and the flowers of Mediterranean forests. You see many people smiling here? That's why."

"I get it," Paul said. "But as for the importing, wouldn't there have been leaks?"

"Yes there were. Two people found out, told some others and, within days, were killed. Others learned about the reason for the crimes but kept their mouths shut. Now, no one here knows who's aware of the exports because they *all* keep their mouths shut. It's an unwritten given.

"So getting back to the shipments, it was all part of a mutual bribery scheme. Napoleon called it 'Beauty in Exchange for Beauty'. So the deliveries have continued, not the women part but the flowers part."

The travelers watched as the curator used his finger to underline several notes before speaking again. "As I said, Napoleon and Lord Elgin hated each other in spite of their business/sex arrangement. And some historians believe that in the end, the emperor contrived to have Elgin poisoned. Not killed but poisoned. It caused widespread skin damage, eventually eating up a good part of his face!"

"He lost his entire nose," Sylvie said, her lip curling in disgust.

Paul had been thinking about informing Clive of Maurice's and the prior's comments about bioterrorism and believed this was as good a time as any. After listening attentively, Clive indicated he had a different opinion about the subject.

"You know," he said, "so many people get it wrong. Pure folly. Bioterrorism isn't the same as biological warfare." He reached down to the bottom drawer of his desk and pulled out a twelve-page newsletter, *The Star Beacon*, dated March, 2003.

"This gets mailed to me from your country. I read every issue religiously," he said, "and I saved this one all these years. Cripes, you'd think I knew back then that we'd be talking about this very thing, but there's a very interesting article in it. Worth saving, I thought."

"What very thing?"

"Bioterrorism. It's the lead article, titled 'The Real Deal About Nuclear, Bio and Chem Attacks.' Written by Red Thomas. Military man. Good writer. You think he's talking to you rather than writing for you. I want you to hear part of it ... let's see, page 3 ... here it is. The heading is 'Biological Warfare'. I've read it more than once since it came out. I hope you'll get the distinction I was referring to. The important line is at the end, as I remember."

There's not much to cover here. Basic personal hygiene and sanitation will take you further than a million dollars. Wash your hands often, don't share drinks, food or sloppy kisses, etc. with strangers. Keep your garbage can with a tight lid on it, and don't have standing water (such as old buckets, ditches or kiddie pools) lying around to allow mosquitoes breeding room. This stuff is carried by vectors, that is bugs, rodents and contaminated material.

If biological warfare is so easy as TV makes it sound, why has Saddam Hussein spent 20 years, and millions and millions of dollars trying to get it right?

If you're clean of person and home, you

eat well and are active, you're gonna live. Overall preparation for any terrorist attack is the same as you'd take for a big storm. If you want a gas mask, fine, go get one. I know this stuff and I'm not getting one, and I told my mom not to bother with one either. (How's that for confidence?) We have a week's worth of cash, several days' worth of canned goods and plenty of soap and water. We don't leave stuff out to attract bugs or rodents, so we don't have them.

These people can't conceive of a nation this big with this many resources. These weapons are made to cause panic, terror and to demoralize.

"There's the line: 'to cause panic, terror and to demoralize. Terror as in 'bioterrorism.' Get the distinction?"

"Sure do," Paul said. "Great way to put it. But you know what, Clive? Bioterrorism, panic, simple terror, biological warfare, whatever ... Maurice spoke about it ... the prior spoke about it ... and now you and I are speaking about it. I'm beginning to get spooked."

Clive put aside his referral sheet as if that would convey more spontaneity to what he was about to say. "My role in all this? The flowers-in-exchange-for-women-scheme, not the biological warfare thing. I'm sure you're wondering about it. I'm neutral. On the one hand, I'm all for progress and profit, but on the other, if I detect dishonesty, I back away. It may have been dishonest centuries ago—during Napoleon's and Elgin's days—but I don't see it as that today. Rest assured: I have no complaints living and working here on this land. To quote one church's rite: 'This fragile earth, our island home.' I do my curator thing. I do my flower and garden thing. I do my therapy thing. What more can I ask for?" He punctuated his words by counting on his fingers.

Paul was inclined to agree with the curator. In any event, such an issue as flower importation, he felt, shouldn't spoil what he might gain from him relative to his current treasure hunt. Wasn't he hired to do a job, not pass judgment on an island's practices? He had already gleaned all he could and felt they should call a halt to the visit. He slid his chair back, slapped his knees and said, "Well, we've taken enough of your time …"

"Not at all," Clive said. "I hope I've helped. But one last thing. About aromatherapy? As I'm sure you know, it's the art and science of treating human illness with essential oils. These volatile essences of plants and flowers have been used for thousands of years—again dating back to Cleopatra's time. There's not much more to say about it within the context of your assignment, Paul, other than to point out that this place—Elba—is a haven for such a discipline."

The session broke up with smiles, expressions of thanks and wishes for good tidings. "To coin a phrase," Paul said, "until we meet again."

Upon landing at the airstrip back in Paris, Paul noticed Leon pacing back and forth faster than usual. The chairman, visibly shaken, walked toward them.

"I hope all went well with Clive, but I have bad

news," he said.

"Oh?"

"Yes. I got a call from Dom not an hour ago. You know Tomi Morita at *Perfumes by Pierre?*"

"Yes, the president."

"He's been murdered."

"Murdered?" Paul shouted. "How? When?"

Garroted. Ligature never found. Sometime this afternoon."

On the drive back to the hotel, Paul thought he could hear his blood flowing in the silence. He didn't know about the others—nor did he dare try to elicit their thoughts for the time being—but he knew about himself. Possibly as a distraction, possibly as a matter of practicality, he became caught up in his next move, and not in the consequences of the murder itself. Question the man's employees? His relatives? The other two Japanese presidents? The local police? He would wait till the most logical of his thoughts sank in. Maybe by morning.

THE EGYPTIAN CONNECTION

Chapter 9

Before retiring the night before, Paul had forgotten to draw the curtains, probably a result of the confluence of travel fatigue and shock over Tomi Morita's murder. And now in the morning, he didn't want to look outside but couldn't help it, and saw that the weather was just as dismal as his mood. A typical morning sky lay hidden behind an overcoat of ashen clouds and the rain looked fierce as it pelted down on what he could see of the cars crawling below. He wanted to return to bed but had promised Leon that at 8:00 a.m., they would meet for breakfast to iron out the implications of the murder and what the next moves should be.

At the hotel's coffee shop, each ordered only a cup of coffee. It took Paul three sips to realize he'd forgotten to add sugar.

"Scatterbrain sometimes," he said.

"You've a right to be," Leon said soothingly. "So what do you make of it?"

"The murder? Nothing yet. I just hope it's not somebody after Japanese entrepreneurs."

"That crossed my mind, too. If so, the other two better watch their backsides. But we'll get back to it—there's more to tell you. What about the trip? Everything go according to plan at your end?"

"More so. Good advice, good leads, so much to do that's just got to get done." Paul's voice felt lifeless, like old wood. "You know a Nadim Maloof?"

"In Rosetta? Yes, very well. He's the one I spoke of before. Good man. Honorable. Among the histarians, he's called the 'informant', not in a negative sense but because he never fails to locate certain bits of information, filling in the blanks. It may be a person's name, a location, a forgotten event. Why? Did Clive recommend contacting him?"

"Sure did. Said I'd gain plenty. That he'd talked to him recently and asked him to check out the past histories of Kuroda, Yawashita and Morita. Gave him the background on perfumes and flowers. Talk about timing!" Paul drained his coffee before asking: "What's this Nadim guy do for a living?"

"He's a medical doctor specializing in nutrition and bioengineering—at the Faculty of Medicine of Alexandria University. Spends most of his time lecturing there, but lately has gotten interested in bioterrorism. Even when undergraduates are on summer break, he continues to lecture graduate students. They say he's always oversubscribed, if that's the best way to say it. They turn away some students every summer."

"There's that term again!" Paul said.

"What term?"

"Bioterrorism. At least he stuck with the 'bio'," Paul said, hoping the seriousness of the moment hadn't gotten lost in his feeble attempt at humor.

Apparently it hadn't, for Leon continued, "He knows more than most about the subject. Published some articles on it in many scientific journals. A brilliant guy and well respected, not only throughout Egypt but here in France, in Japan and even in the U.S. Wasn't he on loan at Yale awhile back?"

"I'm not aware of it, but maybe. So many guest lecturers come and go."

"Even if he wasn't at Yale long, I do know he lectured there once and was invited back several times."

"Come to think if it, that rings a bell," Paul said.

"And I know he's had some training in Japan and even stayed on to teach there for a spell. He's been around."

Paul took out a pocket-size memo pad. "Ran out of cards," he said, this time managing a smile. Lopsided, but a smile nonetheless. He entered several lines on its first page. "The med school's a stone's throw from Rosetta, right?"

"Right. So you're going?"

"I've got to. Remember, nothing's given out except in person? But we're talking a long way. I'll bet over 2,000 miles."

Leon signaled for a coffee refill—Paul refused—and was obviously searching his mind for something specific. "We can do it like last year when you all went to St. Helena," he said, like someone who'd just inserted the final piece into a jigsaw puzzle. "Ansel can fly you to London. I'll have a car ready to drive you to the Brize Norton Airbase and my friends in the R.A.F. can fly you to Alexandria. Shouldn't take more than four or five hours. Six at the most. And I'll make sure you can take your pistols along. How's that sound?"

"Perfect," Paul said, reversing his slouch and adding another word or two to his memo pad. "What d'ya know.

I can smell the coffee now."

"When do you want to leave?"

"Today, if possible."

"I'll *make* it possible. When we finish here I'll place a few phone calls and get back to you. Like for Elba, I'll alert Vincent. You want me to do the same with Sylvie this time?"

"Yes. Please do."

Then, as if the conversation centering on the murder hadn't been interrupted, Leon stated, "So as I was saying, there's more to tell you. Later last night Dom called me again after learning more about the murder. Apparently Tomi left a note on his dresser—discovered after he was found dead." Leon took out a slip of paper. "I wrote down what it said, according to her: 'Let us not be deceived. Don't they know Mohammed did not intend to have religion involved in mass murder on a grand scale?'"

"Hmm," Paul responded. He wrote the two sentences on his pad, then folded his right arm over his chest and crossed a finger of his left hand over his lips. "What was his religion?"

"Most Japanese practice Shinto or Buddhism, but he practiced Islam, I'm told."

"Told by whom?"

"Nadim."

"Nadim? How did he get into the act so soon?"

"Remember I said he was researching those three Japanese perfumers? He called yesterday when you were gone. Told me what he'd learned so far. Tomi's pals—those other two guys? Same thing: Muslims. In other words, Islamists."

"They sure had a lot in common," Paul stated with

a conviction he hadn't shown in some time.

They got up to leave and on the way out, Paul said, "One more thing. Where was the body found?"

"In his driveway, near his car. A neighborhood kid saw him on the ground."

"And saw no one else?"

"Apparently not."

There were three issues that continued to burden Paul: the fact that all three Japanese perfumers had the same Islamic religion, the jetty incident and the reference to "poison" in the latest note left in the doorway. With regard to the first issue, he believed his mind would be put at ease by discovering the extent of Islam in Japan and how many Muslims are immigrants and how many Japanese-born citizens have converted to that Islamic religion. Regarding the second, he relegated its importance to a lower priority status as compared to more current issues. And as for the third, he recalled once skimming through an article about *Sharia,* or Islamic law, and being distressed by its tenets and its forms of punishment. Was "poisoning" included?

At the lobby computer, he downloaded three relevant articles. The first was one that sketched the history of Egypt's Alexandria University. He read it carefully on the screen but didn't bother to print it. The second, with reference for IslamicAwakening.com, was titled *Japanese Muslims Face Fear and Doubt.* He printed it, then read selected sections:

> **At the pavement café in central Tokyo where Samir works, small groups of gangsters often take their seats.**

Their clothes, ostentatious jewelry and swagger mark them out as the "yakuza" gangsters who oversee the city's drug and sex trades, its protection rackets and extortion scams.

Yet more Japanese look at Samir with thinly veiled suspicion, even alarm, than at these underworld thugs.

Samir has dark hair and eyes as well as the aquiline features of his native Morocco. He has been granted permanent residency in Japan, has a full-time job and his daughter is half Japanese.

But still the assumption for some is that he is a terrorist.

"I used to have a beard and on one occasion a customer told me I looked like a terrorist," he said.

"If I were blond and had blue eyes, I wouldn't have any problems, but because my name is Samir and I have a beard, I'm a terrorist." He shaved the beard off shortly after the invasion of Iraq.

Passport to prejudice

Although born and raised in Morocco, Samir has dual nationality. "I always use my French passport," he says.

"If I used the Moroccan one, it would be terrible. I wouldn't be able to do anything. I've learned not to say that I'm Moroccan because that just causes problems."

An estimated 200,000 Muslim immigrants

presently live in Japan, as well as around 10,000 Japanese who have converted to the religion.

The last sentence was exactly what Paul was looking for. He underlined it in ink and read on:

Potential target

"Attitudes among Japanese people towards Muslims have definitely changed," said Khalid Kimio Kiba, a Japanese who converted to Islam 40 years ago and who is presently director of finance at the Islamic center in Tokyo.

All Japanese people's opinions of Muslims changed after the 11 September 2001 attacks in the United States and we are afraid," he said. "We spend a lot of time telling people that we are a sincere group dedicated to peace, that we are neither al-Qaida nor the CIA, but we have to be very careful nowadays."

Surveillance

Every week, an officer from the Tokyo Metropolitan Police visits the Islamic center in the western suburb of Setagaya to ask questions in a "very nice" manner, he says.

And, working with immigration officials, police have introduced other checks, he says, particularly on individuals renewing visas, those involved in transferring large sums of money either abroad or within Japan, or anyone with a criminal record.

"Muslim people are very afraid because we have a bad image," said Kiba. "I ask my Japanese friends whether they believe I have links to al-Qaida and even they say they can't be 100% free of suspicion.

They believe rationally that I'm not bad, but they say they can't be absolutely sure as long as I am a Muslim."

Community facilities

There are around 30 purpose–built mosques around Japan, as well as more than 200 temporary places of worship, according to Abd al-Rab Shaji, who helped found the Islamic center in 1974.

"We concentrate on preaching and the promotion of Islam," said Shaji, a Pakistani national.

Other efforts are under way to get the message across to the Japanese public that Islam does not equate to terrorism. Idris No Madjid founded Ummah Media and began publishing Wawasan Kepulauan just days after the 11 September attacks.

"I did it to make people here understand, to give the other side of the story," says Madjid, who arrived in Japan from Indonesia 30 years ago. "The news here is not balanced with Islamic news and people just don't understand Islam. It doesn't explain the details, but only shows violence and terror."

Paul found the piece informative but believed it shed

no light on why three Japanese perfumers had converted to Islam. He wondered if this was yet another example of what he had labeled "a wild goose chase", but still one that had to be carried out. As for the other nagging question, the one bearing on the message, "I'm talking poison", he read through and printed the third article he had downloaded, the one titled, *The Voice of Sharia:*

> These are the laws that we will enforce and you will obey.
> All citizens must pray five times a day. If it is prayer time and you are caught doing something else, you will be beaten.
> All men will grow their beards. The correct length is at least one clenched fist beneath the chin. If you do not abide by this, you will be beaten.
> All boys will wear turbans. Boys in grades one through six will wear black turbans, higher grades will wear white. All boys will wear Islamic clothes. Shirt collars will be buttoned.
> Singing is forbidden.
> Dancing is forbidden.
> Playing cards, playing chess, gambling, and kite flying are forbidden.
> Writing books, watching films, and painting pictures are forbidden.
> If you steal, your hand will be cut off at the wrist. If you steal again, your foot will be cut off.

Attention women:
You will stay inside your homes at all times. It
is not proper for women to wander aimlessly
about the streets. If you go outside, you must
be accompanied by a mahram, a male relative.
If you are caught alone on the street, you will
be beaten and sent home.
You will not, under any circumstance, show
your face. You will cover with burqa when
outside. If you do not, you will be severely
beaten.
Cosmetics are forbidden.
Jewelry is forbidden.
You will not wear charming clothes.
You will not make eye contact with men.
You will not laugh in public. If you do, you
will be beaten.
You will not paint your nails. If you do, you
will lose a finger.
Girls are forbidden from attending school.
Women are forbidden from working.
If you are found guilty of adultery, you will be
stoned to death.
Listen. Listen well. Obey. Allah-u-akbar.

After the readings, Paul's main thought? An awful
lot of beatings for things trivial to non-Muslims. *But no
mention of poisoning.* All in all, he felt the time spent was
probably not worth it, and he had to settle for remaining
stymied. But whether it was a premonition or whatever,
he believed he might be prompted—even provoked—to
review the second article sometime in the near future.

The phone rang. Leon stated that all was ready and in place for the Alexandria junket. Vincent would pick him up at noon. Leon would meet the three of them at the airstrip before their flight to London and their hooking up with the R.A.F.

Before hanging up, Paul apologized for leaving the country at the same time as Tomi's murder but underscored the significance of meeting with Dr. Maloof as soon as possible. He reminded Leon that while he was on Egyptian soil, he would initiate some kind of research into the life of Cleopatra, but didn't specify what that included. Nor did he share with the chairman what he was anxious to put into words but believed was too premature to do so. It concerned Paul's strong feeling that the number of missed opportunities was directly proportional to the number of important happenings, particularly new ones. The more things happened, the more likely errors could be made. Errors of omission. In private moments of self-evaluation and worth as a treasure hunter, he had sometimes downgraded his effectiveness based on a failed investigation or two, but then would find new resolve by shifting the blame onto sluggish follow-up or—one time—onto the existence of "spies." He pondered the possibility of spies or moles operating in the midst of his investigation. But this was hardly the time to broach such a sensitive subject.

What he did suggest to Leon, however, was for him to contact the two remaining perfume presidents plus the Grasse police to see what he could find out: verifying the two presidents' religion; Tomi's recent actions; visits by strangers; known threats on his life; specifics concerning the crime scene; any other forensic details.

"I'll do my best," Leon said.

"Good. Wish I could be in two places at the same time. See you at the airstrip."

Chapter 10

Among the three travelers and Leon, there wasn't much said at the airstrip that hadn't already been said over the phone in the previous hour or two.

And between the flying of Ansel and that of the R.A.F., Paul, Sylvie and Vincent arrived at the Alexandria National Airport at 7:35 p.m., Egyptian time.

They checked in at the Four Season Alexandria Hotel. It occupied seventeen of the twenty-nine floors of a luxurious seaside tower, located within walking distance of the medical center which overlooked the waterfront's Corniche Promenade and the Mediterranean.

They chose separate rooms, but at the check-in counter, Sylvie whispered in Paul's ear, "But not for the whole night, I hope."

Paul made sure Vincent wasn't watching as he gave her a provocative look, then winked.

They soon convened at Byblos, the hotel's main restaurant, all of them famished, and ordered the same Lebanese herb-infused cuisine, its specialty. They agreed to turn in early and reconvene for a breakfast buffet at the hotel's Kala. As they reentered the main lobby, Paul and Sylvie lagged behind and Vincent said in a nonchalant way, "You're too slow for me. See you in the morning — eight okay?"

"Okay with you, Syl?" Paul asked.

She nodded.

"Eight then, Vincent. Sleep tight." Paul lowered his voice, "And I'll keep those pistols handy."

Paul led Sylvie to the side of an ornate staircase and said, "Look, I have a little preparation to do before we meet with the doctor tomorrow, maybe a half-hour's worth. But after that, care to come next door?"

Sylvie, her voice deepening, answered, "Do roosters go cock-a-doodle-do?"

Alone in his room, all Paul wanted to accomplish was to write out a list of items to hand to Nadim, hoping the doctor would address them. He had difficulty concentrating but wrote:

1. The Rosetta Stone article and its sentence, "This enabled scholars to translate inscriptions inside the Egyptian temples"
2. Temples and inscriptions
3. Past history of Ken, Junzo and Tomi. Their religion. Ties to Japanese rainforests
4. Poisons
5. Cleopatra
6. Napoleon
7. Talleyrand
8. Lady Beckett
9. East India Company
10. Japan

There was a soft knock on the door.

"Yes?" Paul said, walking over.

"It's me," was the reply. It was Sylvie's voice, one

Paul hadn't expected to hear for another fifteen minutes. He unlocked the door and she came in. She wore a red robe, high heels and black stockings. Paul detected a perfume more enticing than he had ever experienced. They smiled at one another roguishly.

"Why the heels and stockings?" he asked.

"Thought you'd like to see me take them off"

"Not a bad idea," he countered, removing his shirt.

She undid the sash to the robe and let them drop to the floor—first the sash, then the robe. She stood nude—uncomfortably, he thought—except for a garter belt, the stockings and the high heels.

Sylvie rushed into his arms, kissed his ear and breathed into it, "We're in Egypt. Can you believe it? And it's unrealistic, I know, but do you know what I would like? To make love to you at the foot of a pyramid."

Paul didn't respond to the statement but did to the kissing—in like kind.

"Oh, Paul," she said, "You mean so much to me! It's as if I've known you all my life?"

Paul couldn't resist. "Even as toddlers?" he said.

She pulled away slightly. "You're making fun of me," she pouted.

"Well, you said all your life. But tell me, why near a pyramid?"

"As a symbol of our eternal love."

"Eternal? But after we die…" He never had a chance to finish the sentence.

"Oh, be quiet," Sylvie said, nudging him toward the bed.

They stayed awake for another twenty minutes.

The next morning, after having had their fill of an

elaborate breakfast in the Kala, the travelers entered the main door to the Faculty of Medicine building. Paul felt underdressed in his open collar yellow shirt and brown blazer. Vincent's blazer was blue as was his striped tie. Sylvie wore a plain brown blouse and matching tight pants.

The door opened into a sprawling square anteroom that had nothing in it but two umbrella stands. Bare masonry walls, hardwood floor with no carpeting, no furniture, no noise, no smells—nothing. They would eventually understand why it was called the "Nothing Room" and even asked several passersby why the room was there. No one had an answer.

The adjoining room, however, was quite the opposite: crowded with employees, women technicians primarily—all wearing scarves of yellow, pink and white; all bustling with activity. At the entrance, the trio paused, and in unison, rubbed their eyes. Sylvie handed the other two a tissue to help rid their nostrils of pungent chemical odors. Some technicians were hard to identify as women, clothed as they were in loose-fitting green scrub suits, and white caps and gowns. Some worked silently and swiftly at benches below suspended fume hoods—benches of Bunsen burners, beakers, wire loops, petri dishes, scales, centrifuges, microscopes, incubators, chemical jars, rubber hosing, glass tubing and oxygen tanks. Others deftly manipulated extension rods through glass partitions, transferring the dexterity of their hands to metal claws inside. Each person seemed to have a purpose as she finished one task and quickly began to tackle another. One seemed out of place, the only one smiling in the room. She greeted the travelers at a reception desk near the door.

It was 9:10 a.m.

"We're early," Paul said, "but we have an appointment with Dr. Maloof for nine-thirty."

"Yes, oh yes … yes, indeed … ," the receptionist said, opening an appointment book. "You must be Paul, Vincent and Sylvie. Sorry, I don't have your last names."

"I can give them to you, if you wish," Paul said.

"No, that won't be necessary. We use first names very often in our Faculty of Medicine. Even Dr. Maloof prefers to be called Nadim."

"Okay then," Paul said. "Would Nadim be available, or are we too early?"

"No, you're not too early. I don't know how he came to suspect it, but he said if you arrived early, to direct you to the central amphitheater. I guess it's affectionately called the 'pit' in every country. Our regular students are still off, but he has an advanced summer class for graduate students every year." She glanced at the clock on the wall. "We all know it's unusual but he lectures in fifteen-minute segments with five minutes off between them. Says it gives students a chance to go over their notes and make changes or additions. So if you'll have a seat for three or four minutes, he'll start again at nine-fifteen. You can use our shortcut over there. Just go through one more room and you'll see a hallway at its far end. Down some steps and there you are: the pit."

They sat on a three-person settee. Paul had a choice of trying to dissect what he'd seen and heard in the last few minutes, or just letting thoughts tumble through his mind. He chose the latter.

He began with something innocuous. He knew the history of the university fairly well, having read that brief article about it once he'd decided to confer with Dr. Nadim Maloof. He was described as one of the luminaries within this Faculty of Medicine, its medical school. When he read the article, Paul had wondered why the facility was so named. Teaching started there during World War II and within fifteen years, a dentistry school, a pharmacy school and a school for nurses, midwives and physiotherapists had been added. Paul remembered that the Faculty of Medicine served a population of over five million people, offering educational opportunities for about 7,000 students annually, and that the teaching component was divided into basic science and clinical science departments. Nadim was associated with both departments.

However Paul didn't think his mind would lead to something disquieting. It had been several days in the making but was too vague to capture his full attention until now. He was coming to an uneasy realization that the focus of his assignment was beginning to change. He was drifting away from flowers and perfumes and the primary goal of locating a stolen packet— to murder with an international flavor. As both simple and complicated as that. Under the present circumstances, he forced his mind to go blank, waiting for two more minutes to pass.

The receptionist finally rose. "I think it's time now. Don't mind the distractions in the next room. It's really our main lab complex but we call it Confusion Room Two."

"Thank you," Paul said. "By the way, what do you call this room?"

"Confusion Room One."

They navigated their way into the next room where there were far fewer technicians, all in more conventional clothing. The air had an entirely different smell as well.

From his not infrequent visits to Yale's various laboratories, Paul had learned about a variety of odors, some sweet, some acrid, some stimulating his taste buds.

The complex consisted essentially of a collection of smaller labs, all beneath separate overhead cameras. Paul was puzzled by the need for such monitoring. Moving forward, they passed a large laboratory outfitted with what he was sure were DNA sequencing machines—devices that resembled the photo processing units at retail photo centers; then a section labeled "Imaging Network"; a larger one labeled "Peptide Synthesis Facility"; a conglomerate of rooms assigned to Radiology, Ultrasound, Nuclear Medicine, Spiral CT Scanning and Open MRI; and a closed cast-iron door with a sign above that read, "Sample Evidence Control." There was a similar door back at Connecticut's Forensic Science Laboratory. Paul was once informed that the room inside was used to coordinate labeling procedures to assure that a legal chain of controls for forensic evidence was maintained and to help avoid anything that could thwart proper DNA identification. Paul's interpretation? It prevented screw-ups.

They made it through to the steps, many more than expected. At the bottom, Paul carefully opened a large door an inch at a time, and peered into what looked like any other "pit" where he'd lectured. The room was still and filled to near capacity—some three hundred students. Below, a man at a pulpit was arranging some papers. Nadim, no doubt. Scattered around him were various audiovisual materials: maps, flip charts, opaque and overhead projectors; and off to both sides, tables burdened with audiotape and compact disc recorders,

VCRs and computer screens. From Paul's vantage point Nadim looked tall, sixty or so, and certainly muscular. Paul walked in quietly, the others followed and they took seats in the last row. The man looked up at them, flashed an animated smile, then announced with great gusto, "Well, ladies and gentlemen, they're here—our visiting friends from Paris: Paul, Sylvie and Vincent." He had not used any notes to check on the names. "I am Nadim and these are my graduate students—my young heroes." Every student rose, turned around and looked toward the center of the back row. The amphitheater then erupted into loud and sustained applause, as if the legendary King Faruk had made an appearance. The travelers were strangers but, in those several brief moments, they found themselves welcomed as heroes.

They exchanged glances, rose to their feet, and waved with enthusiasm.

The doctor, his eyes locked in their direction, said: "I'm near the end of today's talk—perhaps ten minutes more. My study is nearby. Please join me there when I finish?"

Paul nodded for the three of them while giving the thumbs-up sign.

"Bravo. Same in French and English. We have much to discuss based on what our mutual friend has told me."

By this time, Nadim had made more of an impression on Paul. He wore a long white laboratory coat, both chest pockets and both side pockets overstuffed with pens, pencils and slips of paper, undoubtedly lab reports. A burgundy shirt and bright floral tie were barely visible as the coat was buttoned completely to the top. What showed of his pants was black and too long, the pant legs draped over most of his tan moccasin shoes. His snappy moves were at odds with his large frame. Paul believed they were symptomatic of a lifetime of impatience, as was his own habit of chewing on his lower lip. His complexion and eyes were distinctly brown; a foreshortened mustache gray; and for all intents and purposes, he was bald. More than once he dabbed at the perspiration on his scalp, careful not to disturb the three or four strands of gray hair plastered from side to side. He appeared to know their exact location. His face, round and fleshy, devoured his eyes when he smiled. But it was that very smile that Paul knew could dominate a room: easy, full, genuine. The former Yale academician had interacted with many men and women over the years, and he could always separate out those smiles that took shape purely for selfish reasons. Disingenuous versus genuine.

Like a car switching gears, Nadim ran over the slope of students before him and said, "Let us proceed. I want to tell all of you about what genetically modified foods are and then I want to discredit them. And you have heard, I am sure, about my relatively recent interest in terrorism, especially bioterrorism. I won't take up much of your time on it, but we'll end up with that.

"For some time now, genetic engineering has been making headlines in the field of nutrition and so-called food safety. It's the process of altering foods by removing a gene from one type of organism and inserting it in another type. Proponents of the process claim that the result is greater quantities of a food product plus a fresher one." With an upward roll of his eyes and a poorly disguised snicker, the doctor made no bones about his personal view of the subject.

"Let's give you a simple example: genetically altering a tomato. Let's say it's too soft to begin with. It so happens that a naturally occurring enzyme, polygalacturonase—PG for short— makes tomatoes go soft. So through the genetic engineering process, the gene responsible for making PG is isolated and copied. It can then be ... quote ... reversed ... unquote, which serves to cancel its softening capability. This altered gene is next put into bacteria which are placed into a container with tomato leaf pieces. Little do the leaf pieces know that when the bacteria are absorbed, so is the new gene." Nadim smiled at his subtle hint of humor. "Well, the upshot of it all—if you'll forgive the pun—is that when the leaf pieces sprout, they're eventually transferred to soil. Then the seeds are collected from the sprouted plants and, voila, the next generation will produce the altered tomatoes.

"I won't elaborate here, but I have problems with the whole approach and so does this country. In fact, it's banned importing or exporting any genetically modified foods. Implementing that in its entirety is a problem in itself, but that's another story involving politics, ethical concerns, the size of our food supply and so on. My own reservations concern food safety, transfer of food allergens, tampering with nature, domination of the world's food production by a handful of companies, and even the simple process of labeling: confounding the labeling of genetically modified crops with the non-modified.

"So that's enough of that. I've presented it only because so many of you have asked about it. Now how does any of this relate to bioterrorism? It doesn't. And why and how did a medical doctor become interested in the subject? During my earlier training in Japan, especially when I was on duty in a hospital there, I saw so many patients who had died or were near death as a result of some crazy people experimenting with biologicals that could do harm. I vowed that someday I would get involved—not in the way they did, but in the opposite way. I knew then and I know now that one person can't stop people like that. Some call them 'terrorists'. I call them 'malcontents' because I believe a malcontent blossoms first and then he or she may evolve into a full-blown terrorist. So nutrition, genetic engineering, and bioterrorism. Taken together, they form my 'interest model'."

He dismissed the class without further elaboration.

Nadim's study was appropriately named, for besides serving as his official office, it was a study in rich furniture pieces and accessories. Most were upholstered in leather: chairs, sofa, the base of a tower clock, desk and table moldings, even some lampshades. The room was not small—perhaps thirty-feet square—but the number of books lining its walls and the many journals piled high on tables and overflowing onto the corners of its orientally carpeted floor gave it a compact feel. Even some of its windows were partially blocked by books and journals.

To Paul, the doctor looked the same face-to-face as he had in the pit. Maybe somewhat shorter and softer in voice. His handshake was strong even as he commented on Paul's.

"That is what I would call a legitimately firm handshake," he said, shaking his as if in pain.

"Lots of practice," Paul said. "Sorry."

The other two indicated they had heard most favorable remarks about the doctor and his scientific work. Nadim praised all three for their academic achievements, in every case citing specifics that only one who had researched their lives would know about. Paul thanked him for his hospitality and his willingness to confer with them.

The travelers took seats on a sofa that faced Nadim's desk, Paul in the middle. The doctor sat on a large chair that he pulled over and positioned between the desk and sofa. He reached back for a pad which he then balanced on his lap, allowing his arms freedom of movement as he spoke.

Paul handed Nadim the list he'd prepared and, in an apologetic tone, said, "I hope you don't mind lists. I'm a big 'list man' and even my friends think they're too restrictive."

Nadim took the sheet of paper. "Don't be silly," he said. "We scientists like lists. They keep us on course." He perused it, saying, "I spoke with Leon last night. He fairly much knows what's on this list and, moreover, what you're probably aware of regarding each of these items. And in our talk, he relayed that information to me. I hope I can fill in the blanks for you."

"I've been told that's what you excel at," Paul said.

Nadim laughed so hard the pad fell from his lap. Before retrieving it, he said, "That's me, the Egyptian blank filler."

He folded the list and put it in his pocket. Then he straightened up and followed with, "I wish to begin with something that's not on the list because Leon tells me it's been preying on your mind, and he wishes you would concentrate on more immediate problems. I believe I can bring most of this to a conclusion and you'll be done with it. I'm still working on other parts of it, but I expect to have them resolved soon."

Paul had no idea what was coming up, and Vincent's and Sylvie's expressions showed they were just as much in the dark.

Nadim went on: "Let me give you the name Leon used: 'The jetty incident.' And I must preface what I know by admitting … no, that's the wrong word because it implies possible guilt and I assure you I'm not guilty of breaking any law. Let me explain. For many years now, I've kept up a friendship with some organized crime figures, mainly those in Japan. I trained and worked there for eight years. But I've kept my distance. I use them only as informants. The nature of their work makes them *reliable* informants. We all know they deal in corruption, extortion, prostitution, drug-trafficking, murder-for-hire but, at the same time, they're reliable. Isn't that something? If they weren't used to being totally reliable in dealings with others of their kind, they might be killed. Then, in return, I help them with health matters. Many don't dare show their faces in doctors' offices or hospitals, so I make it easy for them. Some mobs are enemies with other mobs, but some individual members do cooperate with other individual members to a certain extent. I'm treated, I suppose, as such a member. And the more friendly I became with the Japanese Yakuza, the more often I was put in contact with their counterparts all over the world: the Chinese Triads and Tongs, the Sicilian and American Mafia, the Viet-Ching and so forth. All sorts of criminal syndicates. I'm not necessarily proud of it, but as long as I don't participate in their racketeering, I have nothing to be ashamed of. So I've kept up the friendships. It's a strange arrangement, I know, and some—not all—of my friends and colleagues here at the University are aware of it, and they don't hold it against me. It's actually like an unspoken secret, I suppose—a secret that most everyone knows about."

The room's ensuing silence hummed with intensity.

Finally, Nadim said, "To wrap this part up, let's just say I have some underworld ties and that's how I secured many answers regarding the jetty incident. After speaking with Leon last night, I made some calls to my usual sources. Even got the details about the shooting of that fellow during what Leon referred to as the chase before Paul's eyes. I have the whole scenario written down here and the players he named." He tapped on his pad. "I assume he got it all from you, Paul?"

"Yes," Paul replied, still stunned by the doctor's revelations. "I told him the whole thing."

"Okay then." Nadim peeked at his notes. "That man tailing you? Rico Cretelli? He was shot by a mobster hired by someone who thought he was your bodyguard. I'm not sure yet who that someone is, but I'm working on it. And the mobster disposed of the body somewhere; however I don't think that's important. But why was someone after you in the first place? Remember, that was Rico Cretelli. Because you were hired to solve the riddle of who stole the packet. Yes, Leon covered all of that. He was quite thorough.

"And the people in the car that sped away? Entirely different story, There were three men in it, all related to the Talleyrand family who still has it in for you. But I think

that can be diffused, one way or another. You'll understand
when we get to them and Napoleon, Lady Beckett, the East
India Company, Yale, and all of that. But I must admit, it's
difficult for me to understand, so many characters being
involved. Or maybe Leon left some things out."

Paul was amazed at what the doctor knew and
told him so. He also told him either he or Sylvie would
summarize the Talleyrand story as they understood it. "She
was a part of it, to a degree, so maybe she should do most
of the talking," he said.

"Yes, that would help." Nadim adjusted his tie and
suppressed a yawn. Then he said, "Leon and I talked for
over an hour and I took copious notes as you can see." He
tilted his pad toward Paul. "He ended up by elaborating on
your entire career, including Yale's firing you because they
said you spent too much time on mythology, and so forth.
So between talking to him and to my various informants,
I must have been on the phone till well past midnight.

"Now 'the chase before your eyes' incident: why
was that fellow shot? Incidentally, I was told you refer
to his assailant as 'the street shooter'. Well, that victim
also dates back to the Talleyrand family and their various
gripes, but the shooter didn't know that. Instead he thought
the guy was trying to take over his paid-for-hire territory.
So for either or both reasons, he was shot. If he were
still around, you might have cause for concern over your
safety. But he's been taken care of, so don't worry. All
very complicated, I'll give you that.

"All right, let's get to the list." Nadim said. He
removed it from his pocket, unfolded it and read sections
of it aloud, editorializing as he went along: "The Rosetta
Stone and the sentence in the article that you feel has

meaning; our temples and inscriptions here in Egypt; the histories and religion of the three big-time perfumers; any ties to Japanese rain forests—I presume you mean on the part of these three men; poisons—when we get to it, we'll determine in what context; Cleopatra; we'll eventually combine Talleyrand, Napoleon, Lady Beckett and the East India Company; and we end up with Japan"

He looked at Paul expectantly, and Paul addressed Sylvie, "You know it better than I do, so just repeat what you once told me, Syl. I'll fill in here and there."

She nodded and her face brightened as if she were thrilled with the opportunity. "I've run it through my mind so many times this shouldn't be a problem, but stop me if you need clarification." She leaned forward and lowered her voice like one revealing a secret.

"In the late 1790's," she began, "Talleyrand was deported from France for reasons that have no bearing on anything right now—and he fled to the U.S. Two years later, he was allowed back. The Institute of France was just starting up at the time and it was struggling, financially and otherwise. Somehow he came to its rescue and from that point on, he developed a strong bond with the Institute and all its branches, including the one I work for, the Academy of Sciences. This bond still exists today through his relatives, who have terrific pull with the Institute."

Paul couldn't help interrupting. "And they were very upset that I had the nerve to write what I thought at the time—that if Napoleon had been murdered, Talleyrand had to be a prime suspect because of the deportation. And how did they even know that? It was in one of my yet-unpublished manuscripts."

Sylvia took over. "That's where Yale came in. Oh

yes, this gets more intriguing by the minute. You still with us, doctor?"

Nadim's eyes narrowed speculatively. "Yes, so far," he replied. "I knew about some of it, but not all."

"Well," Sylvie said, "We've still got Elihu Yale, the East India Company, Lady Beckett and spices to cover."

It was Paul's turn. "But what do spices and the man Yale was named after have to do with it, you ask?"

"The family, to a person, was afraid that you, Paul, might come to a definite conclusion that Napoleon was murdered," Sylvie said. "They wanted the public to think it was a natural death and have been pushing that for years. You see, an unnatural death suggests an ancestor as a possible killer. But a natural death? They can forget about the ancestor as a killer. And as you might imagine, I was caught in the middle — my job, for instance."

Nadim, now taking notes, asked, "Would they resort to murder?" For the first time, the doctor appeared flustered, his smile strained. "Wait," he said, "forget that question. I already said they were after you."

"Yes, you did, and yes, they would," Paul said. "But only through the mob. Signals could get crossed though, or the hoodlums could get careless. They all walk a fine line and one of them never knows what another one is thinking. Even blood relatives can't trust one other. When drugs, prostitution, money laundering, territories controlled, kickbacks and all those money things are concerned, they can throw loyalty out the window. Only they're clever at disguising it. And I should have included murder in there, too. You know all that better than we do, doctor."

In an effort to divert attention from what might be heading toward a tense situation, Paul kicked in again. He switched to another subject. "What I don't understand, though," he said, "is how did the Talleyrands know what I said about that case? Remember, my manuscript was still unpublished. I know the answer, Nadim, but we're presenting it in a rhetorical sense. Sylvie and I have been through this several times before, privately. The answer, Syl?"

"*I* told them. It was part of what I had to do at the time, right Paul?"

"Right."

"Okay," Sylvie said. "Now to Elihu Yale and spices. The university was named after him because he was its largest benefactor. But he was also an official with the British East India Company, just like Lady Beckett. And Talleyrand was not only a great statesman but also a renowned gourmet and wine connoisseur. He once owned the fancy Chateaux Haut-Brion and hired the finest chefs around. He also bought the finest tea and spices from the East India Company. Anyway, that's how Talleyrand and Beckett happened to strike up their friendship and to develop the covers used for her to see Napoleon. And all the rest."

"So Yale University and the Talleyrand clan are close?" Nadim asked.

"Hand in glove, even to this day. And that's how the clan knew about what was in Paul's manuscript. When the Yale people read the names on his suspect list, I'd wager they contacted them on the spot. In fact, I've got to believe that's why they fired Paul. The mythology excuse was entirely secondary."

Nadim's face hardened. "So the remedy for this is very clear," he said, staring at Paul. "I'll arrange for the Talleyrands to learn, via Yale's various publications, that you've discarded your original theory entirely and apologize for any embarrassment you may have caused the family." He shifted his attention to Sylvie. "And if what you say is correct—that Yale let Paul go because of such a theory and not because of the mythology views—I'll go so far as to say that Yale might ask him to rejoin their faculty. Perhaps in a different capacity—say, conducting a class on the perils of international treasure hunting or something like that. Interested, Paul?"

Paul was bowled over by the suggested remedy. More so by its estimated consequence on the part of Yale. And instead of answering, he nervously flicked his finger at motes of dust in a stray shaft of sunlight.

"So would you be interested, Paul?" Sylvie queried.

"You mean in an offer like that?" Paul asked, biding some time. "I'd have to think on it. 'Interesting' and 'interested' can be miles apart, you know."

"Vincent," Nadim said. "You haven't said a word. What do you think?"

"Me? I think it's interesting and merits some interest."

"Way to go, Vincent," Paul said.

"No," Vincent said, "what I mean … er … what I should say is not that Paul should jump at such an offer, if it comes, but that maybe the doctor's idea of having Yale retract Paul's earlier belief—that's where the possible merit comes in … in my opinion."

Paul nodded somewhat reluctantly. "I agree, Vincent," he said. He looked at Nadim and although Paul tried to smile, his face didn't cooperate. But he said, "Let's go with it. You can arrange all this, Nadim?"

"Yes. Certainly."

Paul reached down to tighten a shoelace although it didn't need it. "Please go ahead then," he said. He gave Nadim the name of his Paris hotel.

"Fine, fine," Nadim responded. "It's worth a try. I strongly believe they'll want you back. Who wouldn't? I'll be in contact with you. As you know, we historians don't like to conduct — shall we say, business by phone — but this isn't a brand new topic, so I have no reservation in calling you."

Paul felt like a teenager who had just been patted on the back. "Thank you, doctor," he said. "And may I say something about phone conversations?"

"Certainly you may."

"And you won't be offended?"

"I'm not easily offended."

"Well, I've never fully understood the reason why some historians won't discuss much by phone."

"Neither have I."

Nadim's laugh drowned out Paul's.

Dr. Maloof phoned for tea, coffee, a variety of juices and some pastries. Each one in the study partook of something, undoubtedly to alleviate anxiety more than satisfy hunger. It worked, for within fifteen minutes they were joking about weather, upcoming birthdays, types of clothing and other innocuous subjects.

When the conversation showed its first sign of dwindling, Nadim announced, "Time for the list again. And let me say that unfortunately I'll have the floor most of the time, but don't hesitate to contribute."

He examined the list and said, "Of the ten here, we've

already dealt with Talleyrand, Lady Beckett and the East India Company. As for the Rosetta Stone article and its sentence about enabling scholars to translate inscriptions inside the Egyptian temples—yes, I'm aware of such a sentence—do I know of any inscriptions that might apply to the case? Yes but I can't remember which one came from where. Among the temples are Kom Ombo, Edfu, Esna, Karnak and Luxor. But Paul, I don't think it's necessary to visit them. Regarding their inscriptions, many refer to death in general but there's only one that suggests the possibility of outright murder, and I know it word for word: 'Beware of hidden poisons'. This, of course, is consistent with that last note you received, 'I'm Talking Poison'. We have it from two sources as divergent as they could possibly be: the paper note left at your door and the inscription in an Egyptian temple. But don't forget the third source. Remember the note Tomi Morita left? Leon read it to me and I have it written down." He leafed through the first few pages of his pad. "Here it is," he said. 'Let us not be deceived. Don't they know Mohammed didn't intend to have religion involved in mass murder on a grand scale?' If we interpret 'mass murder' as poisoning—and I realize that's a big 'if'—then that makes a total of three sources. I would call them our 'poison model'. You have your lists, Paul. I have my models."

The trio was thoroughly engrossed in Nadim's words, Paul occasionally jotting down one or two, Sylvie writing complete sentences, and by this time Vincent, borrowing a page from her pad and following suit. Paul was so absorbed in what he was hearing that he didn't want to break his concentration by peering at the reactions on either side of him. He was positive, however, that his colleagues were similarly absorbed.

"And speaking of Tomi Morita," Nadim continued, "let's cover the other two perfumers too, the ones still alive." He gave a concise history of all three: that they were born and raised in Tokyo; all were brought up in the Shinto religion but changed to active Muslims while in college; they preferred to be called Islamists rather than Muslims; they met in college—the University of Tokyo—and eventually became good friends; they were considered brilliant students and even more brilliant in their first jobs—Tomi as a computer programmer, Ken and Junzo as chemists at separate companies. Then suddenly they left their lines of work and turned to perfumery, strangely at about the same time.

"I understand they have some kind of connection with a private Japanese rain forest," Nadim added. "Some of their flowers are delivered to their individual businesses in Grasse. But here's the interesting thing: they needed permission from the Yakuza who control the rain forest."

Paul thought it was about time to say *something*, at least. "Boy, they're into everything, aren't they?"

"At least in Japan," Nadim replied. He rechecked his notes. "Enough on the perfumers?"

"For now? Yes," Paul answered.

"Then let's skip down to Napoleon." Nadim flipped to another page.

"What can I say regarding the emperor? Napoleon was Napoleon. You know about his agreeing to flowers in exchange for an ongoing relationship with Lady Beckett. You know of his use of arsenic as a recreational drug. You know of the theory he was poisoned with it by someone spiking his food and drink over long periods of time—enough for him to flounder away key battles. But I firmly believe arsenic doesn't fit into the 'poison model'. Think about some of the messages. 'Beware of hidden poisons'? Arsenic wasn't a hidden poison. Perhaps the dose might have been, but not the substance itself. 'I'm talking poison'? Nothing there. The one about Mohammed not intending to have religion involved in murder on a grand scale? That refers to large numbers, not to a single individual like Napoleon. So I'd be hard pressed to include arsenic in our three-faced poison model. Wouldn't you?"

Again Paul fumbled for words. He settled on: "You certainly sound like a scientist."

"I should hope so," Nadim responded. "But don't you agree?"

"Absolutely. So arsenic is out."

"Absolutely."

"Doesn't count. I said it last."

They shared a brief laugh before the doctor switched to completing the list.

"Two more to go," he said. "Cleopatra and Japan. Talk about two subjects as far apart as one could imagine! And by your including the queen, I assume you meant visiting her tomb. I see nothing to be gained by it. In fact, no one's certain of where it is. The last I heard it's near the temple of Taposiris Magna here in Alexandria, but who knows for sure? And as for Japan, that's a different story, but you can visit there through me. I know all there is to know about the country and that, together with your interpretation of more information from me will prove to be extremely beneficial. And I mean extremely. We'll talk more about that another time.

"For now, I'd say that on balance, the biggest contribution I can make is to stress the 'poisoning' aspect. How it fits in, I'm not entirely sure yet. With respect to the other matters still hanging, I'll be in touch unless I feel they have no significance in the greater scheme of things."

Nadim was the first to rise. They chatted for a few minutes about what each had learned from the visit.

At the door Paul said, "You've been more than helpful and we thank you."

"It's been my pleasure to participate in this historic challenge," Nadim said. He hesitated before adding, "and the bulk of it is yet to come."

He then expressed the same sentiment to each of the travelers as he shook their hands: "It was good of you to come all the way to Egypt."

Paul was at a loss to explain why the doctor had referred to only one of the three notes left at his door. But then it dawned on him—they weren't on his list.

Chapter 11

As they strolled through the courtyard of the Faculty of Medicine building, a flash of lightening illuminated a fast darkening sky.

"Is that an edification burst for what we learned in there?" Vincent asked.

"Good," Paul said, turning. "Very literary." He was leading the way out.

"But not necessarily appropriate," Sylvie said. She tapped Vincent's shoulder. "I'm not being critical of you, Vincent but …"

"But you have reservations, I know," Paul said. "I sensed it in there, and I'm afraid Nadim did too." He asked that they not stop to confer, as it was starting to drizzle. He looked up at the sky, stroked a few raindrops from his nose and said, "It smells and feels refreshing but from the looks of it, a torrential rain's not far off. We'd better hurry. We'll have our postmortem in due course."

A pelting rain never developed and by the time they reached their hotel, the drizzle had stopped completely. It was eleven-twenty-five a.m. Paul phoned Leon, characterized their trip as hugely successful, and said he'd elaborate in person. Leon indicated that he and Ansel would be waiting for them at London's Heathrow Airport.

Paul, Sylvie and Vincent gathered in Paul's room,

the two men on easy chairs, Sylvie on the edge of the bed. Paul's face held no particular expression as he said, "Okay, Syl, let's hear it. Why the reservations?"

"I hope I'm not upsetting you, Paul, but some things disturbed me over there." She pointed in the direction of the Center. "Disturbed and frightened me."

"Go on," Paul said, his manner amiably composed.

"He's an intelligent, nice guy and so forth but ... well, for starters, all that talk in his lecture about terrorism; his ties with organized crime; discouraging any visit to Cleopatra's tomb; and the fact that he didn't make eye contact with any of us very often."

"But you do agree with how he handled himself on the other issues, especially his 'poison model'?"

"Yes, I thought that was the keynote of the whole session. But getting back to the negatives, or at least what I believe were negatives, I think I had more to say about Talleyrand and Yale and the East India Company and Lady Beckett than he did."

"But I asked you to talk about them, remember?"

"Yes, I do."

"And you don't think it was generous of him to say he'd try to settle the Talleyrand and Yale fiasco? That would be a godsend incidentally."

"Yes, I do. I'm acting foolish, I guess, but take it as coming from a devil's advocate who is very much on your side, Paul."

"But you don't trust him, I take it."

"I didn't *say* that. I'd just be careful." She crimped her mouth in annoyance.

He left his chair, sat beside her on the bed and held her hand. "You know, Syl—and you Vincent—maybe I'm the one who's foolish. It's simply that I believe we learned a great deal from someone who I think doesn't have any particular stake in this—other than doing his best as an historian. He didn't have to lecture on those topics in front of us. He didn't have to admit to connections with the underworld. He wasn't trying to hide anything. As for the eye contact, maybe he's always been that way. Maybe he was shy as a child. Who knows? The only thing I disagree with is his opinion that I needn't visit the temples. I happen to think I should, especially when we're talking poisons. Even *he* admitted to being a bit weak on the inscriptions there. I'm going ... eventually. I'll ask Leon to find the best translator around so he or she can accompany us."

Paul returned to his chair and rolled his neck a few times.

"What do you think, Vincent?" he asked.

"I was impressed. Sorry, Sylvie. Impressed with what we got and with what I believe will come of it. There was just one thing: he never said whether or not you should pay a visit to Beckett Gardens and Lady Beckett's tomb. Was that intentional or unintentional?"

"Makes no difference," Paul replied. "Some time ago, I'd already made up my mind, to go. But not yet."

"Why not, as long as we're already in London?" Vincent asked.

"Because I want to hear first how he makes out with Yale and the Talleyrand family. Don't ask me why but if that issue gets resolved, I have a sneaking suspicion that the trip to Lady Beckett's tomb can be more beneficial. Remember Talleyrand and Lady Beckett were very close, not romantically as far as I know, but as devoted friends.

So reasoning tells me that if his descendants change their mind and look more favorably on me, and if they know something about the tomb, the casket, what's in it, et cetera, then maybe, just maybe, we might find something important if we have it dug up and opened. That's it in a nutshell, but first we have to hear back from Nadim."

"You're so analytical, Paul," Sylvie said. "And I do so hope I didn't put a damper on things by my being odd man out at the beginning. I was just trying to be truthful."

"Understood, Syl, and no, you didn't put a damper on anything. Let's just agree—if you both do—that we're better off now than we were, say, when we first woke up this morning."

Sylvie shot him a sidelong glance but refrained from giving anything away, and Paul added with a straight face, "Come to think of it, I usually feel lousy when I first wake up, but not this morning for some reason. You get my point though, don't you?"

They both nodded, Sylvie a tad less forcefully.

"Good," Paul said, "So let's freshen up, then go unwind during lunch. I might even have a wine."

"Now you're talking!" Vincent exclaimed.

"Me, too." Sylvie said.

At Heathrow, the travelers, Leon and Ansel opted for coffee and doughnuts in a small café instead of meeting at one of its long benches. It wasn't quite dinnertime, 4:20 p.m., yet the airport wasn't as crowded as the several dining areas that ringed the main aisles. Their meeting didn't last long, since Leon anticipated much of what Paul was trying to get across.

"Excellent job, excellent result," the chairman said. "What more could we expect?"

"That the Talleyrand-Yale card is a winning one, and that Yale will take me back," Paul said sheepishly, almost as if he hoped they hadn't heard him. He stood because he couldn't stay seated with the tension.

The four others looked at one another in surprise.

"Paul!" Sylvie shrieked, drawing attention from nearby booths. "*You want Yale to reinstate you?*"

"I suppose. I could still treasure hunt, maybe write another book and teach a class. It all depends on how Nadim makes out." His eyes betrayed a desire to stay on the subject. "Yeah, I've been thinking about it, and do you know what I miss the most about Yale?" He didn't wait for a response. "The students. They're so eager to learn or they wouldn't be at a place like that. Forget sports or other extracurriculars. Sure, they can round out a person but they're definitely secondary in New Haven."

"It wouldn't interfere with your treasure hunting?" Vincent asked.

"It didn't before and I had plenty of administrative duties then. This time I'd just be teaching on a limited basis. We'd have to work it out. Maybe only as a visiting lecturer, maybe an adjunct professor."

"Sounds like you've given it plenty of thought," Sylvie said. "Well, I'm all for it. But again, it depends on what Nadim learns—if Yale cooperates on those publications, and if the Talleyrands accept your apology."

"My view," Leon added, "is that it's obvious you miss being there. Frankly, your pride was hurt when they let you go, a man of your caliber and reputation, but they had their reasons, which I don't accept as fair. And now, if all the preliminaries go well, they'll have their reasons to welcome you back. Am I stating it too bluntly?"

"No," Paul said, "that about sums it up. Bottom line? We'll just wait and see. Hell, I might even change my mind; who knows?"

They were back in the lobby of Paris' Montparnasse shortly after 6 p.m. Paul suggested they have dinner at a side street bistro not far from there. The other three men begged off for understandable reasons. Paul praised the men who returned the compliment, then took their leave after a promise to be at Paul's disposal as necessary. That left Sylvie.

"Let's change into fresh clothes first," she said. "Then we can go rehash as we dine."

"Rehash? You haven't had enough? I have, that's for sure. At least for now. And Syl, I want to apologize again for being so ... so outspoken with you. You must know me by now. Much of it has to do with my typical role-reversal questioning."

Sylvie appeared to pounce on an opportunity. "Well, you were a bit nasty. So you'll just have to make up for it."

They left for the bistro more than an hour later.

Throughout dinner, Paul and Sylvie tried to limit their conversation to things other than the morning's "adventure", as she put it. Neither was successful, but she moderated her stance on Nadim and Paul promised to be cautious in dealing with him. Other than that, they gave surprisingly similar — and swift — interpretations of what had transpired and, following dessert, were anxious to call it a night. Each admitted to exhaustion and, once back at the hotel, they retired to their separate rooms.

As Paul prepared for bed, the phone rang. It was the hotel clerk at the reception desk. "There is a Doctor Nadim Maloof on the line," he said. "He wishes to speak with you. Shall I put him through?"

"Yes, by all means," Paul said. He reached for the hotel's pad and pen, his heart immediately racing.

"Hello. Paul?"

"Yes, Nadim. How are you?"

"Fine. And I'll get right to the point. Yale doesn't have to publish any articles about you."

"I don't understand."

"It's hard to believe, but they were going to contact you before the week was out. And so were the Talleyrands."

"What? You're making this up."

"No, it's true. Between my calls to London and the reports I've received from a few fellow histarians, that's what their plan was."

"But a plan for what?" Paul hoped for the best, crossing several of his fingers for luck.

"Well apparently the Talleyrands and university officials have been talking. They learned of your success with _Vérité_ last year and that you've been retained to solve this latest problem. Long story short, the Talleyrands want a truce and Yale wants you back! See, what did I tell you?"

"I'm confused. Do you mean to say that if they believe a guy names one of their own as a possible murderer of Napoleon, but does a good job in solving a mystery—they're willing to forget the accusation?"

"Maybe not forget, but end the hostilities."

"But there never _were_ any hostilities, at least not

from my end."

"You know that, I know that, *Vérité* knows that, and now they know that."

"You're certain?"

"They said as much. They admitted to being all wrong—that is, the Talleyrands did. They spoke of two things: one, as an author and historian, you had a perfect right to include Talleyrand in a list of suspects, and that wasn't your thought alone but a widely held opinion at the time. And two, maybe more important—the reason he fled to the U.S. and lived there for two years was because he knew he was a suspect and wanted things to die down."

"Why did they let things fester for so long, though? Even to the point of practically getting me killed."

"I'm not so sure about that."

"But what about the car at the jetty scene? You said yourself that the men in it were there on behalf of the Talleyrands."

"Exactly. They were family members themselves, not hired hit men. All they had in mind was to talk to you. Who knows? Maybe to straighten things out."

Paul was beginning to feel convinced.

"And Sylvie was absolutely right," Nadim said. "Yale didn't let you go because of your mythology views but because of its inseparable relationship with the Talleyrands, the East India Company and Lady Beckett. And let's not forget Elihu Yale. They all fit together like peas in a pod and the Talleyrands were calling the shots. Once they decided to make a move toward reconciliation, the rest fell into place."

Paul voiced his feeling. "You're convincing me, Nadim. Yes sir, it all makes sense. I just wish they hadn't waited so long. Some things could have been avoided: misunderstanding, hard feelings, veiled threats, my uprooting at Yale. Who knows what else?"

"Certain things move very slowly," Nadim commented. "Frustrating. If every person, every institution, every government moved as fast as you and I do, they'd take the word 'delay' out of the dictionary. Actually, do you know why I believe we've hit it off so well?"

"Why?"

"Because we're both hyperactive."

"Touché."

"Now, last thing... two things, really... before I finally get some sleep. Yale wants to talk to you. I'd call before too long ... let's see, the blasted time difference — I'd call them at about three, Paris time. That puts it at mid-morning Connecticut time. Ask for Gregory Holliday. He heads up the administrative committee that deals with hiring and firing university staff members."

"I actually know him. Not a bad guy, fair minded. I think he took his orders last year from someone higher up. At this point, I don't give a damn who. Either they want me or they don't."

"Marvelous attitude, Paul. But they *do* want you back. In some capacity or another. I'm anxious to hear what. I'm told Holliday knows the entire Talleyrand background and has been following your career since the dismissal. What's been advertised, anyway. He's expecting your call. Let me know how it turns out. And the other thing? Another call. You're supposed to call one of the Talleyrand descendants, a Miss Thelma Tibbles — now don't laugh — I have it written here. She's apparently the leader of the present-day clan. Very vocal, but instrumental in turning the family's thinking around in your favor. One of my London contacts said she's anxious to talk to you about a secret involving Lady Beckett and her coffin in Beckett Gardens." He gave Paul the phone number.

Paul heard some rustling sounds, like the shuffling and folding of papers.

"There, that's done," Nadim said. He then repeated what he'd said earlier: "And with respect to the other matters still hanging, I'll be in touch if they have any bearing on … oh, you already know that."

Paul knew severe fatigue had set in for the doctor. "You're tired, Nadim, and you should be," he cautioned.

"You might say that, but I'm glad to be of service. Besides, this is interesting. Certainly more so than nutrition. Good night, my friend."

"Good night. I can't thank you enough … and I'll keep you posted." Paul gently hung up the phone.

Exhilarated, he phoned Sylvie with the news. She said she'd be right over. In less time than it takes to open and close two doors, she was at his side for congratulatory hugs and kisses.

But nothing more.

THE YALE
CONNECTION

Chapter 12

Paul was more uplifted by the Yale development than by what appeared to be a resolution of the Talleyrand debacle. In fact, with his understanding that the Yale dismissal had been a direct result of ill-advised Talleyrand assumptions, he confessed to Sylvie that he was inclined to view that family "with utmost suspicion for all of perpetuity."

But there was a call he had to make to one Thelma Tibbles. As was suggested by Nadim, he would place the call after seeing what the Yale overture was all about.

It was slightly after eight when he awoke the next morning, hardly refreshed. He had slept fitfully. Wouldn't anyone with both sides of the Atlantic vying for his attention, and his not knowing the reason why? He lay in bed thinking about his Yale experiences in his undergraduate days. His combined major of history and philosophy; his rejection of varsity basketball, despite entreaties by several assistant coaches who had seen him play in the intra-mural league; his single year on the swimming team which he found too time-consuming. Then four years devoted to private lessons in martial arts: karate, bujutsu, percussive tae kwan do. He thought about the irony of his interest in Japanese culture back then and how it had eventually intersected with the same interest now—twenty-five years later. About his senior year when he was acknowledged to have become somewhat of a master in bujutsu, a form of martial arts that stresses combat and willingness to face death as a matter of honor. He had never been required to confront that situation even though he had begun preliminary classes as a teenager, but he continued to respect the spiritual concepts on which it is based: Zen Buddhism and Shinto. It was through his later pursuits of those teachings—though on a sporadic basis—that he grew to understand Japanese culture in general.

Looking back, it was the karate skills that he honed best and after all these years, he believed that if it ever became necessary, he could call on that martial art again. In this connection, he relived the jetty scene and the "shooter-scarhead chase." He could have used such skills in either of those situations; instead, he had his two pistols at the ready.

But he dwelled most on his years as a faculty member, and his meteoric rise to becoming, at age forty-four, the Nathaniel Bennett Chairmen of the Department of History, and the later charge against him as a "regressive mythologist." He had been forced to step aside not only from the chairmanship but also from the faculty entirely.

Paul was more alert now, the memory of that severance and his handling of it gnawing at him. He had handled it badly and realized it only too keenly in the months that followed. He knew that a tenured professor could not be unceremoniously dismissed without more serious cause such as moral turpitude; but he'd foolishly figured that the university might find ways to make life miserable for him if he didn't cooperate. He had therefore offered no rebuttal and even turned down an opportunity to negotiate for a more favorable financial settlement. What an airhead!

But then was then, and now was now. He leaped out of bed and phoned Leon to give him the good news.

"I knew it! I just knew it!" Leon declared. "Now this time, go easy … er … maybe that's not the right word. Maybe circumspect—that's it, be circumspect."

"Don't worry. I'll evaluate, then reevaluate. Consider, then reconsider. I may be jumping to conclusions in terms of expecting too much but I'll be damned if I give them the breathing room they never gave me. I'll present *my* conditions loud and clear this time around." Paul's voice trailed off into a whisper. "But between you and me, Leon, I haven't the foggiest notion of what they are yet."

"You will, Paul, as both sides talk like civilized people."

"I know one thing," Paul said. "I'm not making any commitment over the phone. I'll see what they're driving at and then I want to sit down with them in person to finalize everything. That's why I've decided not to visit Beckett Gardens just yet."

He informed Leon of Thelma Tibbles and her wish to be called either before or after the Yale situation was clarified.

"Nadim said it has something to do with Lady Beckett and her coffin. So tomorrow, I'll contact Holliday at Yale. If what he says over the phone merits a visit, I'll tell him I have additional work to do here in Paris but can leave for New Haven before the week is out or maybe Monday, and we can discuss it further. Can't appear too anxious, you know. And of course, I'll contact Ms. Tibbles." As an obvious afterthought, Paul tacked on: "See Leon, to me Yale sounds alive whereas Lady Beckett is dead. A few more days before checking her grave won't make a whole lot of difference."

Paul was sitting on the edge of his bed, facing the front of the room and about to receive Leon's response, when he saw a small sheet of paper appearing under the door.

"Uh-oh" Paul said. "Hold on, Leon."

He dropped the receiver on the bed and raced to pick up the paper. It read:

LAST TIME
BACK OFF
WE MEAN BUSINESS

Paul swung the door open. No one was there. He ran around to the next corridor, then doubled back from the opposite side. Seeing no one, he returned to the phone.

"Sorry, Leon," he said, "but the plot thickens." He read the note aloud. "The thing that sticks out like a sore thumb," Paul said, "is the use of the word, 'we'. Remember the last one? It was 'I' — 'I'm talking poison'. I wonder if the change means anything?"

Leon offered nothing concrete other than what Paul had already deduced: that since the Talleyrands, Yale, and even East India Company executives had been virtually eliminated as suspects in the note deliveries, maybe … just maybe … the puzzle might be easier to solve.

Paul suggested they have breakfast together, but Leon declined as he hadn't showered or shaved yet, but offered to meet him for lunch. Paul agreed.

The new note reminded him that he was running behind in writing out summaries of current developments, such as those occurring in Elba and in Alexandria. Therefore, despite an urge to put it off for a while longer, he headed for the downstairs coffee shop. Large pad in hand, he planned on having only orange juice, toast and coffee while writing out the summaries.

The relatively few people there looked elderly or at least innocent to him, certainly incapable of leaving a threatening note anywhere, and most certainly not under someone's door. After only a few swallows of juice, a single piece of toast and a full cup of coffee, he felt free to write:

> <u>Subjects Brought Up in Elba with Clive</u>
> —Said he's become an aromatherapist and the island's administrator of flowers.
> —Reviewed Nap., Rosetta, Beckett, the perfumers, etc.
> —Suggested I visit temples to check on inscriptions.
> —Said Cleopatra very important, that stolen formula may have been her creation.
> —Blue bottle? Just thrown in by Nap. as a bonus.
> —Called the three perfume companies "a strange lot." Their leaders are Japanese with ties to Japanese rainforest.
> —Again, a Japanese linkage.
> —Said Nap. & Elgin hated each other but made a deal: in exchange for flowers & perfume, esp. one handed down by Nap. (stolen formula),

Elgin would supply women.
—Said Elba's flower source began while Nap.
lived there, but was kept secret.
—Said two people learned of secret and were
murdered.

Subjects in Alexandria with
Dr. Nadim Maloof
—We witnessed his lecture on genetic
engineering & bioterrorism.
—Admitted to having ties to organized crime
figures. Called them "informants".
—Gave opinion re jetty incident and "shooter
scene."
—Gave opinion re subjects on my list.
—Sylvie gave details re Talleyrand, Nap.,
Beckett & E. India Co., Yale.
—Said Talleyrands and Yale are close.
—Nadim gave remedy: Yale to publish my
discarded theory of Talleyrand's having killed
Nap. They might reinstate me.
—He mentioned temples and "Beware of
hidden poisons" inscription. Also paper note
at my door plus Tomi Morita's note. Called all
three his "poison model".
—Gave histories of the 3 perfume presidents.
Includes connection to Japanese rainforest.
—Reviewed Nap. Eliminated arsenic as one of
poisons in his (Nadim's) model.
—Said Cleopatra's tomb too hard to find, so
don't bother.
—Indicated no need to visit Japan because he

(Nadim) can provide any info. needed.
— Concluded by stressing "poisoning" issue.

Paul returned to his room and phoned Sylvie. He first apologized for not inviting her to breakfast because he wanted to be alone to bring his notes up to date. She understood. Next, he described the new note to her. She didn't understand.

"I thought we were through with notes like that," she said. "That anybody potentially in the picture has been eliminated. But I guess not. There's still someone out there—or more than one. I'm sure you picked up on that, Paul—the 'we' word?"

"That I did. In any event, it happened again. I've got some serious studying to do because I may be onto something. I'll get back to you. Soon, I hope.'Bye."

He sat at the desk and reached into his briefcase for the other notes. Then he arranged all four in a column and read each one with absorbed attention.

MIND YOUR OWN BUSINESS
GO HOME OR ELSE

FAULT ROSETTA STONE AND ELGIN MARBLES
UNLESS YOU DO NOT MIND A TURNAROUND

I'M TALKING POISON

LAST TIME
BACK OFF
WE MEAN BUSINESS

He read them two more times and tried to reach

some sort of conclusion about each one. Number one and number four? Definite threats. Number three? Unsure. Number two? That one stood out like a new fifty-dollar bill among faded singles. Not a threat at all, but a message. He was convinced of it. "Rosetta Stone ... Elgin Marbles," he muttered. He agonized over how the word "turnaround" fit in. And the word "Fault." He analyzed the four major words every which way: writing them down in reversed order; completely reversing the letters of each word; writing only the *first* letter of each word, and then rearranging the letters in several ways. Finally, when he got to REMS, he felt his mouth sag. He slapped the side of his head and shouted, "That's it! That's it! *REMS*, the company. Of course!"

Now the remaining pieces of the puzzle fell into place effortlessly. Paul expanded the beginning of the message from "Fault" to "It's the fault of", and then reasoned that "It's the fault of the Rosetta Stone and the Elgin Marbles" made no sense, but that "It's the fault of REMS" did. And when he went to the last note and considered the word, "We", and applied it to REMS, he reasoned further that it might apply to more then one employee at *REMS*. The message in effect was targeting employees there as the thieves of *Cleo's* packet. But who delivered the message, and why?

Both relieved and adrenalized, Paul set about to inform his *Vérité* associates of a discovery "that I can't wait to divulge" and asked that they assemble for lunch in the hotel's restaurant in about an hour. He deliberately piqued their interest by withholding the nature of the discovery and intensified it by stating that an immediate trip back to Grasse was necessary. When asked why by each of them—Sylvie, Vincent and Leon—he replied evasively. "Because the *Remsington Company* is there and most everything else is put on hold." He indicated he also wanted to include a brief stop at *Perfumes by Pierre* as long as they were in the vicinity. "There must be a second-in-command who's taken over."

Leon said he would arrange both appointments.

Then Paul called Nadim. The doctor acted shocked at the news and when asked if he thought Paul's assessment of the notes seemed logical, replied, "As logical as logic allows. Even your one or two assumptions seem logical. Good job, as you Americans would say. And another of your sayings: Do keep me in the loop."

Next was the Thelma Tibbles call, one Paul dreaded because of any lingering resentment over the contents of his manuscript. But this feeling was somewhat neutralized by information she might provide regarding Lady Beckett. He was prepared for the worst—perhaps a volley of unfounded accusations or even some profanity. However, she couldn't have been nicer, expressing surprise that he would follow through with the call and indicating she was honored to receive it.

After mutual apologies for what the English lady called "a classic misunderstanding", she said, "Leon Cassell is your number one fan. He says you're very busy so I shan't take up much of your time. You see, Mr. D'Arneau, when I was a teenage girl, my mother told me all about Lady Beckett and her indiscretions, especially with Napoleon Bonaparte. She probably didn't want me to fall into the same trap. Ha, ha. But I remember her mentioning something else that may or may not have significance. She said that something took place at Lady Beckett's coffin soon after she was buried. For a few years, it was common knowledge though nobody did anything about it. But as time went on, it became a secret. At least everyone stopped talking about it. It was that some people had exhumed the coffin, taken out a package, unwrapped it, fiddled with it, and then put it back. Since Leon has told me about your interest in her and that you're trying to learn all you can about her, I thought it wise to contact you. Truth be known, I could have told him and he could have told you, but the atmosphere just wasn't ideal until now when the air has been cleared, so to speak. And there you have it. It may be nothing. It may be something."

They talked for another five minutes, Thelma evidently thriving on the opportunity to comment on her many community activities, Paul verifying his busy schedule. Finally he said, "Thank you very much, Ms. Tibbits."

"That's Tibbles", she said, "but close enough. Everyone seems to make the same mistake."

"Well, I'm truly sorry for the mispronunciation. And I'll definitely check out what you told me. As soon as I can, I'll pay Lady Beckett's tomb a visit, and your information strengthens the reason to exhume the casket."

At lunch, they sat in a booth, Paul and Vincent facing Sylvie and Leon. Paul wasted little time getting to the heart of the get-together, having asked their waitress to delay taking the food orders for ten minutes or so.

He began by placing the four notes before him and reading them just loud enough for the others to hear, enunciating each word with deliberate clarity, each line with precise timing. Next he repeated the second note and discounted it as, "not a note at all, but a message. Someone was trying to warn me or maybe the word 'alert' is better. And who sent the note? I have no idea. The best I can do at the moment is to ask: could it have been Tomi Morita from *Perfumes By Pierre*, and that's why he was murdered?"

Paul's mouth felt dry and he took a generous sip of water. The other three also did, apparently for the same reason.

"I would submit," he continued, "sorry, that sounds like a lawyer … I would *say* that the words 'turnaround' and 'we' have special meaning."

He then described how painstaking it was to turn the words around in every way possible and to duplicate the process with the letters. He even included the slapping of his head when he arrived at 'REMS'.

"That was no slap, I'll tell you," he said with a wry smile. "That was a punch. It would have knocked someone else out, but I felt no pain at all because I was on the verge of shock. From that point on, the rest was easy although I took a couple of liberties."

Paul then emphasized the importance of "we" in the most recent note, and how he reached his deduction that thieves were lurking at *Remsington*.

"It wouldn't surprise me," he said. "But what I don't completely understand is why the sender of the note didn't come right out and identify *Remsington* employees instead of being so coy about it."

"Because of possible retribution by other employees, I would think," Leon said. "Plus it's the old French 'trace and face game', which a prominent attorney once explained to me. If evidence is successfully traced, you might have to face a jury and all hell could break loose against you. A variation of it is if you come right out with a direct accusation and are identified, you might get hauled into the proceedings of a French court of law. No one wants that, believe me. But if you do it the way it was done and, again, if a trace is successful, you can deny everything other than the fact that you're trying to confuse the issue, which is mild by comparison. Also, doing it so indirectly sends *Vérité* and any investigator like you off in another direction—occupying their time elsewhere."

Sylvie swept her eyes over the others and said, "I agree wholeheartedly with what you're saying, Paul, including your questioning, and it gives me the creeps. I also applaud you, Leon, for how you explained 'trace and face'. I've heard of it before but never fully understood it."

"Why steal the formula in the first place?" Vincent asked. "*Remsington* certainly can't put it back on the market."

"Good question," Paul said. "Wish I knew the answer." He stared at Leon briefly. "And you, Leon," he said "Any further comments?"

"Sure," Leon replied. "I must say that what you did was a remarkable piece of detective work. And I hate to use the word 'fault', but I can't fault any of your logic."

"I appreciate that. Let's hope it leads to solving the mystery."

Paul ran his hand over his mouth, a thought flashing through his mind. "You know," he said, "I haven't shared this with you, but lately I've been thinking that the focus of the overall mission has changed. I was retained to solve a mystery—as I just put it—to identify the person or persons who stole a perfume formula and bottle. But what with Napoleon and Lady Beckett and Talleyrand and the East

India Company and Japanese linkages and poisons and Egyptian temples and inscriptions and British Museum pieces and Yale, and so on and so forth, I get the feeling I'm straying. Or is it my imagination?"

"I disagree," Leon said. "These things crop up and simply have to be investigated. No doubt there'll be more, and when you least expect them. But rest assured: your focus is still sharp. What you're definitely not imagining is that your mission has many, many moving parts, let's call them, and in a relatively short time, you've been bombarded with them."

"I guess that's it, Leon. Thanks for the reassurance. And pardon me, all of you. Sometimes I do feel bombarded." He scratched his finger. "But let's carry on. You're probably wondering where we go from here? Straight back to Grasse, as I mentioned earlier. And now you know why. I have to interview the president of *Remsington* and maybe some of his employees. And we'll include a visit to *Perfumes by Pierre*. We defer everything else until those things get done. Except for the Yale phone call. You all game?"

The reply was not long in coming. Their sustained nods reinforced Leon's encouraging words.

Chapter 13

At 3 p.m. sharp, Paul placed the call to his longtime Yale acquaintance, Gregory Holliday. An unusual feature of their initial repartee was when Holliday referred to Paul's current assignment with *Gens de Vérité*.

"French for 'people of truth'," he said. "Not too far off from Yale's motto, 'Lux et Veritas', Latin for 'Light and Truth.'"

"There's a connection there somewhere," Paul said.

Holliday offered that it might be more than coincidence.

When their talk turned serious, Paul leveled with him, saying, "I'm told you might be interested in having me back, and I'm calling to inquire about what you have in mind. Of course you're aware that I'm right in the middle of a case."

"Yes, of course. Dr. Maloof, our mutual Egyptian friend, filled me in on it. Some challenge. You enjoy treasure hunting, don't you?"

"Most times yes."

"Good. You can still do it with what we have in mind. But let me explain first. When the dust settled—and I think you know what I mean—we realized we had treated you unfairly. Our assumptions had no basis in fact once we were convinced that you never … but that's ancient history." Holliday abruptly switched gears. "What's your favorite building at Yale?" he inquired.

"Favorite building? The Sterling Memorial Library. Why, may I ask?"

"We thought so, judging from the amount of time you spent there in the stacks and the way you looked around in awe whenever you were in the main nave. Some observer said it was as if you'd never been there before."

What on earth was he driving at?

"How would you like to become its chief administrator?" Holiday asked.

"What? Of Sterling Memorial?"

"Yes. The library."

"I'd be a librarian?"

"Not quite. You'd be in charge of all the librarians there and of all the affairs of the library itself."

Paul was floored by the offer. "Now wait a minute, Greg. Am I hearing right? As you know, my Yale experience was in teaching. Writing books, yeah, but mainly teaching. Am I really what you're looking for?"

"Let's put it this way. When you headed up our history department, we all thought highly of your administrative skills. But there's another aspect to our offer. The library is falling behind in its number of rare books and manuscripts, especially what we call 'foreign derivatives'. We have a reasonable amount compared to most other American universities, but what we have has remained static, so to speak. In other words, we need new rare books to keep up with our competition. I hate to put it that way, but it's reality. Mostly a matter of pride, I guess. The idea is to allow you certain intervals when you can continue your treasure hunting and maybe, during the course of that, you might come across various rare books. Or at least you can provide us leads and we'll have a special team that can follow through."

Paul, still stunned, said, "I didn't even know such a position existed."

"It doesn't. It's a new position that we'll create for you, Paul. And whenever you're off on one of your missions, we'll assign someone from Administrative Services to pinch hit for you. Of course you can always keep in touch by phone or email. Beyond your salary as top administrator, we can't pay you an additional fee, but we certainly would pick up the cost of any traveling on our behalf. I can envision a scenario where you're searching for a lost or stolen art piece, and while you're in a foreign country, let's say, you can combine that with inquiring about rare book possibilities."

"Well, I just don't know," Paul said. "It would certainly be different. Do other universities have such a set-up? Like Harvard or Princeton?"

"No. And they're our main competitors for books like that. Interested?"

Before Paul had a chance to answer, Holliday gave him two Yale phone numbers where he could be reached plus his home number. "Don't hesitate to call me at home after working hours," he said.

As he had in effect promised Leon, Paul was determined not to make any commitment to the university over the phone. He said, "Interested? Yes. But accept? No. Not yet, anyway. I'll have to give it some thought, Greg, and right now, my mind is filled with details about the trip we're about to take. I'm calling from Paris, incidentally, and we're heading for the Provence area in less than an hour. But I'm glad we've talked; you've honored me with such a unique offer; and I'll get back to you in a couple of days."

There!

In retrospect, Paul thought he might have been somewhat abrupt. Yet, considering the pressures he'd been feeling, he convinced himself that he'd handled the situation judiciously.

Leon was waiting at the airstrip when the travelers arrived. Paul described the Yale offer and received a warm response from all three. When asked what he planned on doing, Paul replied, "Just wait." He repeated the phrase as if unsure of himself: "Just wait."

On the flight to Grasse, Paul was torn between considering the upcoming *Remsington* visit and dwelling on the Yale offer. He even toyed with the idea of contacting Holliday in a couple of weeks rather than days. But before dozing off to sleep, he convinced himself he'd be capable of handling things as they developed at the perfume factories and that the library issue could keep.

They registered at the same hotel as before, had a quick dinner and in the morning, a quicker breakfast. They were running late when they left the coffee shop. Ansel stayed behind.

In contrast to *Cleo's*, the outside appearance of the *Remsington Company* was hardly impressive, looking more like a tool and dye manufacturing plant. Yet inside, one could hardly tell the difference, its barrels, vats, metal tubing and automated machinery every bit the same as in

Ken Kuroda's establishment. Even the scent was similar. The only difference was the overall size of the plant, the number of workers and the noise level. *REMS* was significantly larger on all three counts, although it was only a one-story structure.

At precisely 9 a.m., a secretary ushered the three casually-dressed travelers into President Junzo Yawashita's office, a large room to the right of the main working area. Paul was the first to enter and nearly knocked over the tiny middle-aged man standing just shy of the door as it opened.

"Good morning, Paul," the man said. "My name is Junzo. I hope we can be on a first name basis. My good friend, Ken Kuroda, has told me so much about you that I feel I've known you for a long time. And even you, Sylvia, and you, Vincent."

Sylvie looked irritated, saying, "That's 'Sylvie'."

"Oh, I'm terribly sorry."

"That's okay. Your friend, Ken, made the same mistake."

"Please," Junzo said, "won't you all sit?" After shaking hands, he hurried to pull over three wobbly chairs that were lined against the back wall. The entire room seemed to fit the description of wobbly as in "old, overused, poorly constructed in the first place." There were few furnishings to notice, much less admire, mostly tables stacked with booklets, papers and assorted debris. There were no windows, no photographs, no background music; only a constant, penetrating rattle from the production area. The president's desk was a converted table whose left half was draped in a red silk mantle. It bore a Japanese inscription within a circle.

Junzo's size betrayed a booming voice, perhaps one that had evolved by necessity in such a workplace. His face was not unlike Ken's until he smiled, his teeth noticeably crooked. And he had a mustache, jet black in contrast to a head of hair a shade lighter. He was dressed in a dark brown blazer, solid red tie and light tan pants. Only his black sandals seemed inappropriate.

"It's a pleasure to meet you, Junzo," Paul said. The president bowed before sitting. "I take it," Paul continued, "that Ken briefed you on why we've come here?"

"Yes, he did. And I hope I got it straight, but I'll soon find out, won't I?"

Paul's plan was to lead with questions of some importance but not nearly as much as the one he would hold in reserve.

"First of all," he said, "I assume you know all about the circumstances surrounding the theft of the Vintage formula plus the blue bottle."

"Yes I do, and that's why you were hired. Correct?"

"Correct. Now, may I proceed with some questions that might or might not help in solving the case?"

"Of course. You did the same thing with Ken, and I'll be glad to participate as well."

"Some of the questions may be pointed," Paul said.

"What does that mean, pointed?"

"Sharp. Aimed directly at something or someone."

"Like critical?" Junzo asked.

"Yes, close enough."

"No problem. I can take critical. I'm used to it even though I might not agree. A few reviewers have been critical of some of our perfume lines in the past. Naturally, I get upset all the time, but that soon passes."

"And some questions might be personal," Paul said. "Would that upset you? Or would you say I shouldn't even ask them?"

"It depends on how personal."

"Fair enough," Paul responded, turning up the lower third of his sleeves. "So let's get started."

As usual, Sylvie took out a notebook, tearing out a page and handing it to Vincent.

"Next," Paul said "do you know if there was anything else in the packet besides the perfume formula and the blue bottle?"

"Not that I'm aware of."

"So when you and Tomi looked at the packet six months ago, you saw nothing else, nothing at all?"

"That's right."

"By the way," Paul said, "why did you want to see it in the first place?"

"Because there were relics in there dating back to, maybe, Cleopatra's time and we wanted to see them. Tomi and I were into collecting rare coins... at least *I* still am, and the packet contents seemed fascinating to both of us."

"I get it. Well, is there anything you think we might not know about the theft?" Paul asked.

"I have no way of knowing, but I would imagine you learned a lot when Ken took you up to their junky second story—to show you where the packet was kept and how the criminal cut away the floor."

"That's right. Have you been upstairs there?"

"No, not before—not after."

"Did Ken describe the scene to you?"

"No, all he said was that the packet was missing from where he kept it on the second floor."

"Which reminds me," Paul said. "I notice you have only one floor here. Any reason why there isn't a second floor? It would certainly relieve the congestion out there. There must be a reason for it."

"No special reason, and our workers don't complain."

"Have most of them been with you long?"

"We have over a hundred faithful employees and I can think of only a handful who've left in the past ten years or so."

"You started out as a chemist, right?"

"Yes, both Ken and I did. We double-dated one night and our girlfriends brought up the subject of perfumes. One thing led to another and here we are, perfumers in Grasse."

"Why didn't you go into business together?"

"Good question. We talked about it a lot but finally decided that since we had been with different chemical companies to begin with, and since we had remained friends, let's keep it that way. We're both what you might call headstrong and we didn't want to risk ruining the friendship."

"I see," Paul said, taking out one of his own cards and writing down a single word. "May I ask how old you are?"

"Certainly. I'm fifty-six."

"And you have a family?"

"Yes, a wife and two sons. One of them works here in fact. Been here over three years now and likes what he's doing."

"He chose to do so or did you force him to?" Paul
asked, believing the boy might have been pressured.

It was the first time Junzo hesitated before responding.
"I would say both," he said. "Yes, that would be the most
accurate answer."

"With a little edge to 'forced', maybe"?

"I'd say I was a bit guilty. Yes—I would say that. But
understand, as I told him right after his graduation from
college, he has a lot to gain from working here. We're a
very successful enterprise and he would naturally stand
to move up the ladder faster than the others. That would
be only natural."

"Is he well-liked among his co-workers."

"Very." The president hesitated a second time. "But
why all the questioning about my son?"

"No particular reason," Paul said. "Just trying to
cover all the bases." Noticing several glasses and a pitcher
filled with water on a small nearby table, he pointed to it
and asked, "May I?"

"Of course. I'm terribly sorry. Shall I send for coffee
or tea?"

All three declined, but Sylvie and Vincent joined
Paul who walked over and poured the water.

"Some for you, Junzo?" Paul said

"No, thank you."

"Now there wouldn't be any perfume in this water,
by any chance?" Paul joked.

"Not a chance," Junzo said. "Although we make the
purest perfumes in the world," he joked back. His straight
face disappeared in a matter of seconds.

So did Paul's. He returned to his chair, consulted
another card and continued on. "Was there ever a time

when you wished you hadn't entered this line of work?"

Junzo grimaced. "What kind of question is that? Sorry, I mean why is that important?"

"I should have prefaced it with, 'since this seems very time-consuming, are you lacking in other interests? Or do you have any hobbies?"

"That doesn't have the same slant, but hobbies? Yes. As I've said, I collect rare coins. And other interests? Yes, again. My wife and I go to the theater quite often."

"How well did you know Tomi Morita?"

"Very well. Poor fellow. He didn't deserve to be killed. And why he referred to religion in his note is a mystery to me. But, yes, I knew him very well. As well as Ken. We were classmates in college. I mentioned 'headstrong' before? Well he—that is, Tomi—he was the most headstrong of the three of us, but he was the best computer programmer I ever knew. Ken and I both agreed he should have kept that job rather than switching to perfuming."

"Why?"

"Because he was tops in his field with computers. But as a perfumer?" In a gesture of doubt, Junzo rolled his hand back and forth. "Maybe *near* the top."

"Do you have any idea why he was murdered?"

"None whatsoever. Mistaken identity? Jealousy? Who knows?"

"He was married?"

"Yes. No children."

Paul allowed a few seconds to pass before the next question. "You brought up Tomi's reference to religion. Care to tell us yours?"

"I'm a Muslim but I prefer being called an

Islamist."

"Why is that?"

"Because Islam is the religion of Muslims as set forth in the Koran."

Paul pressed on. "We obviously did background checks on various people and I read that your parents brought you up in the Shinto religion. Why the change? By the way, this is one of those pointed questions."

"I know, and I don't care to answer it," Junzo replied.

"Why not, may I ask?"

"Because it's private—personal."

"Understood," Paul said. "Now on a completely different subject. We were informed that you—and Ken—have a relationship with a private rainforest in Japan and that's where some of your flowers come from. Care to comment?"

"Yes. First, it's perfectly legal. And second, their price is right."

"In that connection, though, apparently the Yakuza control the rainforest. That doesn't bother you?"

"They may or may not, but in our business with the Tokyo owners, the Yakuza are never anywhere in sight."

Paul took advantage of an opening. "If I were to take 'never anywhere in sight' literally, it signifies that you visit Tokyo frequently. Is that a fair assumption?"

"Completely."

"Is it too nosy to ask why?"

"Ah, another pointed question. Let's just say personal business."

Finally the time had come. Paul said, "I'm not at

liberty to reveal why, but we have reason to believe that one or more of the employees here may have had a hand in stealing the packet."

Junzo leaned forward on his arms, fists on his knees. "That's ridiculous!" he declared. "Then is it just as ridiculous to include *you* as a possibility?" Paul asked.

"As a possibility in what?"

"In stealing the packet."

The president eased back in his chair and took a deep breath before answering. "Me? You're not serious are you? Why would I resort to stealing the formula of a product that's already in the marketplace? We have a very successful company here as it is, and wouldn't such an act be worthless from a business standpoint? Under such foolish conditions, wouldn't it be obvious who was the guilty party?"

"Is your operation here as successful as you'd like?"

"No, it never is, and never will be."

"As in 'always striving to improve'?" Paul asked.

"Yes, you said it better."

"Is it as successful as others in Grasse?"

"More so. At least I think that's the case, but maybe others feel the same way."

"Or *felt* the same way," Paul said.

"I don't get it."

"Tomi. Maybe he felt the same way."

Paul was about to follow up further when Junzo said, "And one additional thing. Getting back to that other question—I'm not into collecting treasures."

"Except rare coins," Paul said.

"Except rare coins."

Paul put on his most apologetic expression. "When we get accusatory information like this—that is, about unidentified employees here—we have to check it out. In fact, we have to go one step further."

"Well, Paul, I'm personally offended that you believe I could be the guilty party, and I applaud myself for not losing my composure entirely."

Paul ignored the comment. "You'll notice," he said, "that I spoke of 'employees' before. Is there any chance we could speak briefly with two or three, say, middle management people here?"

Junzo ran his fingers through his hair before responding. "We have three such individuals, and yes, that would be fine. You've come a long way, you have a responsibility and I can appreciate what investigators have to do: follow up on evidence or potential evidence." Essentially composed, he had framed his answer like a student answering a forensic science question during a final examination. "I'll contact them and you can use this office. I'll make myself scarce, maybe go get some coffee. Sure you don't want any?"

"No, thanks," Paul said. Sylvie and Vincent shook their heads no.

"And I'll do you one better, Paul. If you have the time and if you wish, I can announce over the loud speaker that you're in the building because of an interest in perfumery, and that you'll be circulating around to meet with some workers on a random basis. I can either accompany you or the three of you can do so alone."

"That's very considerate of you," Paul said, "but just middle management will be fine."

The travelers spent the next hour lightly interrogating

two men and a woman, one at a time. They were the most neatly dressed of all the employees, obviously people in authority. All were fully cooperative and revealed nothing new to Paul. He had resorted to this method of seeking information before—using people in authority to obtain information about those in their charge—especially if the number were large. A hundred or so, in this case. He'd found it was the least time-consuming and most productive, describing it as "resourceful sampling" to some, "the best bang for the buck" to others.

The three sessions over, he rose and opened the door. He noticed Junzo speaking to an employee nearby. The president also saw Paul and they met halfway.

Paul grasped the president's hand firmly. "Thank you very much. Sorry about the pointed questions."

"Quite okay," Junzo said. "They had to be asked, especially when you're on the receiving end of interesting information." He twisted his mouth like someone who'd made a bad mistake. "Correction—'questionable information'."

"And if more comes in that I'd have to check on, it's all right for me to contact you again?"

"Yes, that wouldn't present a problem. I'm used to pointed questions now." Only *he* smiled.

"Would you mind if I called you even on a Sunday?"

"That wouldn't present a problem either." He handed Paul a business card after writing his home phone number on it.

By then Sylvie and Vincent had joined them; there was another round of handshakes and the travelers left.

They decided not to compare notes until they reached

their hotel. Ansel had stayed behind in the lobby and before the travelers got to their comparisons, he reported seeing a "funny looking" man pacing back and forth in the lobby and acting strangely.

"Then," he said, "he finally marches up to the desk clerk and I thought I heard him ask if any Americans were staying here. But I'm not absolutely sure of their conversation, and I'm not sure it means anything anyway."

"What do you mean funny looking?" Paul asked.

"Oh, I don't know. Maybe not in his looks as much as in what he wore. Yellow pants, bright shirt with stripes up and down, big fluffy handkerchief in his pocket, huge bowtie."

"Sounds like a clown," Sylvie said.

"Maybe he is and was just taking time off from work," Vincent added.

"But why inquire about Americans staying here?" Paul asked. "Americans stay here all the time. It's probably nothing though. Thanks, Ansel."

The four sat together at a round table. Sylvie voiced some suspicion regarding the interview, but it was mild compared to that leveled at Dr. Nadim Maloof in Egypt.

"You're getting more tolerant," Paul said, winking in Vincent's direction.

"Well," Sylvie retorted, "not completely. I don't see why he couldn't have given you better answers about religion and his returning to Tokyo so often. Unless there was something to hide. And he was too pat in answering some of the other questions."

But she and Vincent agreed that, everything considered, the president and middle management people had handled themselves relatively well.

"You, Paul?" Sylvie asked.

"I reserve judgment. Remember though, even negative results have significance. Didn't some famous scientist say that a long time ago?"

At Paul's hotel door he inserted the card into its slot and as the door opened, he felt something pressing him between the shoulders. He was sure it was the muzzle of a gun.

In less than an instant, his past training at Yale in karate and bujutsu flashed into his mind. He had toughened his hands by pounding padded boards; progressed through back stance, cat stance and forward stance; mastered the front kick, hook kick, roundhouse kick and side kick; learned the two-finger and knife-hand punches; became an expert in proper blocking, striking and falling. He had earned a brown belt and was well on his way to black belt status when he strained some back muscles and had to abandon his lessons, never to return.

He took a step to the rear, rammed his elbow back into what felt like an abdomen, twisted around while falling to the floor, and in *tomoenage* or circle throw, swung a man over the top of him. A gun tumbled off to the side. The man—wearing yellow pants, a striped shirt and bowtie—landed on his feet and fled. Paul would have given chase had it not been that—in a maneuver he hadn't tried in years—he wrenched his lower back.

He decided not to inform the front desk or call anyone about the incident. As for the gun, he used a handkerchief to pick it up, then walked gingerly to the elevator and into the lobby where he located an unmarked trash can. When no one was looking, he dropped the gun into it and returned to his room where he mulled over what had just taken place. As usual, the number of questions outweighed the number of answers. *How do threatening people know where I stay, where I am at any one time? Why didn't this guy shoot? He certainly had the time and opportunity. Scare me off but don't kill me? What would have happened if I hadn't acted fast? He follows me into my room? Then what?* Paul cursed himself for being so out of practice.

He hobbled to the bathroom sink and splashed away the sweat from his face. Then he put in a call to Leon. The chairman answered with a sleepy hello.

"You sound tired," Paul said. "I've called at a bad time?"

"No, no. Just got up late. I think I'm coming down with something, maybe a cold. How did it go?"

"It went fine, I suppose I could say. But I'm left uneasy about the guy. One minute too pat; the next, fumbling for words. I guess uneasy is the right word."

"Well, uneasiness is a good thing when you're in this sort of business. Keeps you alert."

"Good way to look at it, Leon, and I'd go into particulars but remember we said we'd withhold them unless something definitive arose and you needed to know about it."

"Yes, it's the best way to handle it. Remember I hired you. However, you're in charge. I like being regularly posted, but how much information you relay to me is at your discretion. You've got enough on your hands and don't need the added burden of sorting out what to reveal about this or that. Later is a different story. That's when it all comes together—hopefully—and you share what you've found out."

"I'm glad you look at it this way. Speaking of that," Paul said, "I sometimes think I'm pursuing parallel paths, one that's obvious—the perfume and flowers bit—and another that's deeper, hidden. On my most confusing days, I tend to believe that the entire perfume thing is a ruse, a cover-up for something else, something dangerous. But I tell myself I've got to follow through with whatever presents itself, seemingly unrelated or not."

Leon didn't respond.

The travelers had a meager lunch that ended at one-fifteen. Paul's back felt better. They then taxied to the next perfumery on their schedule. Its outside appearance was a far cry from the other two they had visited. One could easily have missed the recessed building sandwiched between a postal branch office and a diner, especially on a day like this, clouds thickening, a fine mist rolling in. The building lacked a well-kept lawn, a tree or any variety of shrubbery except for a cluster of weeds that blocked one's view of a small sign in the ground: *Perfumes by Pierre*.

Inside was a different story, for it looked like an imitation of the other giants of the industry: *Cleo's* and *REMS*. The set-up was identical, only smaller—from its equipment to its complement of employees. A miniature *Remsington*. The scent was the same, however.

A male receptionist was seated at a desk just inside the front entrance. He greeted them warmly, referred to them by name and said, "Mr. Carpenter just returned from lunch. He should be waiting for you in his office by now. I'll take you there."

On the way, a distance of no more than twenty feet, Paul said, "Sorry to hear about the loss of Mr. Morita."

"Thank you. We're all upset about it, of course. He was a good man in more ways than one."

The newly installed president's office door still had its old sign:

Nicholas Carpenter
Vice-president

The receptionist knocked once, opened the door and left.

"Do come in," a slim, red-headed man said. "You must be Paul and Sylvie and Vincent. I'm Nick." He circled his desk and reached the trio before they had a chance to respond. Handshakes and introductions complete—first names agreed upon—they took seats around a small table near a large window.

"Looks like we're in for a nasty storm," Nick noted.

"Maybe it'll come and go before we finish," Paul commented. He rethought what he'd said. "Not that we'll take up much of your time, and many thanks for having us here."

"You're entirely welcome. You're friend, Leon, explained the whole situation and I'm only too glad to cooperate."

"Thank you. Our condolences on Tomi's passing."

Nick, visibly upset, simply stared out the window for a moment, and then, as if jolted back from the past, said, "I won't do as good a job as he did, but I'll try my best."

With his long neck, narrow head and ears pressed against his temples, he appeared taller than he was. But the thirty-something president was nonetheless handsome—and impeccably dressed: solid light blue tie over white shirt; checkered dark blue jacket; tan pants. He wore no jewelry save for a wedding ring.

"Again, this won't be a long interview," Paul began, "and hopefully not a difficult one at this sad time for your company." He put one of his index cards on the table. Sylvie took out her notebook as if his action had ignited a reflex.

"As you no doubt know, Nick," Paul said, "we've interviewed Junzo at *Remsington* and Ken at *Cleo's*. And we understand your Tomi completed the triumvirate that began a friendship a long time ago." He paused to determine how to phrase his next thought. "Please forgive me," he continued, "if I sound like a prosecutor or a defense attorney. We hardly view you as a witness, believe me. But my questions will be direct and I hope your answers will be too."

"Certainly. Go right ahead."

"Both Junzo and Ken said they often go back to Japan and that it's been their habit for many years. Did Tomi go with them?"

"Yes and no," Nick replied. "He went with them regularly at first but then about six month ago, he stopped. Never said why, at least not to me."

"Why did he go in the first place?"

"He said they attended seminars."

"On perfumery?"

"Yes. And to compare notes with other perfume leaders."

"So Tomi never said why he stopped going?"

"No, never. And it might have been my imagination, but since then, his relationship with the other two seemed to suffer. Before that, practically every time I walked into this office, he was on the phone with one of them. But that stopped completely."

"So you'd say he abruptly discontinued the trips and never gave the reason why to anyone around here?" Paul asked.

"Yes, as far as I know."

Paul thought aloud. "I wonder if his wife knows why."

"He was a widower," Nick said. "For about five years. Automobile accident. Tragic. Tomi took it real hard. Never got over it. Stopped socializing for the most part."

"I see," Paul said. "So unfortunate. Then he gets killed, himself. Any children?"

"None."

Paul loosened his tie and gazed out the window. The storm seemed to have changed its mind and never came.

Nick, observing Paul, said, "In case you're wondering what's happening out there, that's the way it is in Grasse. One minute, gray, the next, clear as sunshine. We're used to it."

"I'd hate to be a local weatherman," Vincent said.

"Actually," Sylvie said, "it might be easy. Every day just say something like, 'It's going to be both sunny and rainy.'"

Vincent scowled.

Paul returned to the questioning after entering the usual word or two on his card.

"This might be a tough one," he said, "but do you think there ever was a time when Tomi wished he had never become a perfumer?"

"You mean—and had gone into something else?"

"Yes."

"I doubt it. What I *can* say is that it never showed, if that were the case. He was trained as a computer programmer, you know—and even worked at it for a time."

"Yes, I do know. That's why I've wondered if he had any regrets about switching fields." Another notation.

"Hobbies?" Paul inquired.

"You mean him or me?"

"Him. Do you know of any?"

"Yes. He liked to collect rare coins."

"Rare coins—yes, I heard. That's Junzo's hobby too."

"I know. They often used to exchange them."

Paul looked at Nick, half-smiling. "Let me interject here," he said. "It must be very difficult for you to answer questions like this, not only because your former president was recently murdered, but also because you're speaking for him. So I'll bring this to a close in a minute." He glanced at his card, then returned it to his pocket. "Only two more subjects and you don't have to elaborate. You're aware of the note Tomi left, referring to religion?"

"Yes, I am."

"Well, in that context, do you know if he was a practicing Muslim?"

"Yes, I believe he was."

"And he considered himself that?" Paul asked.

"As far as I know."

"And not an Islamist?" Paul asked.

"That, I can't say. But if I may—aren't they both

the same?"

"To some, yes," Paul said. "To others, no."

Both Sylvie who had put away her notebook and Vincent who had taken no notes, eyed Paul with blank expressions.

"Last question then, I promise," Paul said. "Did Tomi ever bring up the subject of the theft at *Cleo's* and if so, did he ever share any theories about it?"

"As I recall, he spoke to me about it one time but not after that. As for theories, he never expressed any."

Their meeting ended as graciously as it had begun and the travelers returned to the hotel in weather that looked as though it still couldn't make up its mind.

At dinner, Paul leveled with the others saying Nick Carpenter appeared to be a "straight shooter" and a guy "who'll be in a tough position for awhile." But he stated it was simply too premature for him to offer an opinion of Junzo. What he didn't state, however, was that Junzo's performance bothered him.

"Any change in your interpretation of the second note left at your door?" Sylvie asked.

"None whatsoever."

On a more personal note, he was also silent on what he believed was the most important thing he'd learned on the trip: that people were still out to get him.

They raced through dinner, admitted they were behind in sleep, set a 10 o'clock time for breakfast and retired to their individual rooms.

Within minutes, Paul decided to phone Sylvie. "Did I wake you?" he asked.

"No, but I'm dog-tired. I think I'll shower and call it a night."

"Why not take it here?"

"Take what there?"

"The shower. I'll join you."

After a brief pause, Paul heard a click over the phone and a knock on the door almost simultaneously.

"That you?" Paul asked, his ear against the unopened door.

"Yes, I'm here," Sylvie replied.

Paul let her in and upon seeing a pink nightgown folded in her hand, said, "You won't be needing that."

"If you insist." She cast the gown onto a nearby chair.

They removed their clothes, staring at one another.

With hot steam enveloping them in the shower, there was a flurry of kissing and petting that climaxed into what had been obvious all along. Then they washed and crawled into bed.

"You know," she whispered in his ear, "that made me even *more* tired."

"Not me," he said, "I'm wide awake now." He bunched up the pillow beneath his head and launched into a non-stop retrospective of all that had occurred at *Remsington*, and was about to do the same regarding his conversation with Yale's Gregory Holliday. But he stopped talking because she stopped listening. She had fallen asleep.

Chapter 14

Twelve hours later, Paul and Sylvie gave Vincent a cheery hello at the coffee shop. "Sleep well?" Vincent asked.

"*Very* well," Sylvie answered.

"Not so well," Paul said, covering a yawn with his fist. "Too much on my mind." He was anxious to bring up a sensitive subject and got right to it.

"On most future trips," he said to Vincent, "if you're looking for us at night, we'll be in the same room. Is that all right with you?" Paul avoided direct eye contact.

"Hell, yes," Vincent said. "You're both legally unattached, so why not? I'm glad to see it. It's obvious how you feel about one another. Come to think of it, why have an extra room to begin with. See? Two happy people and no room charge."

Paul and Sylvie joined hands over the table, a thank you to Vincent reflected in their eyes. Paul had wanted to bring up the subject at least a week before, and if he had anticipated Vincent's understanding comments, he would have. He so informed him. That out of the way, there was little additional talk about the *Remsington* and *Pierre* visits. Paul in effect ended the topic by stating, "I feel it in my bones that I or we will be talking to Junzo again. I woke up in the middle of the night thinking about his relationship with Japan. Tokyo particularly. He said his frequent trips there had to do with personal business—which told us *nothing*. But let's leave it at that for the time being."

Vincent indicated he received an email from a colleague at the Sorbonne. It said he was needed for an unspecified period of time to complete an important project that the colleague had started and then he took sick.

"I'm really sorry about this," he said.

"It's not your fault," Paul stated. Sylvie's reaction was about the same.

"I'll have to get going shortly," Vincent said, "but I'll rejoin you as soon as possible."

Once alone in his room, Paul prioritized his next moves with phone calls at the top of the list. It occurred to him that he hadn't kept in touch with Maurice, Guy, Dom, Clive or Nadim. Nor had he heard from them. He called them all and although each call was protracted, he learned nothing new except from Nadim.

"I was planning on calling you today, Paul," Nadim said. "Yesterday I heard from one of our histarians—Tarek Ronque in Cairo. He runs the Cairo Chemical Company there. We keep in fairly regular contact and last week I told him about you and what you're doing. He'd like to meet with you about two things, but he didn't want to elaborate. I said I'd let you know about his call. Perhaps you can look him up if and when you visit the temples down in those parts." There was a long period of silence. "Will you be going to the Cairo region?"

"Eventually, yes," Paul answered.

"Good. I think it's a wise move. When it comes to

remembering inscriptions, I really can't trust my memory." He gave Paul the histarian's address and phone number.

Aside from that brief exchange, Paul had done most of the talking, bringing them all up to date on what had occurred at his end. To the man, each repeated that Paul would be notified, directly or through Leon, if anything significant developed.

Next was the call to Gregory Holliday at Yale. Paul had debated about whether or not to call so soon. He concluded that on the one hand it might signify he was ready to accept the position, but on the other, he needed a distraction from constantly querying person after person and analyzing their responses. Sleeping in his own bed in New Haven for a night or two would also be helpful. And in his heart of hearts, he *did* want the library position. Again promising himself he wouldn't commit by phone, he was prepared to hear Holliday out again and if a trip to Connecticut came up, he would have tomorrow, a Sunday, to make it.

"Hello, Greg?"

"Well, hi there, Paul. You accept?"

"Not so fast now," Paul responded, forcing a laugh.

"No, you're absolutely right. Not so fast. But I'm glad you called. There's been a new development."

"Oh?"

"Yes, there's a man named Ahmad Khalil. Works for the East India Company. He's the one who created most of the fuss about you before. Born and brought up in Iran but now calls Japan his home. Lived there half his life."

"*Japan again!* " Paul thought. "The name sounds familiar."

Holliday continued. "He's on our faculty—teaches a course in Asian Affairs—and also happens to be on our 'Hire and Fire' Committee. We research and then act on candidates for appointments here. I've been chairman for years. There are eight of us; we meet ad hoc but it amounts to plenty and that's why we work through the summer months even though classes aren't in session. Anyway, when Ahmad heard about our interest in your return, he blew his stack. I called a meeting yesterday, all eight showed up and he was the only one who opposed it. We decided to postpone the vote."

Suddenly Paul exclaimed, "Hold it right there! That's the guy on the card!"

"What card?"

Paul pulled out his wallet and removed the card he'd found on Rico Cretelli at the jetty scene.

"That's it," Paul said, "the same guy."

"You're losing me, Paul."

"Oh, sorry."

Paul then went on to explain, leaving out the murder. "I'll just have to think on it some more," he concluded.

"All I can say," Holliday commented, "is that I'm surprised Ahmad keeps such company."

Paul brushed imaginary lint from his trousers. "Getting back to your meeting. Do all decisions have to be unanimous?"

"Usually, but not always, and all we need for a vote to stand is a quorum. In a non-unanimous vote, the outcome depends on how far a nay voter wants to take things. In this case, I really don't think Ahmad has a leg to stand on, but there may be a delay in confirming your appointment."

"If I acknowledge wanting it."

"Of course. That's a given. Tell you what, Paul. Are you willing to come to New Haven soon? I think we can iron this out better—and sooner—that way. You can still say no if you choose, and all you'd lose is the time coming and going, and meeting with committee members. You probably know most of them anyway."

"Would it include our Mr. Khalil?"

"No. I think I can take care of that. The only problem is the East India Company still gives money to Yale, but I can look into it, possibly today. I'll have to make a few calls to see how much we're talking about, but if it's negligible, we're golden. If it's sizable, there are solutions I can resort to. It all depends. I'd have to make some other calls. Either way, I think it's better if you're here."

"You'll phone me if you find out?"

"Yes, indeed. Hopefully within an hour or two.

"And if you don't mind, Greg, try to have Khalil there. I'd like to meet him."

After sitting on his bed while making six long phone calls, Paul's ear hurt and he felt whipped. He had anticipated writing the two summaries dealing with Junzo Yawashita and Nick Carpenter but fell back on the bed and dozed off.

It was nearly four o'clock when he was awakened by the phone's ring.

"Got good news for you, Paul," Holliday said. "The company's yearly donation has been less and less during 'these bad economic times', as they put it. It's under ten thousand right now and I assure you it won't be missed."

"That's *definitely* good news," Paul said, rubbing his

eyes. "What now?"

"Can you leave tomorrow? And we can meet Monday morning. I shouldn't have any trouble rounding up a quorum, especially given the nature of the agenda. They're all fond of you, Paul."

"I'll do it. Where shall we meet and what time?"

"Right at Sterling Memorial. You're familiar with the Linonia and Brothers Room?"

"Familiar? I practically lived there for special meetings," Paul replied.

"Of course. Leaving France tomorrow, then?"

"Yes, tomorrow. I'll leave from Nice, arrive at J.F.K. and take a train to New Haven. I'll even get some shut-eye on the plane."

"Fine. Let's make it for ten Monday morning."

Paul could feel his face turn pensive. "I'll be there," he finally said.

He called Leon with the news and said he'd return to Paris in about forty-eight hours. "Don't kill yourself over the timing," Leon said, "and good luck. If it works out, it'll be an excellent way for you to operate."

In Paul's next call, Sylvie's response was different. "Why not finish the assignment over here first, and then work on the Yale thing?" she asked.

"I was going to, but now I think I might get to meet a person who could be hiring guys to scare me, or worse. He comes from Iran but works at Yale."

"How did you learn that?"

Paul went into the business about the card he found in Cretelli's wallet and the assumptions that ensued. "At this point, I'm reasonably sure the Iranian's not behind the notes at my door, although I wouldn't swear to it. But he could be the guy directly after me, somehow knowing where I am at all times." Then he indicated he would skip dinner, have a snack later, arrange the flight for the morning and turn in early. He realized he was way behind in sleep requirements and that his attention span had suffered; his unexpected nap was the tipoff. And he was well aware that the jet lag he'd experience in the States would add to the problem.

"Promise me one thing?" Sylvie asked.

"What's that?"

"Be careful," she answered, her voice cracking.

Paul had no trouble booking a first class flight on Air France, the trip from Nice International Airport to J.F.K. to take nine hours, with a 4:10 time of arrival. If things ran smoothly, he hoped to be in his New Haven home by 7 p.m., Eastern Time.

He boarded the plane at 6:30 a.m. The early morning air had tweaked his senses and a stale aisle smell was unusually annoying, but at least he felt more alert. There was one other factor at work here, one that, even alone, would have raised the level of alertness: an opportunity to confront Mr. Ahmad Khalil. To discern the extent of his rancor; to explore the possibility of his involvement in the theft of the formula and in the jetty affair; to learn what he knew about the notes at his door. In short, to size him up. Paul now considered this Connecticut journey as having a dual purpose: possibly securing a new position at the university and possibly identifying a key player in the attempt to obstruct his overall assignment. And as he thought about it further, it became clear that the two were related. Another bit of irony!

Invigorated, Paul removed his most current notes from his briefcase. He wanted to summarize the topics covered in talks with Junzo and Nick, just as he had done for talks with Ken, Dom, Clive and Nadim. Most of what he remembered about the perfumers was still vivid in his mind, the notes serving more in getting the sequences straight. He first checked the passengers around him. No one was looking over his shoulder. No one appeared suspicious. He had plenty of time to write and was in the mood to do so. There would come a point on the plane, however, when he would rather sleep than write—or even eat or drink. It always arrived during a moderately long flight and he considered nine hours moderately long.

<u>Subjects Brought Up at Remsington with Junzo</u>
—Said he knew all about circumstances surrounding theft.
—Claimed he didn't know if anything else was in packet besides formula and bottle.
—Said when he and Tomi looked at packet 6 months before, they saw nothing else.
—Stated they wanted to see packet because it contained relics. Mentioned he collects rare coins.
—Said that regarding theft, only knows what Ken told him.
—Claimed he has never been upstairs at *Cleo's*—where theft occurred.
—Said he's proud of his employees, nearly all of them loyal.
—Said he and Ken started out as chemists. Decided not to go into perfumery as partners

because it might have ruined their friendship.

—Has wife and two sons. One works at *Remsington.*

—Peeved when asked about regrets re going into perfumery.

—Hobbies are collecting rare coins and going to theater.

—Said he knew Tomi Morita very well. Believes he should have remained a computer programmer. Would have been best in field.

—Didn't know why Tomi brought up religion in note.

—No idea why Tomi was murdered. Mentioned jealousy, mistaken identity.

—Said he is Muslim but prefers being called Islamist.

—Refused to answer why he changed from boyhood Shinto to Islam.

—Confirmed he and Ken receive flowers from private rainforest in Japan.

—Denied any contact with Yakuzi element that allegedly controls the rainforest.

—Stated he visits Japan frequently on personal business. Wouldn't elaborate.

—Got upset when asked re possibility of his employees stealing formula. But more upset when he was included as possibility.

—Willingly gave permission to question 3 middle management people.

—They were fully cooperative but revealed nothing new.

<u>Subjects Brought Up at *Pierre* with Nick Carpenter,</u>
<u>Newly Installed President</u>
— Visibly upset over Tomi's murder.
— Said Tomi often visited Japan with Ken and Junzo, but stopped 6 months ago. Didn't know why.
— Said relationship among the three cooled after that.
— Was told reason they went was to attend seminars on perfumery.
— Is a widower with no children. Wife killed in auto accident.
— Said he was never aware that Tomi regretted being a perfumer.
— Verified that Tomi collected rare coins and often traded with Junzo.
— Believes Tomi was a practicing Muslim. Couldn't say if Tomi preferred the term, "Islamist."
— Stated Tomi brought up subject of theft only once and offered no theories about it.

The first thing Paul did when he got home was to notify his next-door neighbor of his arrival because he thought his home lights might cause some concern. He mentioned he would be returning to Paris in a day or two, pending the results of a morning meeting at Yale.

The Sterling Memorial Library at Yale's Cross-Campus never ceased to amaze Paul. Its Gothic revival architecture reminded him of a cathedral, and he had often jokingly answered those who asked where he was headed with a simple, "to pray." His family and colleagues knew that the translation was "to roam among the stacks." Hundreds of stained glass panes and a main circulation desk that resembled an altar did little to impugn the impression of its being a place of worship, a fifteen story one.

The weather was crisp for a July 2nd and Paul regretted he hadn't taken along his trench coat. The previous evening's light fog had lifted, morning had broken to a clear cerulean sky and he could feel the sun's rays through his windshield on the way to the meeting.

He wore a brown jacket with suede elbow patches, button-down yellow shirt and a matching striped tie. He hadn't thought substantively about the meeting but had mentally prepared himself for a showdown of sorts if Khalil showed up.

He was aware of a bounce to his step and twice checked his watch as he walked the several blocks from where he'd parked his Mercedes on College Street. It was five to ten when he pushed open the heavy oak door of the library's main entrance and entered its vestibule. He paused at the near end of Sterling's cavernous nave which he perused in a single sweep, noting three or four staff personnel, several study carrels and, off to the left, an area housing a massive card catalogue system, now made obsolete by modern computer technology but still maintained for historical reasons. He was curious about what was in one of the elongated display cases on the opposite side. Did it still feature the writings and memorabilia of the nineteenth-century scientist, Thomas Henry Huxley, as it had for years? Was the single sentence that Paul had memorized still there?

He took soft steps in a failed attempt to minimize

the echoes as he walked over to the case. Even now, the sentence on a piece of rag paper gave him goose flesh: "The great tragedy of science [is] the slaying of a beautiful hypothesis by an ugly fact." Paul thought of the investigation at hand and the several hypotheses he had accumulated. Would an ugly fact surface to negate them all?

He turned and headed for the Linonia and Brothers Room. He saw Greg Holliday waiting just outside its only door and, giving a two-finger wave, took larger steps. They shook hands eagerly.

"Thanks for coming," Holliday said. I'm expecting this to run smoothly. They're all in there." His smile was engaging and prolonged.

"Even what's-his-name?"

"I'm afraid so, but he's only one vote."

The committee chairman was of average height and weight and had white curly hair, a ruddy face and droopy eyes. Loose folds beneath his chin vibrated when he spoke, and save for an animated voice, he looked as if he should have retired years ago.

"Before we go in, Greg, would it be possible for me to speak to him out here? You can listen in."

"You think that's a good idea?"

"Why not? You yourself said he's only one vote."

Holliday nodded, entered the room and soon returned with a man who appeared half his age.

"Ahmad Khalil, this is Paul D'Arneau," Holliday said.

"Ah, Mr. D'Arneau, we meet at last."

"We do indeed", Paul said sternly.

Their handshake was tentative.

Khalil was bigger than Paul had pictured, perhaps because of his double-breasted jacket. He had a characteristically Asian face, a full head of straight black hair, long sideburns, a small beard and a tuft of hair beneath his lip.

Paul would just as soon have decked the man with one of his patented chops but decided that would have been disastrous if he'd intended to learn anything from someone he already branded as dangerous.

"Thanks for coming out ahead of time … ah … may I call you Ahmad?"

"Yes, I'm Ahmad."

"And I'm Paul."

They shook hands again, awkwardly but more fervently.

"The reason is," Paul said, "I have a few questions for you that I don't believe are appropriate to ask before the full committee. Would that be okay?"

"As you wish."

"I understand you're against my being rehired."

"Not against rehiring altogether," the Iranian said. "Just for this particular job."

"It's a newly created one, and do you know why?" Paul then explained how his role would bear on the secondary reason for the new position: Yale's need to replenish its rare book collection.

"That's not a good reason," Ahmad said.

It was about what Paul had anticipated but he believed the ice had been broken. He let no time pass. "Well then," he said, "now that we know where we stand, may I ask you a few other questions?"

"Fine to ask. To answer? Depends."

Paul expected that type of response as well. But his next statement was the one he'd been setting up. He said, "Maybe I won't need your verbal answers after all. How you handle the questions might be good enough. And for your part, you'll be able to see what's running through my mind. Fair enough exchange?"

Had Paul revealed too much?

"Fair enough. I have nothing to hide," Ahmad said. He folded his arms across his chest in a defensive pose.

Holliday, who was standing near both men, looked decidedly uncomfortable.

"I didn't say you did," Paul continued, "but if you'd merely listen to the questions, I'd be satisfied at my end. And if you don't give an answer, I'll move right onto the next one. Would that be satisfactory at your end?" Paul had learned long ago that in an interrogation, the reference to "ends" as in "at your end" and "at my end" created the impression of a battle, and that two men thus engaged felt a greater need to win.

"Go ahead," Ahmad said.

"*Bingo!*" Paul sneered inwardly at the man. "Why don't you care for me?" he asked.

"I never said I didn't but if you must know, it's not too far from the truth."

"Want to say why?"

"Not particularly."

"Do you know anything about the jetty incident?" Paul asked.

"What jetty incident?" Paul noticed Ahmad swallowing hard.

"When a man tailing me was shot to death."

"News to me."

"Do you know anything about the theft of the perfume formula at *Cleopatra and Her Perfumes*?"

"No, but I've heard about it." His expression was indifferent as he looked down at his shoes while waiting for the next question.

Paul believed the man was trying too hard. "Do you know anything about the notes left at my door?" he asked.

"Afraid not."

"I'm not getting very far, am I?" Paul commented. "So, only one more. What's your religion?"

"That's none of your business, sir!" Ahmad snapped. He turned and said to Holliday, "I think we'd better go in and start the meeting, Mr. Chairman."

As they walked through the door, Paul concluded he'd learned more from the Iranian's evasive demeanor than from his verbal responses. Had Paul just talked with Mr. X and with the person who had planted the notes at his door? He doubted it. But the one who had arranged to have the jetty man shot and later, Scarhead? Possibly.

The room was one of Paul's favorites at the library. On the far side, four casement windows opened out onto the Selin Courtyard. There was a window seat below, three walls lined with books, several small tables with lamps, a long center table with green leather chairs and off in a corner, a small red leather couch.

Six Board members were seated at the table: three male, three female. All were impeccably dressed. They rose in unison when the three men walked in. Holliday made introductions as Paul circled around the table shaking hands and exchanging pleasantries. He recognized the entire group from his teaching days. Holliday took his seat at the head of the table while Paul and Ahmad sat next to him but opposite each other.

One of the other members said for all to hear, "You've made quite a name for yourself in your new career, Paul."

"Good or bad?" Paul responded.

"*Very* good," was the almost unanimous reply.

The chairman opened the meeting with a rambling review of Paul's credentials, the needs of the library and the opportunities his appointment would offer. There was a brief discussion about salary, coverage when Paul was out of town and other technical matters. Very few questions were raised. Ahmad was totally silent and appeared bored.

For the first few minutes of the proceedings, Paul's thoughts were elsewhere, all centering on the Iranian: his lasting resentment had to have some meaning; his role, if any, in each recent unexpected development; the possibility of Ahmad's feelings toward him—and vice versa—interfering with his new job performance.

Before the vote, Paul brought up a sine qua non: if he accepted the position, the Board must give its assurance that he be given the leeway to accept treasure hunting assignments as they materialized.

"Any objection to that?" Holliday asked. There was none. Ahmad simply gazed into the courtyard.

Paul was allowed to remain in the room while the vote was taken. "In favor?" Holliday asked. Seven hands shot up. "Opposed?" No response. "That leaves one abstention. Is that correct, Ahmad?"

"Correct," the Iranian replied.

There was a hard knock on the door. Holliday looked

puzzled as he went over to open it. A uniformed security guard whispered something in his ear. Holliday signaled for Paul to join them.

"He says there's been a fire at your house, Paul—no, not the house but in your garage and workshop and part of the laundry. The main house is intact."

"Oh, Christ!" Paul tried to muffle his reaction but was unsuccessful.

"Fire marshal says there's evidence of an accelerant," the security guard said without lowering his voice. "You're lucky your neighbor was home, sir. He smelled smoke, looked out and saw the flames. Called 911. The fire department arrived in a flash and it's all under control, so don't break your neck getting there."

By then, members of the Board had lined up at Paul's side expressing their concern. He thanked them and said he'd be in touch with Holliday later in the day. Before rushing out, Paul raised up on his toes to make eye contact with the Iranian who was last in line. But he was checking the courtyard again.

Paul brought his car to a screeching halt behind a red truck marked "New Haven Fire Marshal" and raced around to the side of his house. He smelled smoke and could see some rising above the chimney.

"You're the owner?" a burly man in a black uniform asked. His shirt and cap bore the insignia of a fire marshal. Bill Dawkins, Paul's neighbor, stood off to the side.

"Yes, I am," Paul replied, his face blotchy. "Thanks, Bill, for making the call." Bill nodded.

"Definitely set," the marshal said. "He or she entered through the side door. There are obvious signs of an accelerant from the door to the sidewall of the garage and into your workshop. Appears as though your metal equipment slowed down the flames some, but I'm afraid a good deal of the laundry room was destroyed. That's the only damage to the house itself, but it'll take quite a bit of airing to clear away the smoke odor. All in all, it could have been worse."

"Okay for me to walk through?" Paul asked, "or would I be ruining evidence?" Still stunned, he began walking into the garage before waiting for an answer.

"It's okay. We're through."

Both the marshal and Bill accompanied him through the rubble. The marshal carried a clipboard and asked Paul some routine questions. Paul was disinterested but cooperated. And instead of inspecting, he seemed to be searching.

"You're heading back to France?" Bill asked.

"What's that?" Paul responded.

Bill repeated the question.

Paul stopped and ran a finger over his lips. "Actually I planned on leaving in the morning," he said, "but with all of this—and especially the smell—I'll try to catch a flight today."

"Well," Bill said, "I have a large tarpaulin. I'll cover the opening to the laundry room. Want me to contact a carpenter?"

"No. Nice of you, but I'll take care of it before I leave. Thanks so much for all your help." His eyes darted about.

"You're looking for something?" the marshal asked.

"Yes, a note."

THE JAPANESE
CONNECTION

Chapter 15

Before booking an early afternoon flight to Paris, Paul arranged for a carpenter friend to repair the damage from the fire. He also informed Yale's Gregory Holliday that he definitely accepted the position offered—Ahmad Khalil notwithstanding—but that he couldn't begin until his current assignment was completed.

"And Greg," Paul said, "the fire wasn't that bad, but a set fire's a set fire and these violent incidents are piling up. Whether I'm in Paris or New Haven, they're after me. I don't understand why such a feeble attempt this time, but we'll get to the bottom of it all. By my calculations, we're halfway there—just don't tell anyone."

"I have every confidence in you, Paul, and rest assured this job will be waiting for you."

"One last thing," Paul said. He believed he was friendly enough with the chairman to ask, "What's that Iranian doing on the Board in the first place? Forget me. He's an out-and-out sourpuss, and from what I can see, he doesn't do the Board any good."

"East India Company. Remember?"

"But what they give now is a pittance."

Holliday had no answer other than, "Tradition."

Paul arrived in Paris at three the next morning, cursing time differences. It had been over an eight-hour flight and for its first hour he'd been preoccupied with his various harrowing experiences and the head-to-head with Ahmad Khalil. Again he wondered whether certain unknown individuals were aiming to kill him or simply frighten him away. He was emotionally drained and though he tried to ready himself for a long sleep, he couldn't dislodge a single recurring thought. It was two-fold and had crossed his mind several times before, but only in passing.

One concerned the four notes left at his door and specifically, the one about poison—"I'm talking poison". He had previously assigned meaning to the other three but not this one. However, his thinking had changed and he had no idea why. It went something like: if there had been an additional item in the stolen perfume packet, could it have had anything to do with poison or poisoning? Or could it have signified that a poison might be used on him? Or someone else?

The second thought was a direct result of the first. If poison or poisoning had become a threat, he had better modify his course. For the mystery might lie not in the theft of a perfume formula—no matter its historical significance—but in something on a grander scale. Much grander.

Paul analyzed these two propositions in every way possible before he arrived at a jarring conclusion. If the mystery concerned something more significant than a perfume formula, then poison or poisoning must take center stage.

He called over a flight attendant and asked not to be disturbed for meals. Convinced that he was onto something, he drifted off to sleep with the locales of Cairo, the Egyptian temples, Beckett Gardens and Japan filtering through his mind. He awakened just short of landing.

Once he reached the Montparnasse Hotel and unpacked, his body's system acted as though it were later in the day. But it was only around five a.m. and he managed several more hours of sleep on the recliner. At eight-thirty he phoned Leon and Sylvie.

Leon said, "Good, you're back. How did it go?"

"In general, okay, I guess. Learned a lot. But in particular, things could have been better. I'll explain when I see you."

They all agreed to meet in the coffee shop in half an hour.

Before their breakfasts arrived, Paul apprised them of what had happened in the States. Leon showed less surprise than Sylvie and agreed with Paul that Ahmad was up to no good. He even used the word "terrorist." Sylvie, on the other hand, was more concerned about Paul's well-being.

"It's a good thing the fire ended up small," she said, "but what if it hadn't? What if it happened later—when you were fast asleep?"

"I may be way off base, Syl," Paul replied, "but I have a hunch it was timed deliberately for that hour, when I was at the meeting. And if so, that S.O.B. Khalil had a hand in it. What isn't clear though is why the fire was so small in the first place. Was the arsonist scared off by something?"

They both expressed delight about the Yale offer and Paul's acceptance.

When asked what was next on the agenda, Paul

rattled off visiting the four locales. "We've got to cover all the bases, especially now," he said. "I forgot to tell you both but I called Nadim a couple of days ago, just to touch base." Paul took out a card and read from it. "A Tarek Ronque wants to talk to you. He's another Egyptian histarian."

"I *know* the man," Leon said, excitedly. "Excellent reputation. Runs a chemical plant?"

"That's the man," Paul said. "I'd like to start with him. And whether or not we travel to any of those places for the sake of solving the perfume riddle or solving something else is immaterial at this stage. In fact, I'm confident we'll solve both."

Leon stated that Paul's comment was a riddle in itself, whereupon Paul assured him that a clarification would be forthcoming.

"When's that?" Leon asked.

"When I wrap things up."

"Of course," Leon said. "So Cairo's next?"

"Yes, and I'd like to leave today."

"So soon?" Sylvie asked. "I mean you're not too tired? The jet lag and all?"

"I slept most of the way back and even another two or three hours in my room. No, I'm fine and raring to go."

Their meals arrived—Paul's, a full breakfast; Leon's and Sylvie's, coffee and doughnuts.

"Now, Syl," Paul said, "an important question. You game on coming with me?"

"To all four places?"

"All four."

"Absolutely!"

"Will you be going from one place to the next or

coming back to Paris somewhere in the middle," Leon asked.

"Depends on what we find. We might even have to add another place or two, but as far as I know now, definitely those four as a minimum."

Paul gobbled down his eggs, sausages and hash browns before the others had finished their doughnuts.

"You must have been starved," Sylvie commented.

"Lots of sleep," Paul said. "Very little food. In fact I can't remember *any* during the flight."

"But getting back to New Haven," Leon said. "Was the rest of the Board there?"

"Yes, seven of them."

"And they were enthusiastic?"

"Very. At least it appeared that way."

"And Holliday was accommodating?"

"Very."

There was a lull in the conversation until Leon said, "So what was it about Khalil you didn't like?"

"You said it yourself, Leon. Pretty strong words but you're right: he acted like I would imagine a terrorist would act. That might not be totally accurate, but let's just say he was defensive. And what else? Unapologetically rude. His demeanor was strange. His body language stunk. I got a chance to speak with him before the meeting started, and that's when it all came out."

The sighs of the other two reflected a double meaning: unreal and unnecessary.

"There's got to be a reason for that kind of behavior other than his simply being against creating a new position," Sylvie said. "Seems to me he'd just say it that way and then behave like a civil person."

Paul had had enough of the subject. "So, Leon," he said, "can you arrange a flight to Cairo?"

"I'll get right on it. Cairo International Airport. I've landed there myself. I'll set it up through the R.A.F. again. Ansel can fly you to Heathrow first. About five hours total flight time. Can you be ready to leave in an hour? If so, that should get you to Cairo and Ronque's office around four-thirty or five."

"I'll be ready."

"Me, too," Sylvie said.

Leon borrowed Paul's card and wrote down the historian's address and phone number on a scrap of paper. "Meeting at his office okay, or would you rather a neutral site?"

"Probably his office would be better," Paul replied.

Paul picked up the tab and Leon led the way out. He and Sylvie had come in separate cars. Paul stayed behind and watched her wait for Leon to pull out of the parking area, then double back and reenter the hotel. She and Paul unabashedly embraced and kissed in the crowded lobby.

"Well?" he inquired.

Pulling away, she said, "I think you'd better go up and get ready. I'll do the same at my place. You know how fast Leon arranges things. We'll have plenty of time for that during our trips."

"For what?" he asked.

She jabbed Paul's mid-section with her finger and left.

He went directly to the computer room and downloaded a review article about Cairo. Up in his room, he dressed appropriately for yet another important meeting, packed a bag and armed himself with the two pistols.

Within thirty minutes he heard from Leon who gave him directions to Ronque's office.

Paul had never been to Cairo before and didn't know whether they'd be staying there overnight. It depended on the continued availability of the R.A.F. pilots and how he and Sylvie made out with Ronque. If he had a choice in the matter, he'd stay an extra half-day so they could mosey about the city he'd heard so much about. But he had a hunch the meeting wouldn't take long and that the pilots would have to return to London quickly, so he downloaded the review article. On the flight down he read through it, mainly hitting the highlights:

Cairo, the capital of Egypt, has nearly 7,000,000 people, making it the most populated of any city in Africa. It lies in the Nile Valley at the southern lip of the Nile Delta. The Nile River divides into two channels just north of the city. Huge deserts lie east and west of the city. Some famous reminders of ancient Egypt, which include pyramids and the Great Sphinx, are located in Giza in the desert west of the city.

Cairo is a mixture of the old and the new. The oldest and most historic sections are in the eastern part, the newer, more modern sections along the west bank of the Nile; on islands in the river; and on Garden City, a narrow strip along the east bank. Most government buildings, foreign embassies, museums, hotels and universities are on the islands or in the suburbs.

Most buildings in the modern sections were built in the 1900's. Their design is in the style of present-day American and European culture. These sections have many gardens, parks, public squares and wide boulevards — all of which make these areas less crowded and more orderly than the older sections.

In sharp contrast, Cairo's older areas are famous for what's called their "old quarters" — areas of narrow, winding streets and buildings that are hundreds of years old. They're known for their more than 300 mosques (Islamic houses of worship). Minarets (tall, slender towers) are important features of the mosques. Islamic officials called muezzins announce prayer from atop the minarets five times a day. At least one minaret can be seen from almost any place in the city's old section.

Cairo's museums house priceless treasures from many periods in history. The city's Egyptian Museum contains the mummy of Ramses II and the gold mask and other belongings of King Tutankhamen.

The people of Cairo are called Cairenes. Many of them are poor, unskilled workers employed by factories or small shops.

They live in crowded apartments in the old quarters. Some dress in long flowing robes, the traditional Arab garment. But most wear Western-style clothes made in Egypt. Most middle-class and wealthy Cairenes live in Garden City, on the islands, or in the suburbs. These people include doctors, factory managers, government officials, lawyers and teachers.

They dress like Americans and Europeans. Most Cairenes are Arabs and Muslims. The Copts form the largest Christian group in Cairo, tracing their origin back to the Christians who lived in Egypt before the Arabs came. Many Europeans and some Jews live in Cairo, but their numbers have decreased greatly since the mid-1900's. At that time, the government took over most businesses and adopted policies that promoted the economic opportunities of Egyptian Muslims. These policies limited the opportunities of minority groups and foreigners.

The Cairo area is an important manufacturing center. A factory at Hulwan, south of the city, makes iron and steel. Other industries in and near Cairo produce sugar and manufacture chemicals, paper, textiles and other products. Many small companies and shops make such items as jewelry and statues that are sold to tourists as souvenirs. In the mid-1900's, the government took over all but the smallest industries. Many have been returned to private ownership, but the government still owns the majority of them.

Paul and Sylvie followed Leon's directions and approached what looked like a row of three large apartment buildings. They were both smartly dressed, he in a gray suit and patterned tie, she in black pants, high heels and a white jacket shirt with a tuft of red ribbons adorning its chest pocket. The pants had a sharp, single pleat down its legs, creating a strong vertical line. Paul carried his usual briefcase, Sylvie a new frilly black purse.. They entered the door of the middle building. It was four-fifty p.m.

Inside, a young pretty receptionist sat at a desk in an immense but barren anteroom. There were no odors, no noises and it was as clean as the main corridor of a hospital. She rose upon seeing them, said her name was "Sally" and gracefully extended her hand. With her blonde hair, green eyes and captivating smile, she appeared to be more European, or even American than Asian. They gently shook her hand and asked if they were in the right building.

"Cairo Chemical?" Paul asked. "Tarek Ronque's office?"

"This is it. You can enter his office in a moment." Sally pointed to the room's only other door. "First I must ask that the briefcase remain out here, locked in the top wall safe near the door. It's easy. Pick any three numbers. That's the combination to open and close it. The purse is okay to take in. "

"Understood," Paul said. It was the first time he'd

ever been required to do so. He removed a small pad of paper from the briefcase and locked it in the safe using 1-2-3 as the numbers.

"Fine. Thank you," the receptionist said. "You may go in now. Don't bother to knock." They walked in.

The man who bolted from behind his desk to shake their hands and usher them to fancy chairs wasn't what Paul had expected. He wore a well-tailored tan suit and coordinated shirt and tie. Of medium height, he was trim and broad-shouldered, with white wavy hair combed straight back, thick eyebrows, a full mustache and a gap in the center of his front teeth. Momentarily, Paul thought he was about to speak to Omar Sharif, the dark complexioned star of *Lawrence of Arabia, Doctor Zhivago* and *Funny Girl*. Having these roles in mind, he realized the person before him expressed a personality that was both tender and empathetic. With his eyes and his bearing alone, he communicated the essence of romance. What was he doing running a chemical plant? He should be in pictures! And Paul told him so in his very first sentence.

"You're so kind," Ronque responded after returning to his chair. He brushed off the compliment with, "But what we do here is extremely essential, not only in production but also for national security. You see, we have two divisions—the actual chemical plants on either side of us, and our training unit which I'm in charge of. It's right beyond the wall behind me."

"I thought you were in charge of the whole complex," Paul said.

"I suppose you might think that's the way we operate, but not really. I'm the company's founder and president, but two other people are in charge of what goes on in the other two buildings. They certainly know more about it than I do. The most I can say about their work is that it's impossible to imagine a world without gasoline, paper, pharmaceuticals, fertilizers, plastics, synthetic fibers, paint, film or any other chemical product we use and demand in our daily lives. Most of our workers and management here are chemical analysts, including me, and actually our facilities are geared more toward bettering existing products than in creating new ones. For example, we don't make plastics or paint, but we offer ways to improve them."

Paying close attention to what Ronque said and to his initial manner was sufficient for Paul to trust him. And Sylvie's eyes conveyed the same feeling.

"But enough is enough," Ronque remarked. He measured Paul from side to side. "So you're the fellow we histarians always talk about, Mr. D'Arneau?"

"Call me Paul, please."

"And, please, you do the same. I'm Tarek."

Sylvie raised her hand and said, "And it's Sylvie over here."

"Yes, indeed," Tarek said. "I was saving the best for last."

Paul had been this introductory route so many times before, but always wondered how every new one would materialize. He was satisfied.

"Thank you for staying late," he said.

"It's not late at all," Tarek responded. "I usually don't leave here until seven or eight. But just to complete the picture of our three-building enterprise: It's about what I manage here, and this in turn relates to the first reason I wanted to see you. As I said, I deal with our training unit and here's a brief rundown on what we do. Our country has what's called a Non-Lethal Weapons Directive or NLWD. As a result of that, we have a single Advanced Chemical, Biological, Radiological and Explosives Training Program, and it's held right here."

"In this building?" Sylvie asked.

"In this building. The thrust of the program is to allow our scientists and engineers to share their knowledge and expertise directly with students through classroom, special exercise and custom-made programs. Participants can select individual training modules to meet specific mission requirements and the training team will custom design a training program for them."

"So you're saying you offer courses right here," Paul said.

"Correct. But it isn't just didactic. I mean not just a matter of lectures. We have labs back there and sometimes we take the students out into the field."

"Which is where?" Paul asked.

"We have more than enough deserts in these parts."

"And do the courses have names?" Sylvie inquired, by this time taking notes.

"I was hoping you'd ask," Tarek replied. "The general courses do, but they could be modified, depending on the students' special needs. Here, I'll read a few so you get an idea of the subjects we cover."

He slid over a card from the corner of his desk and read from it:

Chemical Agent Production
Biological Agent Production
Improvised Explosive Device Detection
and Recognition

Basic Course for Weapons of Mass
    Destruction
Toxic Industrial Chemicals as an
    Asymmetric Chemical Weapons Threat
Vehicle Borne Improvised Dissemination
    Device Prevention
Improvised Dispersal Device Construction
    and Disassembly

"The reason I invited you here is to talk about the last two. Remember the words 'Dissemination' and 'Dispersal'. But first I must point out that long-range delivery devices may easily be converted for use as biological agents or other chemicals, including lethal nerve gas—like the sarin that was released in the Tokyo subway system in 1995. Although there was nothing like 'long-range' in that tragedy. The important point is that a lethal chemical or biological weapons program might easily be developed by a country without resorting to secrecy. They might just use the buzz-word 'non-lethal' as a cover.

"Now, getting down to why you're here. The other day I received a call from a man who identified himself as a worldwide perfumer. He wouldn't give his name and asked if I was willing to talk to him in spite of that. I almost refused until he mentioned CR-23, AUT-45 and ERE-12. What are they? They're three chemicals that when added to another chemical, can make that other chemical disperse or disseminate better. And the fact is, these three chemicals are only available here, in this facility. We, and we alone, produce them. Anyway, he said his company didn't want any samples but he wanted to buy their formulas. Then his company would manufacture them, use them in its perfume lines, and his products would be more 'dispersible'—it's the word he used—than those of his competitors."

"Sounds logical and innocent enough," Paul commented.

Tarek had been twirling a pencil as he spoke. He tossed it onto his desk and exclaimed: "But Paul, they're too powerful for perfumes! Perfumes are too light. CR, AUT and ERE are fine for heavier chemicals but not for a perfume. And the way he talked, it was obvious he very well knew it. When I refused his request, he hung up."

"Unbelievable," Paul said. He suddenly had become almost as breathless as Sylvie.

"Anything distinctive about his voice?" he asked.

"No, and I don't think I'd recognize it again if I heard it. It was sorta creepy though."

"I'll bet," Paul said.

"Incidentally," Tarek continued, "All the historians I talk to know what you're working on. We call it the 'perfume case', and I thought this might be important for you to know."

"Why do you manufacture those three chemicals?" Sylvie asked.

"It ties in with what I was explaining. Egypt commissioned us to do so, as long as NLWD continues to be operational."

"Non-Lethal Weapons Directive," Paul said.

"Yes."

Paul looked at Sylvie to make sure she was still taking notes. She was writing furiously while he steepled his fingers over his mouth, ignoring a bead of sweat on his brow.

After he and Tarek exchanged questioning glances, Paul said, "That's either a helluva bombshell or an unrelated happenstance. I believe a bombshell, otherwise why would he know the names of those chemicals? Not exactly in the news every day."

"I agree with you, Paul. Now you've heard I had two reasons to see you. The second has to do with Thatcher Drinkwell."

"Thatcher Drinkwell? Down on St. Helena?"

"That's the one."

"We were just there, about a year ago. How did he get into this mess?"

"He and I talk all the time. And as you know, depending on their experience, some histarians talk freely over the phone. Others don't. Drinkwell's one of those. Nothing significant over the phone. That's just the way it is with him. He's a very good friend but please forgive me, he may be a bit paranoid."

"I know exactly what you mean," Paul responded.

"So what do we talk about?" Tarek went on. "He's into flowers and I'm into chemicals. But every once in a while he'll get into something he would ordinarily only discuss in person. And that happened the day before yesterday. He knows I'm more apt to talk freely by phone and asked that I bring this up with you, only scratching the surface of course. He said a man by the name of Inoue called him to get some information about Napoleon and arsenic. Said he'd heard about Thatcher and heard about you too. He read your Napoleon book."

"Inoue? I know that name," Paul said, strumming his fingers on his thigh. "Sure! Hiroshi Inoue. That's the Japanese guy who fancies himself as another Shoko Asaharam, the Islamic extremist and founder of the Arm Shivrikyo Cult."

"Correction," Tarek said, "Inoue's a *military* Islamic extremist."

Paul had never heard the three words put together in that order before. "Even worse," he said. "So what did he want from Thatcher?"

"Wouldn't say. That is, Thatcher wouldn't say. Although it must have been serious because he wants you to travel there again and discuss it."

"To St. Helena? Talk about remote…"

"I know it's a tough trip, Paul, but if you want my advice, I'd go. Thatcher's Thatcher, but I could tell he's concerned about the intentions of this guy. Said he just listened while Inoue went on and on about what he called a 'little known side-effect of arsenic'."

"But the island's a long way off; hard to get to, as you know. You don't think Thatcher would make an exception and explain it all to me over the phone."

"No, I don't. I wouldn't even waste time calling him."

Paul clenched his teeth and looked at Sylvie. She stopped taking notes and tilted her head to accept his stare.

"Well?" he asked her.

"Let's go back, Paul," she said. "Sounds important and besides, we had a good time there last year. And learned what we had to."

"Including Jules Smit's murder."

"Terrible, terrible thing," she said. "All murders are, but it was out of our control."

Tarek interrupted. "I forgot something else. Since Thatcher's the constable there, he has access to all sorts of news coming over the wire services. He's always tuned in and learned that some of Inoue's followers have taken up residence there."

"What the hell for?" Paul asked, torn between going or waiting for Thatcher to cave in, thereby saving him the burden of a two-day-plus journey by plane and freighter.

"That's one of the things to find out," Tarek replied.

Finally Paul said, "We'll compromise. We have to pay a visit to two or three other places first, and if we haven't heard from Thatcher by then, we'll go."

"Sounds workable," Tarek said.

Sylvie resumed her note taking, a tiny smile barely noticeable.

Like one who'd just experienced a heavy weight drop from his shoulder, Paul said, "So that's that." He still felt a second weight on the other shoulder. "At least for now," he added.

"I vowed that during the remainder of this investigation, I'd bring up the issue of poisons or poisoning wherever we went," he continued. "Anything to say about that, Tarek?"

"Only that they're covered in one of the courses I listed: Biological Agent Production."

"Well, I've been told more than once that any historian I consult knows the nature of the assignment *Vérité* gave me. That being said, you know the key part of the assignment is to find out who stole ..."

"The perfume packet," Tarek stated.

"See? Anyway, can you conceive of anything else in that packet, like a poison formula?"

Tarek showed no surprise, no emotion. "Yes," he answered, "I can conceive of it, but I can't offer more than that, because I don't know. There certainly hasn't been anyone asking us to produce a specific poison or to concoct a formula for one."

Paul felt both disappointed and relieved as he turned to get Sylvie's reaction. She gave a ready-to-leave-gesture as she put her pad back in her purse. But Paul wasn't quite ready.

"One final thing, Tarek. We plan on checking your temples for any inscriptions about poisons, and we can't possibly visit all of them. Could you suggest a couple?"

"I'd choose Luxor and Karnak. But what do you have so far?"

Paul took out one of his cards. "The Rosetta Stone sentence: 'This enabled scholars to translate inscriptions inside the Egyptian temples', and the inscription Nadim told us about; 'Beware of hidden poisons'."

"So there you have it," Tarek said.

"You mean that's it?"

"Yup. Not worth another trip."

Chapter 16

Paul's hunch had been right. The R.A.F. unit had to be back in London by midnight to meet another obligation. They made it just in time, landing at an airstrip in northern London.

During the flight, Sylvie dozed for the most part, while Paul reflected long and hard on what had occurred in the past twenty-four hours. He wrote in his pad: "One thing undeniable: although tiring, the time spent in Cairo completely worth it and am confident will pay dividends in long run. Session with Tarek must rank near the top. Learned plenty to help crack the case. Things beginning to make sense."

Next he summarized what had taken place at Cairo Chemical, using Sylvie's notes for technical details:

<u>Subjects Brought Up at Cairo Chemical</u>
<u>with Tarek Ronque</u>

—Said they have two divisions in their complex: two chemical plants and a training unit. He is president of all, but runs only the training unit.

—Said most employees are chemical analysts and the facilities are aimed more toward improving chemical products rather than creating new ones.

—Both Syl and I think he can be trusted.

—His main function is to implement an Egyptian Non-Lethal Weapons Directive (NLWD). They instruct students in an advanced chemical, biological, radiological and explosives training program. Teach them on-site and in the field.

—Listed titles of some of their courses, but stressed two: "Vehicle Borne Improvised Dissemination Device Prevention" and "Improvised Dispersal Device Construction and Disassembly." Emphasized the words "Dissemination" and "Dispersal."

—Used the sarin nerve gas incidents in Tokyo subways as example of long-range delivery devices being converted for short-range purposes.

—In connection with NLWD, said that buzz-word "non-lethal" could be used as a cover.

—Said chief reason why he asked us there was to talk about man who called with unusual request. Man said he was "worldwide perfumer". Wouldn't give name. Referred to CR-23, AUT-45 & ERE-12. Tarek explained they are 3 chemicals that can make other chemicals disperse better. But not suitable for perfumes. The 3 are manufactured only at Cairo Chemical.

—Man wanted to buy formulas for them. Would use them as additives to his company's perfume lines so their perfumes would disperse better than competitors'.

—Tarek refused, saying the 3 chemical additives are too powerful for perfume dispersal. Key point of whole subject matter.

—When asked why they manufacture the 3 in first place, he said they were commissioned to do so by Egyptian government.

—Tarek also said Thatcher Drinkwell wants us to visit him on St. Helena. Still vague over phone but did say concerns Hiroshi Inoue who consulted him about "little known side-effect of arsenic."

—Thatcher insists we go. What a trip! But will go. Eventually.

—Tarek knew all about stolen perfume packet.

—I brought up poison subject. He had nothing to offer.

—I brought up our plan to visit temples. Talked us out of it.

Then using his cell phone and referring to the summary sheet, he called Leon and presented the essentials of the meeting. Furthermore he indicated that since they'd be in London, they would check on Lady Beckett's coffin, as strongly suggested by the Talleyrand descendant, Thelma Tibbles. He asked Leon to contact historian Graham Radford who had orchestrated the exhumation of Napoleon's coffin a year ago and was well paid for it.

"Please tell him, Leon, that we'll need a supervisor and a three-man digging crew, just like before. Only this time we'll be interested in Lady Beckett's resting place, not Napoleon's."

"Any idea what you're looking for?" Leon asked.

"Just going by what Tibbles said—that some people had exhumed the coffin and did something to a package that was in with the body. I think 'fiddled with it' was the way she expressed it. So we'll see." Paul was trying to downplay the significance of the "inspection", as he called it last time, but this time around, he felt ill at ease over what he might discover.

Leon agreed to phone Radford and if he were unavailable, he would call another histarian friend in nearby Chatham.

Paul and Sylvie were within walking distance of a small hotel near the airstrip, so since it was one a.m., they called it a night and shared the only king-size bed in the hotel.

The Beckett estate, once an expansive tract of floral land with mansion, riding stable and assorted outbuildings, was converted into a cemetery by vote of Edenshire Township residents in the early 1900's. Initially it was designated the "Cemetery at Beckett Gardens" but this gradually changed simply to "Beckett Gardens".

Upon her death, her heirs buried her there on the land she treasured and erected a massive headstone. It's inscription read:

Lady Ashley Beckett
Entrepreneur and Friend to Many
1795-1845
May She Rest In Peace

The cobblestone entry drive to the gardens was bordered on both sides by stone pots on rock pedestals, pachysandra, rose geraniums, towering sycamores and plane trees. Far off in the distance were row upon row of gravestones in a sea of yellows and reds and blues of flowers that Paul couldn't identify. Fifty yards in, the supervisor pointed to Lady Beckett's headstone. Paul urged the supervisor to leave while assuring him the diggers would stay only until the coffin was slightly raised and then opened, but not inspected in their presence. They would be asked to "make themselves scarce" for a short while, then return to replace the casket. Paul also stressed that no defiling would take place and that once they were through, the grounds would be restored to their original condition.

The diggers knew where to begin and as they proceeded, Paul felt the blotches come. It didn't take long for the men to reach their target and open its lid. Iron screws dangled from the coffin's rim.

Paul and Sylvie remained speechless as they beheld a mummified corpse before them, but they paid little attention to its condition or to what was left of decayed cloth fragments surrounding its shoulders and mid-section. What they were after was in plain sight to the left of the body—a fairly large tin box. Paul pried it open with a shaking finger and withdrew several sheets of rag paper—stiff and brittle with irregular edges—and a black notebook.

"Do you smell what I smell?" Paul whispered.

"Perfume," Sylvie gasped.

The scent of a perfume seemed to increase as Paul carefully pulled the papers apart, but he wasn't positive until he read what was scrawled on the papers loud enough for Sylvie to hear:

I shall divulge my perfume code in due course. What is widely presumed about the dear emperor and me is true. We have shared our most intimate love secrets for many years. Secrets that have been outshone only by our devotion to each other. Within his battles and without. Within my business affairs at East India and without. No matter, they have endured. I mask this in my favorite perfume which the emperor has named Vintage. Such action symbolizes, signifies and preserves my admission as still a secret. Let our secret about secrets continue to endure. If this is found, so be it. It has endured in our hearts. If it is not found, it is coded both here and in our hearts. In the first instance, if the finder or finders wish to propagate the scent, its formula can be found in Psalm 45 from the Old Testament: "Your throne, O God, endures for ever and ever, a scepter of righteousness is the scepter of your kingdom; you love righteousness and hate iniquity. Therefore God, your God, has anointed you with the oil of gladness above your fellows. All your garments are fragrant with myrrh, aloes and cassia, and the music of strings from ivory palaces makes you glad." Be aware that in the blend, myrrh is aromatic, aloes is of the lilies and cassia's scent is cinnamon. Add whatever, but for what reason? The blend will seep through.

But Paul was more interested in the black book. He snatched it up and with Sylvie looking over his shoulder, he flipped through its pages and recoiled upon seeing what was immediately apparent. Filling at least ten pages were the names of male lovers and a dollar amount on the same line. Still other pages listed the names of approximately twenty-five women and beneath each of them, male names and, again, dollar amounts.

Paul snapped the book shut and hurled it back into the casket. He looked at his hands as if they'd been muddied, then turned to Sylvie.

"I'll be damned!" he cried.

"Mind-boggling," she responded. "Simply mind-boggling."

"She was nothing but a whore!" he declared. "And a madam to boot!"

"I would say the queen of the madams."

"Who would have ever…" Paul's voice had changed back to a whisper now. "I have to think a minute." He walked around the casket and leaned against a corner of the headstone.

He wanted to discuss with Sylvie what his current thinking was all about, but he hadn't yet shared certain thoughts with her. Was this another instance of something serving as a cover? Was all the talk about Napoleon-Beckett alliances just that: all talk? But a definite cover? And he couldn't help but extrapolate. Could a cover — any cover — serve as a disguise for something grander, as on a "grander scale"? He returned to her side in a minute.

"What was that all about?" she asked.

"Only this." He then described how covers can

mask more serious things, and then gave examples. He underscored this one at Beckett Gardens and, in the process, denigrated the note Lady Beckett had left behind.

"'Secrets outshown by our devotion to each other!' he said sarcastically. "Really!"

"But they both had other lovers," Sylvie said.

"And so did everyone else of importance in those days," Paul responded. "But such a black book takes it to a higher level."

"That Tibbles gal said certain people fiddled with the casket later on. Who were they?"

"Who knows? A group of the madams? Maybe they had something against her. Their male customers? Who can possibly know after all these years? The other thing is," Paul continued, "it demonstrates that, given the right circumstances, a scheme can be devised to cover for something terrible. And here's the important point, Syl. The scheme is elaborate, so elaborate that it's believable. While the something terrible is concrete and simple."

"Like the black book?"

"Like the black book."

"Now I feel like going over in the corner *myself* to think," Sylvie said, totally serious and absorbed. "But knowing how you think—God, do I know how you think—would you by any chance be implying that the perfumery business we're familiar with could have served as a cover for something more concrete?"

"You're getting there."

"And such a concrete thing was put into the packet that was stolen at *Cleo's*?"

"Something like that. But we've got a ways to go yet.

Even if that was the methodology, I have no idea what the packet contained—I mean besides the Vintage formula. Or who the perpetrator was."

Before summoning back the diggers and leaving the gardens, Paul moved off to the side and called Ms. Tibbles, spending considerable time listing most of what they'd found. But he made no mention of the black book.

"So I've been helpful?" she asked.

"Exceedingly. Many, many thanks. I can't stress strongly enough what this visit's provided. As a result of it, I'm definitely closer to cracking the case."

"Good. Perhaps I've made up for all the trouble my family has caused you."

Paul decided to sidestep the issue. "Thank you once again, Ms. Tibbles."

It was not yet noon when they returned to the London hotel and plopped down into the only two chairs in their room.

"So we're going, right?" Sylvie asked.

"St. Helena? Yes, we'd better. And I think it would be silly to return to Paris first. Why don't I just call Leon. I want to tell him what we found here anyway, and ask him to put the trip together. And since the R.A.F. is key again, we'll leave directly from here."

"You have my vote," Sylvie said, leaping from her chair onto Paul's lap. She yanked his head toward her and planted a loud, hard kiss on his lips.

"Hey there, Syl!" he said, pulling back and grinning. "More gentle, please."

"Why? I'm so happy."

"Because you're shaking up the thoughts in my head."

Sylvie returned to her chair. "Remember our last trip there?" she asked. "When I made a fool of myself a couple of times?"

"You had too much to drink."

"But I hardly knew you, Paul, drinks or not."

"It's because I'm so alluring," Paul retorted.

"No, really, can we relive it, and I'll act more sensibly?"

"It's a given. But let's not forget our mission goal. And I'd better notify Leon." Once again Paul took out his cell phone. "I'm growing tired of these calls," he said.

"You'd have to make a lot more if you didn't have him," Sylvie said. "Hotel bookings, flights, taxi rides, meetings. I'd call it leg work or dirty work, but he seems to enjoy it."

"You're right. Of course you're right," Paul said. "He does my dirty work so I don't get bogged down and can plow ahead."

He described the Beckett Gardens visit for Leon in as much detail as he'd given to Ms. Tibbles, but once again, withheld any mention of a black book. He'd already decided to reveal its existence only during a last get-together with the entire *Vérité* delegation—after the investigation had ended. It was one of several things he was holding in reserve, including what he characterized as "logic points." He had used the phrase when he told Sylvie what he'd just said to Leon.

"You have a lot of them," she said.

"A lot of what?"

"Oh, your little headings like 'logic points', 'probabilities and possibilities', 'germane or not germane', 'Phase One', 'written listing', 'reflective listing'.

"You know them all, don't you?" Paul asked, impressed.

"Of course. I hear most everything you say, but I didn't hear you tell Leon about the black book."

"I didn't as a matter of fact."

"How come?"

"Because I want to save it for my wrap-up, hopefully in a few more days. And speaking of days, do you know that today is the Fourth of July in our country?"

"Well, happy Fourth of July," Sylvie said. "We'll have to celebrate."

"When?"

"Tonight."

"Promise?"

"Promise."

They began their long and arduous journey to St. Helena within two hours. Leon had arranged the one-hour car ride to Brize Norton airbase where they boarded an R.A.F. plane which landed at Wideawake Airfield on Ascension island three hours later. It was a joint facility of the United States Air Force, the Royal Air Force and the BBC World Service Atlantic Relay Station. Paul remembered it was used extensively by the British military during the Falklands War. After a six-hour wait, they set sail on the Royal Mail ship, *St. Helena,* bound for the capital city of Jamestown, seven-hundred miles and thirty-six hours away. They were offered separate cabins but chose only one, an unexpectedly roomy space that contained a lower and foldaway upper birth, large window, two wardrobe units, an armchair, a dressing table with over-lighted mirror and a bathroom with shower. The upper birth remained undisturbed during the entire voyage, and before July Fourth became history, they celebrated the United States holiday in their own special manner.

"We're in the middle of nowhere," Sylvie said. "But who cares? We're with each other."

Well into the trip, Paul picked up a flyer from a table outside the ship's galley. Titled *St. Helena and Napoleon,* it was in a pile available to all the ship's forty to fifty passengers. Other piles dealt with services on the island such as transport, banking, communications, immigration, shopping and medical care. He recalled browsing through a similar flyer on his last trip to St. Helena and though he knew nearly everything it covered, having written so extensively about the emperor, this time he read its contents word for word:

> St. Helena, a British Island in the south Atlantic, is situated 1,200 miles off the coast of Africa and 700 miles southeast of Ascension Island. The Portuguese discovered St. Helena in 1502 but it became part of Great Britain in 1673. The island is approximately ten by seven miles in size or about half the size of Napoleon's former home-in-exile, Elba. Rough and mountainous, it is composed mainly of volcanic wasteland. The highest peaks— Diana's Peak and Mount Actaeon—rise more then 1,000 feet above sea level. An area of past volcanic activity is Sandy Bay which contains fertile soil, ideal for the island's fruit and vegetable production.

Three columns of Basalt in this area are called Lot, Lot's Wife and Asses Ear.

The island's only port and village is Jamestown, the capital. Its population is about 5,600, principally Europeans, Africans and East Indians. Its main bay is called James Bay.

The chief crops are flax and potatoes. For a century or more, the flax was used to make mailbags for British Post Offices but this process has declined because of the availability of cheaper synthetic materials. Other industries there include fish curing and the manufacture of lace and fiber mats.

For many years, it was an important port of call for Portuguese sailors to replenish their supplies and to receive medical attention. At one time both the British and the Dutch claimed the island as their own as they visited it on their voyages to India. In 1659 the East India Company colonized the island. Fourteen years later, the Dutch attacked and took over the island but the British retook it within six months.

Napoleon Bonaparte of course was its most famous resident. After his defeat at Waterloo, he signed a second abdication at the Elysee Palace. Three weeks later he surrendered himself to the captain of H.M.S. *Bellerophon* which took him to

Plymouth. From there, he embarked on the H.M.S. *Northumberland* bound for St. Helena, arriving October 15, 1815. He was allowed a retinue of thirty people. Napoleon stayed at a small house, the Briars, while his eventual home, Longwood House, was being readied. Shortly thereafter he moved into Longwood and lived there until his death.

Three frigates and eight other vessels continually patrolled James Bay or were kept on standby. Gun emplacements and guard posts were established throughout the island.

A year later, Sir Hudson Lowe was appointed governor of St. Helena and it quickly became apparent that he and Napoleon had little respect for one another.

Napoleon died there on May 5, 1821. The cause and manner of death remain in dispute. Some claim he was poisoned by arsenic, either intentionally or by accident. Others state he died of stomach cancer as did his father. He was buried in the island's Sane Valley where his body remained until 1840. It was then transported to Paris and currently lies in the Hotel des Invalides.

Paul was on deck as the ship headed into its southerly approach to James Bay. Taking the time zone difference into account, it was Friday July 6, eleven a.m. From a distance, the island looked ominous in the hazy light, just as it had a year ago. How can a massive black iceberg change in only a year? As they sailed closer, he could make out its irregular upper border and what appeared to be a thin valley down its middle, with whitish buildings on either side.

They disembarked on Napoleon Street, the main and only street in town. It was quiet, narrow and congested with all makes of cars, their bright colors in sharp contrast to the light buildings hugging the curbs. Most of the buildings were one-storied with sturdy cement facades. Sidewalks were similarly crowded with dawdling people. Paul made it a point to check, but none looked suspicious.

They walked into the center of town and registered at the Consolate Hotel. Leon had reserved a single room for them. It was a mid-18th century building with old, colonial wrought- iron balconies, a public bar and surprisingly, a computer room off the main lobby.

The receptionist was a stout, jovial man who introduced himself as Jeremy. It didn't take long for him to tell them he had lived in Jamestown for all his fifty-two years and had rarely met visitors he didn't like.

"Of course there are exceptions to everything, you know."

"About visitors?" Paul asked.

"Yes, I'm afraid so."

Jeremy didn't give Paul a chance to inquire further, instead saying, "See, it's like this. Before we had these certain groups arrive, it was all peace and quiet around here. Then about three years ago, the Saints and the Fish Truck moved in and there's been fighting ever since. Not all the time mind you, but enough to … shall we say …

upset the equilibrium." He smiled, obviously proud of
his last statement, but before he could resume talking,
Paul said, "Yes, I've heard of the Saints, but what's the
Fish Truck?"

"Well the Saints deal in prostitution and the Fish
Truck got their name because they operate out of a
big black truck with a high canvas cover in the back.
Sometimes they haul fish. Other times they haul men, their
own men. They're into gambling, the numbers, loans, but
mainly they offer protection."

"So if both sides do different things, why do they
fight?" Sylvie asked.

"Because they don't stick to what they do. They
wander into each other's activities and territory. They're
just dumb."

"Interesting stuff," Paul said. "But look, we're in a
bit of a hurry. While we go to our room for a few minutes,
could you call us a taxi? We have an appointment at the
Police Service Building."

"Thatcher Drinkwell's place," Jeremy stated. "Sure,
I'd be glad to."

"You know him?" Paul asked.

"Who doesn't? Practically runs the island."

It was almost noon when they arrived at the island's
Police Service Building, its outside resembling a one-room
schoolhouse in rural New England. The inside contained
two rooms—front to back. The first one appeared barren
with little more than a gray metal desk and chair, several
wooden straight-back chairs, a filing cabinet and a single
holding cell. The room was the larger of the two and
smelled at once musty and antiseptic. From the ticking
and clicking in the back room, Paul assumed it was a

command post that held the usual electronic equipment associated with police departments.

A man of average height and weight sat at the desk, rifling through several folders, his expression pinched. He had closely cropped brown hair and a fair complexion with a small scar on his chin. A pistol strapped to a leather holster was attached to the right side of his belt. He inserted the folders, turned toward them and froze. "Paul!" he exclaimed. "Sylvie!"

Paul eyed Sylvie as if asking who should speak first. "Hi, Thatcher," Paul said solemnly. Sylvie followed with, "Hello, constable."

Thatcher came around, gave her a hug and kissed her on the forehead. Then the men wrapped their arms around one another, squeezing hard.

"Give up?" Thatcher asked.

"Not a chance," Paul answered.

"So you made it after all," the constable said. "You know, no one ever got back to me about whether you were coming or not. So I'm delighted you're here. Much to tell you, unfortunately none of it good."

They sat down. "But first," Thatcher said, "how was the trip?"

"The usual," Paul replied.

"Which is?"

"What can I say? Treacherous. And you? Still active with birds?"

"Absolutely, but don't get me going on that. We'd be here all afternoon."

"But generally copacetic?" It was Paul's version of baiting.

"Yes, I'd say copacetic." Thatcher twisted his mouth

to the side. "Oh we have the usual problems, but all in all, things aren't too bad as long as we keep on top of them."

Paul thought it was the perfect time to broach the subject that had been gnawing at him. "I hear there's a mysterious Japanese contingent on the island now."

"That's right. They have a spokesman and he claims they're hiding from something going on in Tokyo, but he refuses to say what. Meanwhile they're bothering everybody with questions, including me. Frankly I think the hiding business is a lot of bunk especially after he began pumping me about Napoleon and arsenic."

"What did he want to know specifically?" Paul asked.

"First if Napoleon was using it here."

"Was he?"

"I don't know. And secondly, did he die because no more arsenic was available to him."

"Did he?"

"Again, I don't know. But that's when I became really suspicious. I mean the intensity of his questioning. I think it represents something serious and that's the reason I asked for you to come down. But there are other reasons too."

"Before you get to that, Thatcher, could I ask why don't you like to say things like this by phone?"

"Because I've had some bad experiences. Like one time when a person's phone was bugged and there went an entire case I was working on. No, it's too risky and I simply won't do it. I'll continue as an historian but I refuse to share what I learn with scumbags. Electronic communication simply has some drawbacks, especially where sensitive information is concerned."

"And I assume that includes shortwave radio?"

"Shortwave radio? That's even worse! With that, signals are bounced off the ionosphere—I mean a hundred miles off the earth's surface. So things can get intercepted by people all over the world. In other words, anybody can tune in. No, I'll have nothing to do with that except for routine stuff."

After the constable ran his hand over his forehead and then straightened his badge, Paul thought it advisable to change the subject. "Okay that's that," he said. "I didn't mean to press you on it. You were about to mention other reasons."

"Yes, two or three others. Some of this might be old news for you but I have it on reliable authority that the Japanese men here are really followers of that Hiroshi Inoue guy. You know—the Islamic extremist over in Tokyo. We've already touched on it, but there's a little-known side- effect of arsenic that those new arrivals here are interested in. Napoleon is probably the best example of that effect taking hold."

Thatcher reached into a desk drawer for a card and handed it to Paul. "Here," he said, "this describes it best. It's a very concise statement from an historian in Romania—a molecular biologist. Why not read it now? Maybe you can read it together." Sylvie shifted her chair closer to Paul so they could share the card:

> In Europe arsenic was used by some as a mind-altering drug. In small doses it produced a feeling of well-being and strength. When a man has once begun to

indulge in it he must continue to indulge
... or the last dose kills him. Indeed, the
arsenic eater must not only continue his
indulgence, he must also increase the
quantity of the drug, so it is extraordinarily
difficult to stop the habit; for, as the
sudden cessation causes death, the gradual
cessation produces a terrible realization
that the user must continue to take arsenic
until he dies.

"Now," Thatcher continued, rubbing his hands together. "This ties in with the next reason for asking you to make this long trip. I've been told that you know about the effects of CR-23, Aut-45 and ERE-12. They're dispersal agents. But CR-23 is more than that. Dangerously more than that. In a sense, it acts like arsenic. Say a person survives a biochemical attack, like by sarin, the nerve gas, and that CR-23 had been added to the gas to make it disperse better. Well, he must have more of the additive to live. Just like arsenic! Can you imagine the chaos? People killing people to get supplies of it. Utter, utter chaos. It would lead to a cruel Armageddon."

The constable was breathing as though he had just chopped a pile of wood. Sylvie moved her chair back to its original position, also breathing harder. And Paul tried to remain composed although he was lost for words.

"I suppose I'd better look into it," he finally said in a shallow voice.

"Funny you should say that," Thatcher said. "It's the last reason. In a recent talk with Guy, he spoke about a journalist colleague of his who happens to be an historian."

He checked in one of his desk's top drawers. "Name's Shapiro. Harry Shapiro. Writes for *The New York Times*. Normally works only out of New York, but three months ago was sent on assignment to Tokyo to cover the fifteenth anniversary of the subway sarin attacks. Back in New York, they liked the piece he wrote, made it a feature article and asked him to stay on in Japan for a couple of months. Had something to do with researching the Aum Shinrikyo cult that's still active there. Parenthetically, Shapiro hates to give out important information over the phone as much as I do, so Guy and I both feel you and he should meet. He's back in New York now."

"I read that sarin article. It was excellent," Paul said.

They decided to skip lunch but planned on having dinner at Ann's Place, the site of a meal or two the year before. At Paul's insistence, Thatcher said he would contact Leon and between the two of them, they would arrange a voyage back to Europe. They would set sail later that night and their final destination would be Paris. Paul had thought briefly about a direct trip to Japan and mentioned it to Sylvie, but it didn't take much for her to talk him out of it.

"Too much travel in too short a span," she said. "We've got to collect ourselves."

Thatcher concurred and said he would have Guy notify Shapiro that Paul would contact him. "You can probably learn as much from him as you would by visiting Tokyo. And it would save you from another long trip."

"Definitely a plus," Paul said.

The three of them decided to meet at the restaurant at six p.m. and Paul indicated they would be ready to leave the island four hours later.

"I'm sorry we have to cut this visit short, Thatcher, but there's so much on my plate that has to be tended to," he commented. "You've been extremely helpful and I promise to take everything you've said into consideration. It's a no brainer."

Ann's Place was exactly as Paul and Sylvie remembered: quaint, near the pier in Jamestown, in the middle of an expansive garden. It boasted a variety of popular "Saint" dishes such as curry, pumpkin stew, fishcakes, pilau, black pudding and coconut fingers. It was noisy, jammed to capacity and filled with pleasant food aromas.

Each ordered fishcakes and black pudding and raced through the meal as though they were late for a job interview. Their conversation, what there was of it, centered on the issues Thatcher had raised at his office and Paul's assurance that he would follow through in implementing any suggestions, real or implied.

Paul and Sylvie said their good-byes to Thatcher at about seven-fifteen. Her reciprocated and said he would stay behind for an after-dinner drink. "I'll toast the air in honor of your great sacrifice in coming here. I'm not kidding, I mean it. Do keep me informed and I'll try my best not to be so secretive on the phone."

About a half-hour later, Paul left their hotel room to download some information about Tokyo's sarin attack in 1995. He put the two-page article in his briefcase and left the computer room at seven-forty-five. He noticed that the reception desk was unattended. As he crossed the deserted lobby, four men appeared out of nowhere. Two staggered on either side of him, one of the pair grabbing hold of his arm. All were Japanese and each man had his hand in a jacket pocket. They reeked of alcohol, their expressions slimy. One of them yanked the briefcase from Paul's hand, threw it behind a chair and whispered in his ear, "You won't be needing this anymore, dead man." The words were slurred.

Paul felt his face blotch and his finger itch. He was afraid his judo moves would be useless against four men. Could he break away and make a run for it? Could he pretend tripping and falling to the floor, hoping someone would come by?

They escorted him out a side door.

The alley was dark, dank and smelled of old garbage. Small shafts of light shone from the upper windows of a next-door apartment house, and only one car passed by on Napoleon Street, about sixty feet to the left. The distant yapping of a dog broke an otherwise deadly silence.

Paul's abductors tied his wrists behind him, applied duct tape tightly over his mouth and patted him down for guns. Paul felt as though all the air had been sucked out of his lungs. And what about Sylvie? The mission?

The rub of firearms against his waist became more pronounced as they marched him across the street and into an opposing alley. Their gait was faster than Paul would have expected. The men switched from English to the staccato of Japanese as they argued among themselves, presumably about their next move. They walked behind a row of buildings and, after covering a distance of about a quarter of a mile, Paul feigned fatigue and they dragged him for another twenty-five feet. There, one of the men pointed to a metal railing below which a restless sea slapped against the rocks. They nodded. Paul struggled as they lifted him up, shoulder-high, and tossed him over the railing.

He could have gone limp and sunk far enough to gauge the level of the sea but didn't want to chance it. Instead he immediately put his legs in motion with a kick that brought back memories of the pool at Yale's Payne Whitney Gym. He flipped over onto his back, his bound arms relatively unnecessary for such a maneuver. And he floated, just long enough to get his bearings. In that position he took a hard look up at the railing he'd been thrown over. No one was in sight. How careless! How inefficient! And how drunk! Yet he knew they would still be around on the island and was glad that he and Sylvie would be leaving soon. At least he hoped so.

But his more immediate concern was to get on dry land. He kicked as he floated, shifting shoulders from side to side to provide some balance. He spotted a wooden ladder up ahead, quickened his stroke and was soon able to straighten up and wrap his body around it. Then he used his chin and knees to elevate himself until his feet reached a rung below water level. The rest was easy by comparison, though he knew his chin would be bruised and bleeding. At ground level, he found a split in the metal railing and used one of the sharp edges to free his hands. Then he ripped the tape from his mouth.

He shuffled back to the hotel. Luckily the lobby was still deserted, no one was behind the registration desk and he even recovered his briefcase from behind the chair. The whole ordeal had taken only twenty minutes and aside from his bruised chin, drenched clothes and look of disbelief when he walked into their room, Sylvie would hardly have noticed anything unusual.

But before she had a chance to say a word, he began stripping off his clothes while uttering a stream of questions: "How did they know I was on the island? Recognized me at Ann's Place? Was my picture in a Japanese newspaper? If so, why?" Totally nude, he dropped onto the bed.

"What's going on?" she screamed, hopping beside him and twisting his head to get a closer look at his chin.

After a series of deep sighs he related what had happened—referring to the four men as "drunken goons"—and said he had better notify Thatcher.

"Thank you, Lord," Sylvie said loudly. And then softly, "for looking out for my man."

She embraced him until he reminded her of the Thatcher call.

She handed Paul the phone after reaching the constable.

Paul repeated what had happened, ending with, "It's a good thing they were looped or I wouldn't be talking to you right now."

Thatcher apologized for what Paul had gone through and said he would check around to see if he could determine who the "bastards" were.

"It's not your fault," Paul said.

"I guess not, but I made you come here."

"We learned a lot," Paul added.

"But you didn't have to learn *this*."

There were several more minutes of talk about the attack and then Thatcher indicated their ship would be at the pier by ten p.m.

The vessel was named the Argos, a small Greek freighter that hauled roll-on/roll-off vehicles, packaged lumber and containers. It had cabin space for twelve passengers in square units that were surprisingly well furnished and comfortable. They set sail at ten-fifteen. There were no other passengers on board.

Paul and Sylvie filled the next thirty-six hours at sea primarily with frequent naps, chats with the crew, considerable lovemaking, and discussions about what needed to be learned, who had to be visited, and who or what had to be flushed out. Whenever the subject of Japan came up, both were thankful that a trip there had been avoided. Instead they would meet with Harry Shapiro of *The New York Times*.

At one point early on, Paul looked at a small calendar in their cabin and said, "I can't believe that after what took place on that god-forsaken island, it's still only Saturday, July seventh. Seems like we arrived there an eternity ago."

Mid-afternoon a day later, he was back in his Montparnasse room, by way of the usual R.A.F. flight and a ride with Leon who had met him and Sylvie at the de Gaulle Junior airstrip. Paul briefed him on the goings-on at St. Helena including the incident involving the four Japanese men.

"Good thing they were drunk," Leon said, "or who knows what?"

"That's for sure."

Paul indicated that Thatcher turned out to be invaluable in his comments and advice, and that the constable believed it important for Paul to speak with a journalist named Harry Shapiro. He described his background and mentioned he'd been an historian for some time.

"Do call me after the meeting—when you get a chance," Leon said as Paul and Sylvie exited the car.

There was a front-desk message near Paul's phone that said Yale's Gregory Holliday had called earlier in the day and wanted to speak to him. The slip was marked urgent.

"Hello, Greg? It's Paul D'Arneau here. You called?"

"Yes. Thanks for getting back to me so soon. I'll get right to the point. It's bad. Ahmad Khalil's been shot."

"Shot? Dead?"

"I'm afraid so."

Paul whispered the news to Sylvie who gasped in disbelief.

Ordinarily, Paul would have been shocked at that kind of information, but found it hard to hide a measure of calm, even indifference. He chose his words carefully. "Well I hate to say it, Greg, because these things are always unfortunate, but I'm not surprised. In my humble opinion, he was the kind of guy who found it easy to stir up trouble. Where did it happen?"

"In a downtown parking lot. Shot in the head, apparently as he was getting out of his car. The police said eyewitnesses reported hearing two shots and seeing a pick-up truck speed away."

"Any leads?"

"Not that I'm aware of."

"Well again, unfortunate. I would suspect he had some enemies at the East India Company, and probably Japan. Who knows?"

"Maybe Iran too. He was born there and moved away, leaving some family behind. I wonder why."

"And let's not forget the jetty scene. Remember his old business card was on the guy who was shot there—the guy following me, Rico Cretelli. It's a good bet the mob had a hand in that job. Maybe this one too."

"Could be," Greg said, distantly. "But who hired them?"

"We may never know."

Paul didn't let the killing sidetrack him. "Anyway," he said, "I plan on returning to New Haven tomorrow. Hope to meet with a New York journalist who's familiar with Japan, its current politics, some problems there and so on. Saves a long trip. Between you and me, this travel is beginning to wear on me. I'm sticking with it, but I'd be happy to take a break."

"And start working at Sterling," Holliday said confidently.

"And start working at Sterling." Paul rethought his answer. "But don't get me wrong, Greg. After some rest, I'll combine it with being on the road again. Have to look for some rare books and manuscripts, you know."

"Now you have it."

Paul dialed Leon's cell phone number and told him about Khalil's murder. Leon offered nothing constructive about the murder. His only comment was, "And the mysteries continue."

Paul and Sylvie sat on the edge of his bed. After some emotional words with her about the shooting and his need to fly back to Connecticut, he tried to comfort her by promising to return to Paris and devote a few days to rest and relaxation. Paul deliberately left out when and she didn't ask. He was quick to change the subject.

"By the way," he said, "what's with Vincent?"

"He's still dealing with that special project at the Sorbonne. Says it's harder than he thought, but he's got no choice except to finish it." Evidently, Sylvie's mind was still on the previous subject. "You know what bugs me about our or your flying from country to country, Paul?"

"Okay, I'll bite. What?"

"You can't take your guns with you. Didn't Vincent say he could arrange for you to have some when you got to another place?"

"Come to think of it, he did."

"That's what I mean."

"How's that?" he asked.

Her response was patently derisive. "Get with it, Paul. Look at the shooting that just happened. Look at those four guys on the island."

"My guns wouldn't have helped in either case, but tell you what. I'll be well armed after I arrive in New Haven."

"Are you sure I shouldn't go with you?"

"I'm sure."

"Why not?"

"Because if someone takes a shot at me, it might hit you instead."

"Now cut that out!"

He thinned his lips in a mocking gesture.

"I mean it!" she said.

They both called it quits as they embraced and fell back onto the bed.

Paul was delighted with the job his carpenter friend

had done on his fire-damaged garage and workshop. Although most of the power tools were not in their original positions and were rusted here and there, the "Furniture Central" bay appeared intact and the other two bays looked better than new.

It was a Sunday and he was certain Harry Shapiro was not at *The Times*. Just as well. He would spend the day catching up on sleep, straightening out the workshop and, time permitting, reviewing where he was on his assignment. Considering the scope of the case, he felt he was ahead of schedule compared to other cases he'd worked on. And when he factored in that more countries were involved this time around, he had an additional reason to be pleased. He celebrated by having more than two wines, his usual quota. And he would phone *The Times* in the morning.

At nine the next morning, he had difficulty getting through to the journalist until he told the newspaper's operator that he was returning Harry Shapiro's call. Which he was, in a way.

"Hello, is this Harry?"

"Yeah, you got the right guy. Who's this?"

"Paul D'Arneau from New Haven."

"Paul, it's you! Well I'll be damned. So many have spoken so highly of you that I feel I know you. Thanks so much for calling." It was as if his manner of speaking had been raised to a salute.

"Well the feeling's mutual or I should say I know *of* you. You have plenty of admirers but Guy Martin and Thatcher Drinkwell are your greatest."

"Again, thanks. Now, I'd like very much for us to get together. I've got plenty to tell you." It seemed to Paul that most of his recent contacts could switch gears with impunity.

"And that's why I'm calling," Paul said, "How's today?"

"Perfect. The sooner the better."

"I can meet you there or you can come here."

"Let's make it there. Too many eyes and ears around here."

"Fine. Private room?"

"Private room," Harry replied.

"Okay," Paul said. "Ever been to the Sterling Memorial Library?"

"Oh, yes. I wrote about it a few years ago. Quite a library."

"Then look, I'll meet you there at two. The Linonia and Brothers Room. I'll phone ahead and make sure they keep it available. I've got some pull in that place now."

"I've heard about *that,* too," Harry said.

The early afternoon was hot and humid with a threat of rain. Paul arrived just before two and waited inside the front entrance. Shortly thereafter, he thought he saw James Cagney walk in. Actually a cross between Cagney and a throwback to a Western Union clerk in a 1940's movie: slicked down black hair parted in the middle, wire-framed glasses, gartered shirt sleeves. In one hand he carried a brown-checked jacket slung over his shoulder, a thick briefcase in the other. His plain gold tie was loosened at the collar and his trousers were wrinkled and too long. He had probing eyes, a prominent forehead and he spoke through the corner of his mouth.

"You're Paul, right?" he said.

"Right. Boy, am I glad to see you."

"But you see lots of people. Are you *always* glad?"

"Hardly. First, you've saved me a trip to Tokyo.

And second, I think I'm correct in saying that what you have to tell me might be the turning point in cracking this blasted case."

Paul loosened his striped tie and took his own jacket off, a gray blazer. He'd left his briefcase home but had a small pad in a back pocket.

Alone in the Linonia and Brothers Room, they sat opposite each other, near the end of the same long table Paul and the Board had used a week before. Harry removed several papers from his briefcase and spread them out.

"Ready to get started?" he asked.

"I'm all ears."

Harry looked around as if he expected spies to be crouched behind chairs and tables. Paul wouldn't have been surprised if the journalist eventually checked outside the closed door.

"First off," Harry said, "did you happen to read my article on the Tokyo sarin attacks?"

"Yes, sir, an outstanding job."

"Well, even so, I'll probably refer to some of the things I included in it."

"That's fine, Harry. A complete presentation is what I'm after. In other words, what did you learn in the three months you were there?" Paul took off his tie entirely. "Am I being too direct?"

"No, not at all. I'm trying to decide what to leave in and what not to bother with."

"Let's say: bother with *everything.*"

"But just so I know. Thatcher told you about CR-23?" Harry asked.

"Yes."

"And I believe Tarek Ronque told you about AUT-45 and ERE-12 and even some about CR-23? And that his company is the only one in the world that manufactures all three?"

"Yes, that's right." *Why doesn't he get on with it?*

Shapiro craned his head forward and quick as a hiccup, said, "Well, you know what the chemicals do and I'm here to say that they plan on doing it and we'd better hurry to stop it before they get their hands on the formula."

"Just a minute," Paul said. "Give me that again. Who is 'they', exactly what do they plan on doing, and are we talking about the perfume formula?" He found himself speaking nearly as fast as Shapiro. Do they all speak like that at *The Times?*

"Jeez, it's hot in here," Shapiro said. He too removed his tie, then rolled up his sleeves. "Okay, let's break it down before I go into details," he continued. "And instead of giving the specific names of those three chemicals—they're just acronyms—let's refer to them as 'those chemicals.'"

"Good enough."

"You see, the extremist group that organized and implemented the 1995 sarin release in Tokyo was called Aum Shinrikyo—and still is. It's also known as Aum and Aleph and is a Japanese cult that combines tenets from Hinduism and Buddhism, and they're obsessed with the apocalypse. It was a coordinated attack on five trains in the subway system that left twelve commuters dead, seriously injured fifty-four and caused 6,000 more people to seek medical attention. Aum's founder is Shoko Asahara who claims he's the first enlightened one since Buddha. At the time of the attack Aum alleged it had 40,000 members worldwide and had offices here in the U.S., in Russia and, of course, in Japan. The group split into two factions three years· ago over attempts to moderate its religious beliefs, whatever that means." The journalist was reading from one of his papers. "And I should mention that Asahara predicted the end of the world was near and that only his followers would survive. Crazy man, for sure."

"But crazy men can kill," Paul interjected, looking up from the notations he was making.

"So we have a guy like that and/or his followers still on the loose," Shapiro continued. "And what are their immediate plans, you may ask? They want to release a stronger nerve gas somewhere in New York City. In fact they have a name for the newer gas. They simply reversed the letters in sarin and refer to it as 'niras'. The group is even preaching that Niras is the name of a Buddhist goddess, which is a lot of hooey."

The journalist pushed aside several papers he'd already referred to and slid a new stack in their place. "Are you following me?" he asked.

"Yes," Paul said. "Please go on. The perfume formula issue intrigues me. Where does that come in?"

"You're psychic; that comes next. Notice I never said it was a *perfume* formula, because it isn't. There may be one, but that's not what they're interested in. They're interested in the formula that strengthens sarin, and that's the formula the thief was after at *Cleo's*, not a perfume one. There were two formulas in the packet, one for perfume and the one that would enhance the potency of sarin. And change it to niras, in other words. The perfume one—what do they call it? Vintage? That was simply a cover."

Paul puffed out a breath. "Just as I thought," he said. "Where'd you get this information?"

"From my contacts in Tokyo, especially disenfranchised members of Aum. And there's more. Those chemicals? They'd be added to niras and would make the final nerve gas more dispersible. I guess you know all about that, though."

"Yes, pretty much. But who would make the niras?"

"Aum scientists in Tokyo. They're waiting for whoever stole the packet to hand it over. I'm told you're calling him Mr. X. So the successful scenario would be: identify Mr. X before he gives Tokyo the packet and therefore the augmented and more dispersible sarin doesn't get used. And that's where you come in, Paul."

"Yes, I know. I suspect a certain someone and have maybe 90 percent of the proof."

"So you're close."

"Yes, but a lot closer because of you."

"Don't reveal his name yet because that might bring bad luck. You see, I'm superstitious."

"So am I sometimes."

"I could go on and on about that fellow Hiroshi Inoue, the so-called military Islamic extremist," Shapiro said, "and CR-23'S arsenic-like side-effect; and special operation forces; and perimeter security; and especially counter-terrorist forces in Tokyo, but I think you have your hands full as it is."

"And my head."

Chapter 17

Paul had to get his facts, assumptions and hunches straight, and he spent the rest of Monday doing just that. He consulted all past notes, summaries, articles and even made new notes. And the more he did, the more it reinforced what he planned to do. In his mind, it loomed heavy as his end game and he would return to Paris in the morning to begin the process.

First thing Tuesday, he phoned Sylvie, summarized the discussion with Shapiro and informed her of the plans. He asked her to call Leon, brief him and indicated it was important for both of them to be at the Montparnasse lobby later in the afternoon, at about five.

Like clockwork, Paul checked in at four-thirty, went to the lobby and they were both there—along with Vincent. They sat inconspicuously in an area tucked behind two massive flower pots that rose halfway to the ceiling.

"Vincent! You're back," Paul exclaimed.

"Actually they couldn't stand me any longer," Vincent said. "Good timing, eh?"

Paul noticed he was carrying a brief case. "What's with that?" he asked. "You never had one before."

"*These*," Vincent replied. He looked around, then reached in and withdrew Paul's two pistols and their rigs.

"Ah," Paul said, "I was wondering about them." He slowly armed himself, making certain no other guests were observing. "Thanks. They might come in handy for a change."

"Paul," Leon said. "Not to change the subject but the three of us were just talking about the latest."

"The latest? Now what?"

"Ken Kuroda's been murdered."

"Ken, the perfumer?" Paul's eyes took on a wounded look that disappeared with his next comment: "Seems like someone's knocking off all human evidence."

"I know what you mean," Leon said.

"Shot or garroted?" Paul asked.

"Shot. Back of the head. Police think there was a bit of a struggle."

"Where?"

"In his office. When he didn't arrive home at the usual time, his wife gave him three or four more hours, then called them. They found his car out back and the side door of the building partially open. Went in and found him."

Paul thought aloud: "First Tomi, now Ken." He searched the others' faces. "Know what I'm driving at?" he continued. "I thought I had more than enough goods. Now this just adds to it. It's a dead giveaway, no pun intended. And that business about *Remsington* employees being responsible for the theft goes out the window. They wouldn't follow this pattern. This is president to president, so to speak. Paying the mob to do one's dirty work. And we should be able to prove it sometime within the next twenty-four hours or so."

The other three glanced at one another and nodded.

"Okay," Paul said. "Here's what we do. Can you all come along to Grasse?"

They nodded again.

"I'll make a date with Mr. X for mid-afternoon, and I think we should all be there," Paul said. "You can make the flight arrangements with Ansel, Leon?"

"Done."

"We confront him," Paul said. "I cover the ground I've been working on for days now. He'll probably kick us out. If not, we should leave anyway, giving him a chance to leave the area. Most likely to leave town. And where does he head for? Tokyo, of course. That's where his allegiance lies—and, he hopes, his safety. So, Leon, in your arrangements, can you add a police contingent at the Nice International Airport? Level with them, including mentioning the packet."

"Also done."

Chapter 18

"To what do I owe the honor of having four of you here this time?" Junzo asked as he lined up chairs before his desk.

"The more witnesses the better," Paul replied.

"Witnesses to what?"

"To what you say and do."

"Do?"

"Yes, your body language."

"You're big on body language, I take it," Junzo said, elevating his chin almost imperceptibly.

"Yes with a capital 'Y'. Sometimes it indicates more than one could put into words. But let's get on with it. You heard about Ken's death?"

"Yes, I did. Absolutely a shame," Junzo said in a deadpan manner. "I wonder if I'm next."

"I doubt it," Paul said.

"What's *that* supposed to mean?"

"I read your facial expression after I mentioned Ken's murder. That's body language too, you know."

"This is getting ridiculous, but I'll play along. And what did you see?"

"Nothing. Blank. Zero. That's like a hundred words."

"I find my expression to things totally irrelevant,"

Junzo responded. "Let's not be deceived."

A look of self-satisfaction crossed Paul's face, but only momentarily.

"Let's move ahead," he said. "Aside from bringing up Ken's fate, I planned on covering only two topics. Number one: Last time you referred to the note Tomi left. But this wasn't publicized anywhere. Only Nadim Maloof and the four of us here knew about it. What's more, it began 'Let's not be deceived' — not exactly an overused phrase. But you used it just seconds ago. I submit *you* wrote that letter, not Tomi."

"Are you out of your *mind?*"

"Care to give me a sample of your writing?"

"The hell I will."

"Let's get to number two," Paul said. He glanced at one of his notes. "During our first meeting, you said you'd never been upstairs at *Cleo's*. Yet you referred to how junky it was and to how the criminal had the floor cut away to steal the safe containing the packet. I asked if Ken had ever described the scene to you and you answered no — only that the packet was missing. And the fact is, sir, the floor's being cut away has never been disclosed publicly."

The perfumer suddenly appeared whipped. "Look," he said. "I've treated you as guests. But you've ended up — twice now — interrogating me as though I'm some sort of villain, and making wild accusations that are completely unfounded. You have no police authority whatsoever and I must ask you all to leave the premises."

With a motion of his head, Paul signaled that they should comply.

Two hours later, Paul and the three *Vérité* delegation members conferred with a contingent of police officers at the Nice International Airport.

"We checked and there's no one with that name headed for Tokyo," the senior officer said.

Paul then noticed four Japanese men stagger through a side door and steady themselves against a wide supporting column. The drunken goons!

All four waved to a man about to enter one of the boarding areas. He wore beige clothes including a cap that was pulled down to his dark glasses. His full beard looked fake. Could it be Junzo in disguise?

Paul alerted the police who dashed toward the man. One officer asked him to remove his hat while another went for the beard. It didn't take much tugging.

"It's Junzo alright," Paul declared as he and the delegation members walked over.

The perfumer was arrested and handcuffed. He put up no resistance as he stared at the travelers, his face a cold mask of menace.

The senior officer opened Junzo's suitcase and withdrew the packet.

"Let's have that please," Paul said, "or it could destroy the world."

He looked around. The goons had vanished.

EPILOGUE

Paul met with the entire *Vérité* delegation to address several things. First and foremost was the disposition of the packet that contained the formula to an enhanced sarin nerve gas. He had simply burned it and hoped there wasn't another copy anywhere.

Next he described what was in the black book found in Lady Beckett's casket. He used it as an example of "something terrible", as opposed to an elaborate scheme devised to cover for it.

This led to what he had branded a "wild goose chase". He explained it this way: "What does nearly every item on the list I gave Nadim have to do with the stolen packet? That is, with a more powerful sarin chemical? My answer is there is no connection at all. That's the important point. *Those items and the references to the past all represented a cover for REMS.* Tomi knew it and was killed. Ken knew it and was killed. The only thing an investigation into flowers and perfumes did was to familiarize me with the characters involved in a plan to release a stronger and more dispersible sarin. And as we all know, the characters were reduced to one: Mr. X himself, Junzo Yawashita. His frequent trips to Tokyo, and preferring to be known as an Islamic, made me suspicious. The perfumery aspect of my mission provided an excuse to broaden my scope. As a by-product of that—and with your indispensable assistance—I hit pay dirt. So, in effect, I went along calling my investigation a perfumery inquiry while all the while using it as a vehicle. As a license to delve into what I thought was more important, albeit more dangerous. I just didn't know *what* until things unfolded."

JERRY LABRIOLA

With regard to Paul's relationship with Sylvie. That flourished. She anticipated resigning from the French Academy of Sciences and moving to New Haven to live with Paul. Possibly to becoming Mrs. D'Arneau. She hoped her experience might earn her a position at Yale where Paul began his job at Sterling Memorial.

Leon was delighted with the outcome and said he would contact Paul for any future high-level challenges put to *Gens de Vérité*.

Finally the matter of loose ends. Not all questions had been answered to Paul's satisfaction but he was content in thinking that the ones that hadn't been were not germane to the case anyway. In this connection, the one that galled him the most was, as he phrased it: "How did some people know where I was at any one time?"